| BETWEEN THE LIES |

by
Marv Levy

www.ascendbooks.com

Praise for *Between the Lies*

"Marv writes like he coached—detailed and thorough, entertaining and successful. He produced a winner on the field in Buffalo and has produced another winner on the pages of this book."

—Rick Gosselin, NFL Columnist
Dallas Morning News

"Having covered Marv Levy for all of his 12 seasons as coach of the Buffalo Bills, I came to know him not only as a tremendous coach, but also as a superb wordsmith. His considerable writing talent shines through on every page of his highly entertaining book. Although this story is the product of Marv's imagination, it contains a great deal of actual, behind-the-scenes perspective that readers will find fascinating as they follow the drama and humor in the telling of his 'fifth' Super Bowl experience."

—Vic Carucci,
New York Times Best-Selling Author & Senior Columnist, NFL.com

"Marv Levy brings his Hall of Fame experience as a coach and general manager to *Between the Lies*. He also brings his Hall of Fame sense of humor and literary ability to this book. For the first time, the average fan (and reader) will experience why it was so much fun to work with Marv on a day-to-day basis. *Between the Lies* will teach you football and keep you laughing. Marv does in this book what he did every day of his career."

—Bill Polian,
Six-time NFL Executive of the Year

"The beauty of Marv Levy is that he was much more than a Hall of Fame football coach. His kindness, perception, sense of humor, and overall keen mind combined to make Marv one of my favorite all-time people. Now, he's combined all of this by putting pen to paper to create *Between the Lies*. It's a perfect combination, whether or not you remember his Super Bowl Buffalo Bills teams. He even has a bunch of nicknames that, of course, make me chuckle!"

—Chris Berman,
Senior ESPN Analyst

"Marv Levy's fertile mind and imagination, cultivated by his experience as a 4-time Super Bowl coach, provide readers with a rich and plausible adventure through the often sordid world of sports, business, media and politics."

—Fred Mitchell,
Sports Columnist, *Chicago Tribune*

Requests for permission should be addressed to:
Ascend Books, LLC, Attn: Rights and Permission Department

10 9 8 7 6 5 4 3 2

Printed in the United States of America

ISBN: 978-0-9830619-3-9
Library of Congress Cataloging-in-Publications Data Available Upon Request

Editors: Lee Stuart and Cindy Ratcliff
Publication Coordinator: Christine Drummond
Editorial Contributions: Eric Tangye
Design: Cheryl Johnson, S&Co. Design

The NFL and The Super Bowl are registered trademarks of the National Football League.

Publisher's Note:
This book is a work of fiction. References to real people, events, establishments, organizations, and locales are intended solely to enhance the fictional story, provide a historical perspective, and give the book a sense of reality and authenticity.

All main characters, events, dialogue, and incidents in the novel are the creation of the author's imagination.

www.ascendbooks.com

DEDICATION

To all those coaches, journalists, and general managers (Bill Polian, John Butler, Jim Schaaf) with whom I have worked (and argued) during my forty-nine years in the game. Wasn't it fun?

BETWEEN THE LIES

MARV LEVY

CHAPTER ONE

No one else knew it yet — not even his wife, Frannie — but when Mel Herbert's outdated Chevy Corvette pulled into the reserved-for-media parking lot on the first day of training camp for the National Football League's Los Angeles Leopards, only the person sitting in the passenger seat knew that this would be Mel's final season on the job. That's because Mel was the person sitting in that seat. Someone else was driving his car.

Mel originally had thought about retiring six years earlier when he grudgingly acknowledged that not just his bad knee, but several other crackling body parts, too, made it too painful for him to meet the rigors of maneuvering his vehicle in the heavy Los Angeles traffic or even of being able, while wrestling with his steering wheel, to deliver a middle finger flip to some of those head-bobbing, boom-box-listening, backwards-baseball-cap-wearing L.A. Raiders goofball fans who always seemed to be on the freeway whenever he was.

Those retirement plans short-circuited, however, when he shared a dinner out one evening with his old friend, Joe Skoronski. Mel had known Joe since they met in Chicago back in 1972 when Mel was working the sports beat for the *Chicago Sun-Times* and Joe was employed as an assistant to the equipment manager with the Chicago Bears.

As their friendship developed during the ensuing years in Chicago, they enjoyed numerous dinners out together. Mel often came away from those evenings with some valuable inside information and frequently in a state of near exhaustion brought on by a mix of too many calories, too many sips, too many cigars, and some outrageous pronouncements from "Malaprop Joe."

In 1982 — as in every other year — some exciting events occurred, and there are many knowledgeable sports gurus who would be quick to inform students of history that it was in 1982 that the Oakland Raiders of the National Football League moved to Los Angeles.

It was during that same year that the *Los Angeles Guardian* made its big move, as well. Determined to enlist the services of the best football journalist they knew of, they came up with one of those offers you can't refuse, and the man who didn't refuse it was veteran *Chicago Sun-Times* sports writer and NFL authority Mel Herbert.

One week after he started on the job in L.A., Mel landed an interview with Dale Bendersen, the General Manager of the other team in town at that time, the Los Angeles Rams. One of the many issues they discussed was the complex task involved in dealing with the constant turnover in office and support staff. When the GM said, "Equipment manager, for example," Mel told him about his old buddy, Joe Skoronski.

Bendersen added Joe's name to his list of candidates. He liked what he learned, and just one month after Mel Herbert had made his way out west, Joe Skoronski, the newly appointed equipment manager for the Los Angeles Rams, followed.

Their evenings together resumed in Los Angeles, replete, once again, with discussions involving topics of interest and with overindulgence in culinary creations, liquid refreshments, and cigars with exotic names. At one of those outings, however, 10 years after they had both moved to the West Coast, they wound up sharing more than just the routine nourishment and camaraderie. It developed when Joe initiated a conversation that moved from the usual to the meaningful.

"Hey, Mel, ya oughta have one more a dem martinis before dey bring out dat disha lobster humidor ya ordered. I read in some magazine at da barber shop dat olives is good for ya."

Mel didn't respond immediately, and so Joe, after filling his mouth with half of the calamari appetizer and spilling the other half on the protruding front midsection of his Los Angeles Rams zip-up rain jacket, addressed a subject that was getting a considerable amount of media attention at the time.

"I betcha wanna know if dat wide receiver of ours, Duane Clarkson, is guilty of dat robbery charge dat dey're trying ta hang on him. Well, I can tell ya; he ain't. He's a real law imbibing citizen type a guy. He wasn't even near da place dat got robbed. Someone's lyin' when dey say dat it was him. He was at home all alone dat night, and so dere ain't even nobody who's gonna be able to step in and supersede on his behalf. Dey can't try ta convict a guy on such circumcisional evidence like dat, can dey?"

"Naw, Joe, I'm not after Duane," Mel said. "Some of the other writers might be because he won't speak to any of us about his contract holdout or about that speeding ticket he got in Las Vegas last winter."

"Geez! Da poor guy goes ta Vegas ta get married; he's hurrying too fast back ta da hotel ta help his bride-ta-be pick up her torso in time for dere pre-nuptials, and den he catches a bad break. It could happen ta anybody," Joe said while waving at the waiter by circling his fork in the air and jabbing with the forefinger of his other hand at his empty snifter of Dewars on the rocks.

"Well, he really ought to get into camp and start catching the ball instead or he'll be piling up a few more bad breaks for himself," Mel said.

"Ya gotta good point dere. Hey, pass dat bread basket and dose pickles, will ya?"

"Actually, Joe, the real reason I wanted to have dinner with you tonight was because I don't think I'm going to be able to keep doing this job, and before I called it quits I wanted to tell you personally how much I always enjoy your company and your wonderful opinions on fine dining."

"Whaddaya mean call it quits?" Joe was so shocked that he actually laid down his knife and fork. "You're still sharp as ever. I know because I read your column every day, right after I look at da racetrack results. And don't give me dat BS about me being some kinda bigwig on knowing what ta eat. Ya know darn well dat when it comes ta eating da right kinda diet, you're da guy who is da real common sewer of good food."

"Gee, thanks for the compliment," Mel said, "but, Joe, even though I still love covering the practices and games, I'm finding it too damn hard to drive anymore. I can't ask Frannie to drive me everywhere. I want her to be glad to see me not be burdened. I love her too much for that. When we go anywhere together now, she does all of the driving. Enough already."

"Ya know what I tink ya oughta do?"

"I never know what you think."

"I tink ya oughta get Billy ta do da driving for ya. He'd really like dat."

"Billy? Billy Zizzo? He still lives in Chicago. You know that."

"He'd be here in a Newark minute if you assed him and told him why. You know how much he'd like ta be hangin' around all dese stadiums and locker rooms doin' sumpthin' real important, don't cha?"

Mel and Joe spent the next several minutes reminiscing—between timeouts to order refills for their respective drinks—about their old buddy, Billy "Zig Zag" Zizzo. Billy had been employed as a driver for the trucking company that serviced the Chicago Bears equipment department during the time that Joe worked for the Bears.

Through Joe, Mel had gotten to know Billy, and, after watching him in action for a while, Mel became convinced that if the Bears players could be as intense and dedicated as Billy was, they would definitely improve their chances of making the playoffs.

The Bears players, too, were aware of and amused by Billy's work ethic, and that is why—after watching him jump, lift, elbow his way by, step up the pace, bark orders at his helpers, get the loading ramp in place without a hitch, shift things around, always seem able to find a parking space, guide his clumsy truck through even the most perplexing of traffic patterns, and talk his way by any obstacle—they anointed him with the nickname he coveted. Forevermore, he would be "Zig Zag" Zizzo.

One day, at the end of a Bears practice session, Mel had spotted Billy unloading some supplies just outside the locker room. The Bears were going into a bye week, and since not much else exciting was happening, Mel thought that a feature story about this unique character might have some appeal to the *Sun-Times* sports editor. Mel invited Billy to join him and Joe for an informal dinner at the Omega Restaurant where it was his intention, also, to interview Billy.

Billy, upon accepting both the dinner invitation and the attendant interview, made one ardent request. "Please call me 'Zig Zag' in the article." Mel made the promise. He kept it, and from that day on, Mel, Joe, and Billy (oops!) Zig Zag became known, in tribute to their facial adornments, as the Three Mustachekateers.

Long after Mel decided to get rid of the needless hair on his upper lip, the designation "Three Mustachekateers" lived on. Even they liked it.

■

In 1982, when Mel, and then Joe, moved on to their new endeavors in Los Angeles, Billy remained behind. Five years later the trucking company that provided services for the Chicago Bears went out of business and Billy found himself out of a job. For a few weeks, Billy, whose tastes and needs were simple, savored the free time and the opportunities he had to pack his fishing gear and head up to the lake country in Wisconsin where he could share wisdom with his fellow anglers.

It wasn't long, however, until Billy realized that it still cost money to buy bait, food, and a night or two at Motel 6, and so he took a nighttime job delivering pizzas for Ranalli's Italian Gardens Restaurant on Chicago's near north side. His tips were a lot better on evenings following wins by the Chicago Cubs or the Bears, which gave him an additional reason to pull for the home teams. He might not have been able to tell you the name of the alderman in his district, but if anyone wanted to know Ryne Sandberg's on-base percentage or Walter Payton's average yards per carry, they didn't have to look it up; just ask Zig Zag.

Billy continued to squeeze out his livelihood in the Windy City, but on this night, 10 years after Mel and Joe had moved to Los Angeles and Mel disclosed to Joe his inclination to retire, Joe persisted in urging Mel to make contact with Billy.

"Give da guy a call, Mel; you'll see."

"It doesn't make sense, Joe. He's lived in Chicago all his life, and he's got a job there. He's not going to leave."

"Wanna bet?"

"No. I never win a bet with you."

"Dat's right; and you wouldn't win dis one, eadder. He's really dere all alone now. His wife, Elma, she left town a year ago ta go find herself, and now even Billy can't find her. And den his only daughter, Meredith — da one dey named after Don Meredith, dat Dallas Cowboys quarterback, remember? — she grew up and got married and den she moved wit her husband ta Carolina last winter when da weather got bad."

Mel felt the seeds of a solution starting to bud. He really did want to continue doing the job that he always loved. He once commented that although he often put in long hours, he'd *never* worked a day in his life. Maybe it was worth placing a feel-it-out call in order to hear directly from Billy whether the proposal had any appeal to him.

"You did it again, Joe. You convinced me to give it a try."

"Hey, dat's great," Joe beamed. "And, oh yeah, I got just one last little bitta advice dat's impertinent ta dis whole matter."

"And that is?"

"When you call him, remember ta say his name 'Zig Zag.'"

On that note, dinner ended. Joe had the waiter bring him a Styrofoam container into which he dumped the remaining half of the massive bread pudding dessert, sticky chocolate caramel sauce included, that Mel had been unable to finish. Then they each headed for home, where, upon arriving, Mel placed his phone call to Zig Zag, and Joe foraged in the refrigerator for a snack to keep him company while he watched *ESPN News*.

■

"Hey, Zig Zag, this is Mel Herbert. How's it going?"

"Aw, not too good right now, Mel. The Cubs are down 7 to 4 in the eighth inning. How's it going with you?"

"Actually, that's sort of what I'm calling you about," Mel said, and then he launched his sales campaign. Four sentences into his presentation, Billy interrupted him.

"Boy, that sounds great to me. Will I be able to be at some of the games with you, too?"

"We can work it all out. Let me get back to you in a day or two with some details. Are you sure you won't miss Chicago? There is a degree of culture there that you won't really find out here."

"Yeah, I know. We got the Cubs, the White Sox, the Bears, the Bulls, and the Blackhawks. But don't forget, you got the Dodgers and the Angels, the Lakers, the Rams, and the Raiders. And then there's that Rose Bowl game with the big parade they have out there every winter, too."

"Okay, Zig Zag, I'll call you as soon as I know more. Anything else before I hang up?"

"You bet! The Cubbies just got a three-run homer to tie it up. You want to stay on the phone for the ninth inning?"

"Not right now, Bi-, uh, Zig Zag. I've got some work that needs to get done. Great talking to you. I'll be in touch."

As soon as Mel hung up the telephone he realized that he hadn't been kidding; there was a lot of work that he needed to get done before the ideal arrangement that he envisioned could become a reality. He feared that the biggest obstacle facing him would be convincing his employers at the *Los Angeles Guardian* that he could still perform his duties at a high level even though he would no longer be doing his own driving.

He was wrong. They not only understood, they were elated. They had become aware of the driving difficulties that their 69-year-old ace reporter and columnist was experiencing, and they were concerned that this deficiency might be leading him to contemplate retirement. They were so elated, if fact, that they solved Mel's main concern regarding how he could sufficiently compensate Billy. As soon as Mel mentioned Billy and his qualifications to his bosses at the newspaper, they didn't hesitate.

"We'll hire him. We'll pay him," they said, "and his main duty will be to serve as your driver."

Was this a happy ending or what? Mel was happy. Joe and Zig Zag were both happy. Everyone at the *Guardian*—his superiors and his cohorts—was happy. The devoted readers of Mel's columns had reason to be happy. But, in truth, it wasn't a happy *ending*. It was a happy *beginning*.

CHAPTER TWO

Add one more person to that contingent of the newly happy: Frannie, Mel's wife, his true love, the mother of their two children. Mel hadn't seen her exhibit this much joy since that day four years earlier when their daughter, Emily, gave birth and presented them with their first grandchild, dear little Amapola.

When Mel told Frannie that Billy was moving to L.A. and would be taking over the driving duties that had been weighing so heavily on her, he was treated to a wide-eyed, open-mouthed look of youthful glee that triggered in him a startling recall of what he had seen 42 years earlier, the first time that he ever glanced her way.

He had been in his second year working as a cub reporter for the *Sun-Times*, and while he was puttering around with his papers up in the press box at Dyche Stadium in Evanston, Illinois, the Northwestern Wildcats football players were out on the field warming up for their season's opening game against the Iowa Hawkeyes.

As Mel was reviewing his roster card in order to make sure that he had memorized all the players' numbers, he became distracted when one of the press box attendants plopped a packet of statistics on the counter in front of his assigned seat. It wasn't this vital new information that caused him to veer off course, however. It was the dimpled smile, the hairdo, the crisp blouse and skirt, the posture, the just-right high heels, the hint of "Hi" in her look, those bright eyes, the nimble moves, and all the et ceteras packaged in that vision that was standing in front of him that caused it.

For a moment, beyond a cursory, "Hey, thanks," he was speechless, but as the sparkling young lady moved on down the line, Mel knew that he was going to find a way to talk to her about a lot more than just press releases.

Once Mel learned that Frances Clovis would be a press box attendant for every home game during her then senior year as a student at Northwestern, he returned to his office where he succeeded in convincing sports editor Norm Edelman that his knowledge and grasp of Wildcats football was unparalleled. Norm assigned him to cover all their games, and by the end of the season Mel proved that he really was the premier media authority on the gridiron sport at Northwestern University.

To Mel, that accomplishment was inconsequential when measured against his attainment of an even more lofty objective that he had established for himself. He and Frances became friends. Then they became more than friends.

On their first date Mel learned, among many other things, that all her friends called her Fran. He made the adjustment.

Two years passed, and then, in the twilight of a summer evening as they were strolling along the winding paths on Chicago's lakefront near Diversey Harbor, Mel Herbert, the man of many words, uttered a mere five: "Frannie, will you marry me?"

She responded with five words of her own: "Yes, my darling. I will." And after a passionate kiss she added, "I love it when you call me Frannie."

Forty years and millions of words later they were still in love. And now, upon receiving the good news that Zig Zag Zizzo, driver extraordinaire, was coming to L.A., she added a few more words. "Melvin, my dear love, you still know how to make me happy, don't you?"

"I learned that skill from you, my darling Frannie."

"When will Billy arrive?" Frannie asked.

"He'll be flying in on Saturday. Joe and I are going to meet him at the airport. He's bringing The Gipper with him, too."

"The Gipper? Who's that?"

"That's his dog. I thought you knew."

"Aw, isn't that sweet. I'm going to come, too."

"Oh, no! That's the day you have your scheduled workout class at the Redondo Beach Athletic Club."

"I can afford to miss *one* session for something like this," Frannie said. "Will you please stop bugging me about exercise already?"

"You're so beautiful, and I just don't want you to ever lose it. And, please, I don't 'bug you.' I merely encourage you to follow a healthful and invigorating lifestyle as prescribed by the leading authorities in the field," Mel said as he concentrated on assuming the best posture that his aching joints would allow.

"Well, missing one little workout for something like this will not destroy me. Fun, too, is healthful and invigorating. I'm coming with you. Case closed."

"Let me tell you something, madam," Mel said. "I'm the person who has the final say around here. And that is, as always, 'Yes, dear.'"

"Oh, Mel, I love you. And you know, too, how much I love it when you get excited enough to write one of your poems. Why don't you write one for Billy?"

"A poem? For Billy? And by the way, when you see him, don't call him Billy anymore. We've all got to call him Zig Zag. Joe never stops reminding me about that."

"Okay. Write a poem for Zig Zag, then."

Once again, Frannie's urgings prevailed, and so the self-appointed Bard of the Press Box went to work.

At the bar nearest the airport where they all assembled to celebrate right after Billy's plane landed, they had a rollicking time as Mel recited his newly created lines of tribute followed by Frannie's presentation to Billy of an attractive plaque that she prepared for the occasion. It was inscribed with these immortal words:

Zig Zag Zizzo Iz Comin' To Town

Zig Zag Zizzo iz zon hiz way,
> *And heez gonna be here by Zaturday.*
When he zoomz into town we'll all zing a zong,
Zig Zag will zero in, and he'll zing along.
From Joe and from Mel he'll hear lusty cheerz,
> *As they get together again after all theze yearz.*
Zig Zag's a guy who will do everything to pleeze,
> *But he better find some time to get some Zs.*
Because once heez here, he'll be in a tizzy

Driving Mel everywhere in hiz old tin Lizzie.
Zig Zag's zo zealous and zo full of zeal
That I can hardly wait till he getz behind the wheel.
Then he'll zip around town with hiz signature zest.
Zig Zag Zizzo, you are the best.

Enthusiasm reigned. Mel plunged back into doing the work he loved so much, and Zig Zag was reborn. At every sporting event that Mel covered, he arranged to get a press box pass for his buddy. Mel was in the press box; Zig Zag was in heaven.

CHAPTER THREE

A little more than two years passed following Zig Zag's arrival out West. And then, Los Angeles was rocked. It wasn't an earthquake. It was Al Davis, owner of the Los Angeles Raiders, and Georgia Frontiere, owner of the Los Angeles Rams, who were responsible for delivering the shockwave. Right after the 1994 National Football League season ended, they both said "bye-bye" to Tinseltown. The Raiders, who had left Oakland for L.A. just 12 years earlier, were heading back to their original hometown, and the Rams were moving to St. Louis.

Mel Herbert, Joe Skoronski, and Zig Zag Zizzo were shocked. Along with the almost 10 million other people living in Los Angeles County, they were seeking to regain their bearings.

"Ya know, I can maybe unnerstan' da Raiders goin' back to Oakland where dey was anyway before movin' here in '82," Joe said. "Den, after dey got amalgamated by dat 51 to 3 score a coupla years ago in dat AFC Championship Game back in Buffalo, tings went downhill real fast from dere. But da Rams, geez, dey've been out here ever since way back in 1946. I was just a real little kid livin' in Chicago in dat Backa da Yards neighborhood at dat time. Football wasn't even on TV yet back den. Dat's how long ago dat was."

Both Mel and Zig Zag knew that they could continue working for the *Guardian*, but it wouldn't be near as much fun without some local favorite NFL team to follow. Joe's situation was more complex. The Rams wanted him to come with them to St. Louis where he would continue to serve as their equipment manager, but they emphasized that they'd have to know within the next few days so that they could move forward with their planning.

Joe was torn. He wanted to remain in Los Angeles, but how could he do it without a job, he wondered. He sought out his good friend, hoping that Mel could provide some guidance as he struggled to reach a decision.

"Mel, it would really be tough for me ta leave here. Dere are too many tings I love about dis place," Joe said.

"Well, then don't go. You'll find something to do here."

"Yeah, but it won't be pro football, and dat's da only ting I really love."

"I thought I just heard you say that there were a whole bunch of things that you loved out here."

"Well, yeah, dat's true. I love dat lady friend a mine, Darlene, for instance, and I'd really hate ta hafta leave her."

"Wouldn't she come along if you asked her to?"

"Dat's annudder big problem. I don't wanta put her on da spot like dat. She's got one son, Ernie, livin' here in El Segundo and da udder one, Bernie, out dere in Anaheim. Or maybe it's da udder way around; I get mixed up sometimes. Anyway, besides all dat, she finally just got dat job she's been after for so long showin' people around dat Museum of Contemptible Art. I don't wanta break her heart on dat one."

"Maybe it will break her heart even more if you run off and leave her," Mel said.

"It's already bodderin her real bad. I see her sittin' dere sometimes wit one a dose real sadistic-like looks on her face. It makes me feel terrible, but man, I gotta earn a livin', too, ya know, and da Rams, dey wanna know real soon if I'm comin' back dere wit 'em or not."

"Can you wait until Friday before you give them your answer?" Mel asked.

"Dey said dey'd give me just ta da enda dis week, so I guess dat Friday would be okay, but why do you want me ta wait til den?"

"I do have a reason, Joe, but I can't tell you what it is right now. Just trust me, please. I know you've got a difficult decision to make, but I'll say one more time that I'll wager you'll be able to find something good if you decide to stay here."

"Boy, I don't know. If I do dat I'll probably be cuttin' off my nose despite my face," Joe said as he walked away even more perplexed than he had been prior to their meeting. Joe continued to vacillate, and through the early part of that week, Mel continued to do everything he could to keep him vacillating.

CHAPTER FOUR

There was a compelling reason Mel had been trying to sway Joe into making a commitment to remain in Los Angeles. Mel had some sworn-to-secrecy inside information that, had he disclosed it to Joe, would have made Joe's decision an easy and an obvious one. It was something that Mel couldn't divulge, however, without breaking a promise he had made to Brant Gilbert, the San Diego Chargers director of player personnel.

Among the members of the media, Mel—and only Mel—had learned that the National Football League owners, aware of the painful void resulting from the Rams and Raiders departures from Los Angeles, were about to grant an expansion franchise to Hollywood movie mogul, Cedric B. Medill, with the specification that the team was to be located in that grieving West Coast city.

Even before the news about the expansion franchise became public, the team's new owner hit the ground running when he scored his first coup by negotiating a verbal agreement with Brant Gilbert. Brant was to be brought aboard to serve as the new team's General Manager.

Brant and Cedric B. pledged to each other that nothing about this arrangement was to be disclosed until the complicated legalities authorizing the new franchise had been resolved. Talking about it prematurely might jeopardize the deal, Cedric B. cautioned. No one else was to know until, if everything proceeded according to plan, NFL Commissioner Paul Rogers announced it at a press conference scheduled for Thursday of that week. It was the same week during which Joe Skoronski was facing his own personal deadline.

■

During the season that had just finished, the San Diego Chargers made it all the way to the Super Bowl Game, and, although they lost it to the San Francisco 49ers, many knowledgeable NFL insiders were impressed by the important role Brant Gilbert had played in helping put together the team's roster. Mel Herbert was, too, and so he arranged a Monday afternoon interview with Brant at the Chargers facility.

Mel arrived at Brant's office and sat down in the waiting area as instructed by Brant's secretary, Margie DeVito, who then informed Brant over the intercom that Mr. Herbert was there.

"Tell him I'll see him in just a few minutes," Brant said. "Right now I'm on an important telephone call."

Mel, hearing that message from Brant, nodded his head in acknowledgement. Margie then excused herself and left the room to attend to what Mel surmised may have been a call of nature. In her haste to leave, she neglected to turn off the speaker system on the intercom. As a result of that oversight, Mel was anything but bored as he sat alone in the waiting room while Brant and the other person with whom he was speaking proceeded with their telephone conversation. That other person was Cedric B. Medill.

During the next five minutes, Mel gleaned as much information about a hush-hush subject as Pulitzer Prize-winning reporters Carl Bernstein and Bob Woodard had been able to garner during their several weeks of intensive investigation into the Watergate scandal 20 years earlier.

Brant and Cedric B., with one more mutual assurance that they would "keep it just between the two of us," finished their phone call. A smiling Brant then opened his office door and invited Mel to enter. Mel took his seat, and knowing that if he was going to level with Brant, it was incumbent upon him to seize the initiative.

"So you and Cedric B. Medill are going to see to it that NFL football remains in L.A. after all." Mel said. Brant's smile disappeared. His mouth was now wide open, instead. His eyes may have been even more wide open.

"What?!" he rasped.

Mel then told Brant what he had heard over the intercom while sitting in the waiting room. Brant's head dropped, and his shoulders sagged. Then he sat there silently, elbows on his desk, hands folded under his chin, staring at nothing in particular. Mel said nothing either, and at last Brant resumed the conversation.

"If this gets out now, Mel, everything I've worked for all my life is out the window. Even if the awarding of the franchise to Mr. Medill goes through, as it probably will anyway, I still would have been responsible for screwing up even before my first day on the job. In his eyes I'd just be a guy who blunders and who doesn't keep his promises. He wouldn't want a jerk like that working for him, and I sure wouldn't blame him."

"I know," Mel said. "But if some other writer breaks the story between now and Thursday and my editor finds out that I knew and sat on it, then, in his mind, I take over the title of 'Dumb Jerk.'" Brant sat there, silent once again, looking like a person who had exposed himself to the wrath of the guillotine and was now resigned to his fate.

Mel saw something different. He saw a man who had always been forthright, honest, and responsive in his dealings, not just with the media but—if all reports Mel had heard were accurate—with players, associates, and fans, as well. He was gazing across that desk at a man whom he believed revered the game and who was on the threshold of ascending to a position that would allow him to apply, for the benefit of the sport he loved, the high ideals that drove him.

Thirty more seconds of silence ticked by, and then Mel spoke. "Brant, I'm going to be a dumb jerk. I'm going to keep your secret." Brant, with his elbows on the desk where he was sitting, folded his elevated hands, pressed the back knuckles of his thumbs against his forehead, and stared straight down at the top of the desk. He just didn't know what to say.

Finally, he spoke. "Mel, I just don't know what to say."

"Then don't say anything."

"How can I not? How can I ever thank you?"

Mel, rather than answering the question, steered the conversation into a discussion of how they would both handle this delicate matter. Mel promised that he would maintain the secret, but they both agreed that the instant the Thursday press conference by the Commissioner began, Mel could pull the trigger and release the carefully crafted story he would have ready to go.

The tension began to ease. They relaxed and allowed themselves to discuss some other items of interest to them both. One of the topics that Mel brought up was the status of Rams equipment manager, Joe Skoronski. When Brant heard that Joe really wanted to stay in L.A., he lighted up.

"I've heard all about him," Brant said. "Everyone I know who knows him says he does an outstanding job."

"That he does, and besides that, he'll keep you laughing."

"I'm sure there'll be times I could use some of that. He'd be my first choice for the job. I'm glad you let me know about his being available. Thank you for that, *and* for a helluva lot more."

"Well, I guess it's time for me to get going," Mel said.

They parted, two men with even greater respect for each other than they had had two hours earlier.

■

Thursday arrived, and just as Commissioner Paul Rogers was making the announcement that there would be a new NFL team in Los Angeles, Mel Herbert, now relieved from his vow of confidentiality, broke his bombshell account of how it had all come to fruition.

For the Three Mustachekateers and some of their newfound friends, it could have been an appropriate time for them to belt out a chorus or two of "Happy Days Are Here Again." Joe was staying where his heart was. Zig Zag would be guaranteeing, 100%, that the new team in town—and his beloved Chicago Cubs, too, of course—would win their league championships. Mel was the toast of Journalismville, and Brant Gilbert was coming to Hollywood where he'd be directing Cedric B. Medill's latest blockbuster production.

Welcome to the era of the Los Angeles Leopards.

CHAPTER FIVE

It didn't take long for Brant Gilbert to learn that putting a new NFL franchise together and getting a team out onto the field in less than a year was:

#1. Fun

#2. A pain in some delicate body parts

"Let's see now," he said to himself his first day on the job, "we've got to get a stadium lease, a practice facility with meeting rooms, locker rooms, and an administrative office complex. Then, of course, we're going to need a chief financial officer, a salary cap expert, a marketing department, a ticket manager along with a ticket office staff, and team doctors who will have to oversee a top-notch group of athletic trainers. Oh, and don't forget the video department and the stadium operations staff and security, also. Remember, too, you need a crackerjack director of media relations and a group of good, smart people to work with him."

Brant granted himself a short pause in order to allow his mounting dizzy spell to subside, and then he continued on with his personal reminders.

"I shouldn't worry, I'm not going to forget about a department of community relations, or about an assistant GM who can help me with contract negotiations, or about another administrative assistant who can handle that endless accumulation of boring details that keep throwing me off the track. We're going to need secretarial help in every department and a bunch of other qualified people, too, like our directors of college and pro scouting and all our talent scouts, and I know that it's essential for me to get to work on lining up a training camp facility and on all the logistics that go with that."

It was time for another deep breath. And then a bolt of realization provided him cause to crank it up once again.

"Oh, yeah! That's right! This team is going to need coaches and players, too, and they are all going to require tons of equipment. At least, we've already got an equipment manager. We're off and running now, baby!"

■

Late in the afternoon of his first day on the job, Brant met in his office with Mel. At the conclusion of their meeting in San Diego a few days earlier when Mel's promise to Brant had been so meaningful, Brant promised, in return, that he would grant this exclusive day-one interview to the *Guardian's* premier sports reporter.

On his chauffeured ride home following that interview, Mel, after asking Zig Zag, who was listening on the radio to the "Maniac Manny and Looney Louie Spectacular Sports Call-in Show," to turn down the volume, pondered how he might be able to lend any support that might help Brant in his efforts to deal with the overwhelming challenges he was facing.

He chose to employ a poetic solution. This time, however, it wasn't *his* pen that he used to provide solace. It was someone else's. In the mail, two days later, Brant received a letter from Mel. Inside the envelope he found a brief handwritten note.

"I think you'll be interested in this little 'pep talk' from a writer you may have heard of. His name is Edgar A. Guest," Mel wrote, "and so, as best as I can recall, here it is:"

> *Somebody said that it couldn't be done.*
> *But he with a chuckle replied,*
> *That maybe it couldn't, but he would be one*
> *Who wouldn't say so 'til he'd tried.*
>
> *So he buckled right in with the trace of a grin*
> *Never doubting or thinking to quit it.*
> *And he started to sing as he tackled that thing*
> *That couldn't be done. And he did it.*

Brant didn't cast the poem aside. He read it again. And then, he buckled right in with the trace of a grin, never doubting or thinking to quit it.

■

When Brant plunged into the process of sorting out all that needed to be done in order to get the engine running, it was the fun part that he had thought about last. How could I have left the *team* until last, he wondered. Football *is* players and coaches, he reminded himself. It's what I know best. It's what I enjoy. It's what I'm good at—I hope. It is where I am going to focus my attention and energies, *and* it's the direction in which I'd better get my butt moving ... right now! There, it's moving. This is fun already.

Out of the chaos that beleaguered Brant during his first few days as general manager of the L.A. Leopards, there emerged for him a clear picture of the anatomy of a pro football franchise.

There is no question that it is a business operation; just ask Cedric B. Medill about that. It is also big-time entertainment; again, ask Cedric B. Medill—and several million beer-guzzling fans—about that. And it is a competitive sport; just ask the men down on the field about that. How the body is structured is important, Brant acknowledged. How it functions is just as important.

If he tried to be the *expert* on everything, he realized, he'd more likely wind up being the *ex-employee* of a pro football team. Hire good front office people and then get out of the way, he told himself. Let someone else worry about the potholes in the parking lot, about selling the rights for sponsorship of the half-time show to some toilet paper company, about writing a letter of apology to some lady in Section D, Row 27 for the language that some bare-chested, potty-mouthed screwball with a painted face in Row 26 had directed toward her and her 9-year-old son. He was going to find and connect with the players and the coaches who made all the other parts work.

And he was going to have fun doing it.

CHAPTER SIX

Brant felt good. He had simplified things. Now for the hard part. First, find the right man to serve as head coach of the team. In reality, the hard part wasn't identifying the person he wanted. He already knew who that was. It was convincing Cedric B. that the coach he had in mind was the one they should hire.

"Brant, why would you have someone who has never been a head coach in the NFL at the top of your list?" Cedric B. asked when Brant told him whom it was that he favored.

"Mr. Medill, I've had Bobby Russell in my sights for a long time now. He's a great teacher, and the players really tune in when he's instructing them. He interacts with all the other coaches on the staff in a very healthy way, and, believe me, that is important."

"If he's so good why hasn't any other team made him their head coach, then?" Cedric B. asked. "He's been around a long time now, hasn't he? And once again, Brant, you can call me Cedric, please."

"Yes, sir, Mr. Medill, I'll do that, but to answer your question, I can't really nail down why. Bobby's not a big self-promoting sort of guy, and that age factor—he's 57—might have something to do with it, too," Brant said.

"I still think we need to bring in someone who has been a winning head coach in the NFL. Someone like that will give us a boost in ticket sales, too, don't you think?"

"It might, but I can tell you that a head coach who has already established a reputation as a winner in this league isn't going to be looking to take over an expansion team in its first year. He'd zero in on a job where the prospects for winning immediately are much more likely. And, as I just said, Mr. Medill, there isn't anyone like that available, anyway."

Cedric B. took in a deep breath, and then he blew it out. "I think I'm going to begin calling you 'Mr. Gilbert,'" he said. "How would you like that?"

Brant blinked. And then, with a smile and with an earnest, but flawed, effort to affect an oh-so-British accent, he said, with lifted chin and half-closed eyes, "That I would deem, indeed, to be most appropriate, Cedric, old bean."

Brant concluded his response by reverting to his more natural, but no easier to decipher, native Texas twang. "I finally do get the message. *Cedric.*"

Cedric B. returned Brant's smile while thinking to himself that Brant had just eliminated himself from any consideration as a candidate for a role in the new version of *Wuthering Heights* that was about to go into production at his studios.

From that moment on, Brant was comfortable being on a first-name basis with his boss, and, as he dealt with Cedric B. on an almost daily basis, he developed a liking and respect for the man. Cedric B. would not hesitate to voice a strong opinion, but he would listen to and honestly evaluate the opinions of others — Brant included — who might have a contrary view. If he made a promise, he kept it. He was no dictator, but he was no pushover. Add to all of that, he had a sense of humor and it would manifest itself often at just the right times. Brant came to think of him as not just his boss, but as his friend, as well.

It was a relationship that would mature during the months that lay ahead, but at this stage in its development they were locked into the process of deciding who was going to be the first head coach of the Los Angeles Leopards. Cedric B. resumed their conversation. "Tell me once again, Brant, what is so special about this Bobby Russell fellow?"

"He is organized like you can't believe. Everywhere he's been the teams have won, and he's been a huge part of the reason those teams have been winners. I've seen that first hand. He was our defensive coordinator in San Diego."

"Defense! We want someone who is an offensive guy, don't we? You've got to score points to win games, and you've got to open it up and air it out to win fans. Even I know that."

"No insult to offense, Mr.—uh—Cedric, because offense really is important, but it is no *more* important than defense *or* than the kicking game. No one understands that better than Bobby Russell, and I don't think there would be anyone better than him at finding the right assistant coaches to handle all three of those areas."

"Okay, let's bring him in for an interview. Before we hire anybody, I'd like to see what he's like myself."

"Oh, of course," Brant said. "That's what I intended to do from the beginning. Also, all I've said is that Bobby is the prime candidate in my mind right now, but there are a couple of other qualified guys out there, too, whom I think we should interview before making any final decision."

"Good," Cedric B. said. "And as long we are going to be looking at other possibilities, there is one other fellow I'd be interested in talking to, as well. I have a friend, a gentleman named Merle Cornish, who is a heavy investor in a lot of our productions. Merle lives in Houston, and he's a big football fan. He's a good friend of Adam Budd, the owner of the Houston Oilers, and he's been a frequent guest in Adam's private box during games or even on the sidelines during training camp every year.

"Anyway, he called me a couple of days ago and recommended one of the assistant coaches with the Oilers for the head job here," Cedric B. continued. "He said that the guy was a fireball and that the media and fans in Houston all thought that he was real head coach material. Merle said he saw all those signs in him, too. At that time, though, I told Merle—just like I said to you a while ago—that I'd prefer some former big name head coach. Now that that's out the window, I'd like us to bring that fellow in for an interview, too. His name is Randy Dolbermeier."

"I've heard his name. He coaches their defensive line. I don't know much more about him," Brant said, "but I can sure find out. And if you'd feel better about it, let's have him come in, too,"

"Fine, let's do that, Mr. Gilbert."

"Okay, Cedric."

Ten days later, when all of their interviews were completed, Brant and Cedric B. had their coach. It was Bobby Russell.

"Cedric, I really am convinced that we've got the right man," Brant said. The two of them were sitting in Cedric B.'s office, and Brant had just hung up the telephone from finishing his seal-the-deal conversation with Russell. Brant and Cedric B. were feeling relaxed and laid back now, but in the Russell household in San Diego there was a raucous celebration going on.

"I'm relying on your good judgment in this matter, Brant. After all, that's why I hired you." Cedric B. said. "Bobby seemed to be very knowledgeable, and I can see that he is also the kind of person who will work well with everyone else in the organization, just like you said. Still, I really did like that Randy Dolbermeier. I can see why Merle was so sold on him. He was really high energy, wasn't he? I know he's coaching on the defensive side of the ball now, but they tell me that he was a brilliant offensive coordinator when he was coaching in college. You could tell that when we spoke with him, couldn't you? I thought he had some very interesting and innovative ideas about what kind of offensive schemes he would use. They sure sounded exciting to me."

"I'm glad that we did get to talk with him," Brant said. "My impressions, too, were favorable, but I'm still convinced that Bobby is the best man for this job."

"Well, we've made that decision already, haven't we? Now, let me ask you this: Do you think Bobby might be agreeable to bringing Dolbermeier onto his staff? As his defensive coordinator, for instance. That would be a promotion, and the Oilers couldn't keep him from accepting something like that, as I understand it."

"Not unless they promoted him to that position themselves, and they won't do that. Corey Walters is their defensive coordinator now, and they really like him. For good reasons, too," Brant said. "When Bobby gets here tomorrow, I will talk with him about it. It might all work out."

The next day, following completion of the press conference where Bobby Russell was introduced as the head coach of the Leopards, Brant and Bobby retired to Brant's office. Hiring a coaching staff was number one on the priority list now.

"It isn't just a good *coach* that makes the difference; it is a good *coaching staff*," Bobby had said a few days earlier during his interview with Brant and Cedric B. Brant smiled and nodded in agreement. They were on the same page already.

They both knew that it was the head coach who had the major responsibility and authority for selecting the members of his coaching staff. That didn't mean that the GM should just bow out. A smart head coach would be open to, and at times would even seek, input from his general manager. This was one of those occasions.

"Bobby, Mr. Medill wanted me to suggest to you that you consider hiring Randy Dolbermeier as your defensive coordinator," Brant said. "That's the only coach he has said anything about, and so he's really not going to meddle in your overall staff structure. I'll fill you in later about why he's so high on Randy, but first, what do you know about him?"

"From what I hear, he does a good job. I know him just a little bit from meeting him when we'd all scout those college all-star games, but I don't know him that well. Why is Mr. Medill pushing for him?" Brant filled Bobby in. As they continued to talk, Brant learned that although Bobby had several assistants in mind already, his thinking was still wide open as far as defensive coordinator was concerned. Here was the opening for Brant to provide some timely counsel. It consisted of: "Interview him. Evaluate him. If he is a good coach, hire him. Do that, and you'll not only add a good coach to your staff, but you'll also score some big-time points, right from the opening kickoff, with the team's owner."

Bobby followed Brant's advice, and one week later the Los Angeles Leopards announced the hiring of Randy Dolbermeier as their defensive coordinator.

CHAPTER SEVEN

The expansion Los Angeles Leopards somehow got it all done by the time training camp opened in July. Provisions for facilities, front office structure and personnel, coaching staff, support personnel, the expansion draft, player signings, the NFL draft in late April, ticket sales, sponsorships—even an occasional timeout for lunch—had all been made.

They weren't the only ones who accomplished this remarkable feat, however. The NFL, in its desire to maintain an equal number of teams in the league's two conferences, had also awarded an expansion franchise to another West Coast city. While the fledgling Los Angeles Leopards of the American Football Conference would be taking the field for their inaugural season that fall, so would the newly created Portland Pioneers of the National Football Conference.

The Pioneers, too, succeeded in getting it all ready to roll on time, and they did it while functioning with an organizational structure that had no precedent. Yves Napoleon, the Canadian technology magnate from Quebec City, paid a previously unmatched ransom-level price to the NFL in order to purchase the rights to his new team.

A few years prior to this acquisition, Yves's son, René, upon receiving his MBA from Stanford, had moved to the Silicon Valley in order to oversee his father's burgeoning business operations in the United States. One evening, while attending a cocktail party in Palo Alto hosted by the owner of the San Francisco 49ers, René met another Stanford alum, Lilly Nanula, the daughter of the 49ers' chief financial officer, Vincent Nanula.

René was smitten.

It wasn't just her vibrant good looks or her happy manner that captured him, although he was keenly aware of those appealing qualities. She was personable and witty, and she displayed a knowledge of football—not just the financial aspects of it—that both amused and baffled him. How would she know, or care, he wondered, who the backup defensive tackles for the Tampa Bay Buccaneers were.

Before the evening was over, René gave Lilly his business card, and she gave hers to him. Good, he thought, now I've got her phone number. He called. They met. They began to date. They began to like each other. They began to fall in love. They did fall in love. He asked her if she would marry him.

"Oui! Oui, mon cher René. Je t'aime avec tout mon coeur," she said.

"Mia carissima Lilly, ti amo," he said.

"I now pronounce you man and wife," the priest said. But that was four months later at a lavish ceremony in Carmel-by-the-Sea.

Lilly's interest in NFL football, and her manner of displaying it, had a contagious effect, and soon René, too, became an avid devotee of the game. Over time, he succeeded in educating his father about the soaring financial growth in value that NFL franchises were experiencing. That contributed to motivating Yves Napoleon's bold entrepreneurial venture into American football, but even that investment wasn't as daring as what he did just two days after attaining ownership of the team. He announced that the general manager of the Portland Pioneers would be ... Lilly Napoleon.

There were countless heel-of-the-hand slaps to the forehead by NFL executives, fans, and members of the media when the news that "Lady Lilly" would be serving in the role that her father-in-law had indicated. He hadn't been joking, after all.

The first female general manager in the history of the National Football League went to work, and by the time all the teams in the league were ready to report to training camp in July, several members of the media were hoping that no one would recall the searing, and at times humorous (at least so far as they attempted to portray it), commentary they had disseminated back when the original announcement that Napoleon had come marching in shocked the football world. It was beginning to appear as if she might really know what needed to be done *and* how to do it.

But the true test lay ahead. How you fare once the regular season games begin is what counts, and, when it comes to an expansion team's first year on-the-field performance in the NFL, it faces obstacles that the fainthearted would deem to be insurmountable. They probably are, but neither Brant Gilbert of the Leopards nor Lilly Napoleon of the Pioneers would ever surrender to that argument.

Yes, they had to begin operations with not a single player on the roster. Sure, there was an expansion draft from a list of players on existing NFL team rosters, but the established teams in the league were required to expose only a limited number of their players, and they were not going to put any of the difference-makers on the available-for-selection list. In many instances, those other teams actually welcomed the opportunity to rid their rosters, in a graceful way, of players whom they planned to replace, anyway.

The new teams had no previous systems of play in place. Their players would not have the benefit of any previous exposure to the terminology or to the playbooks they would be using, of having worked with teammates, or of responding to the teaching methods of the coaches who would most likely all be working together for the first time.

Some pundits might counter by pointing out that the expansion teams would be slotted at the top of every round in the college draft. Wonderful! That meant that they would be bringing in a bunch of overpaid, untested rookies who would soon find out that the difference between college and professional football might be akin to the difference between pedaling a tricycle around the schoolyard playground on a balmy summer afternoon as compared to gunning a Harley-Davidson through a snowstorm in downtown Manhattan at rush hour.

Another distracting complication to which the general manager and the head coach are subjected results from the mounting pressure exerted by euphoric fans, from the "logic" expressed by the media, and even from the enthrallment embraced by first-time team owners to do what "any fool" can see should be done. That is, of course, "draft that glamour *quarterback* with that very first pick in the entire draft, dummy!"

Brant Gilbert and Bobby Russell wanted to pick defensive end Sylvester "Sackmaster" Simmons with the top selection. Cedric B. was aghast.

"How can we not go with that quarterback, Quentin Pye?" Cedric B. asked. "He's a hometown kid on top of that. I hear that he's movie star handsome. The fans here will go wild for him. Also, they tell me that that draft guru, Del Piper from ESPN, says he's the best quarterback to come out of college in the last 20 years."

"Cedric, he says that about the top-rated quarterback in the draft every year," Brant said.

"Yeah, well someone showed me an article about Pye in *The Sporting News*. I read that he threw 51 touchdown passes in his college career and ran it in for 11 more. How many touchdowns has that Simmons fellow scored? That's what I'd like to know."

The discussion went on, but Cedric B. remained adamant. Brant and Bobby recognized that this was an issue on which they were going to have to concede. With the first pick in the first round of their first draft, the Los Angeles Leopards selected quarterback Quentin Thomas Pye from UCLA.

Now it was the Portland Pioneers' turn to pick. Team owner Yves Napoleon was in the draft room on draft day, but after acknowledging that he didn't know the difference between an onside kick and a kick in the backside, he looked to General Manger Lilly Napoleon, to Director of Player Personnel Charlie Navey, and to Head Coach Denzel Jackson to make the pick. The Pioneers then selected Sylvester Simmons, defensive end from Notre Dame. In addition to all his pass rushing and dominant run-stopping abilities, he had also scored not one but two touchdowns during his collegiate career. When Yves Napoleon read that in the newspaper the next day, he was impressed.

Cedric B. had certainly been right about one thing: the L.A. fans were elated by the decision to draft Pye. Reporter Mel Herbert added to the hoopla when, in his morning-after-the-draft article, he reported, at the suggestion of his wife, Frannie, that even all the lukewarm female football fans in Los Angeles were going to be giddy about having Q.T. "Cutie" Pye as the on-the-field leader of their home-town team.

CHAPTER EIGHT

Both the Los Angeles Leopards and the Portland Pioneers were primed and ready to go when the regular season kicked off in September. It was after the games began to count in the standings that things got rough. The Leopards lost their first four games, before pulling off a startling 27–24 upset of the New England Patriots. Then they lost their next three games. At midseason, their record stood at 1–7. The Pioneers fared little better, logging a 2–6 mark by the season's midway point.

It was about what might have been expected from expansion teams in their first year of competition, but it was far short of the expectations that Cedric B. had for his Leopards.

"Does this guy Russell really know what he is doing?" Cedric B. asked Brant during their Monday telephone conversation on the day after their seventh loss of the season. "How can they blow a 10-point lead like they did yesterday? That's what I'd like to know."

"Cedric, our defense has a long way to go yet," Brant responded. "You know how heavily we went for offense in the draft. That was what you really urged us to do, remember?"

"Yes, I do, and I'm glad I did. That's how we got that lead. That's why Q.T. had those two touchdown passes that put us in front until that damn conservative prevent defense that Russell kept calling screwed it up."

"Q.T. also threw three interceptions in the game, Cedric, including the one that set up their last touchdown drive."

"Who sent that play in? And why would he be throwing to a receiver that was being covered by Montavius Boswell? I keep hearing that he's the best defensive back in the NFL."

"It was a rookie mistake, Cedric. Besides, Q.T. was under lots of pressure. Our pass protection isn't what it needs to be yet. He didn't have much time, and so he just unloaded the ball."

"Well, then why are we throwing the ball in a situation like that?"

"It was still early in the fourth quarter," Brant explained. "It was a third-down and eight-yards-to-go situation. We needed to get a first down. We needed to maintain control of the ball, and, at that point in the game, it would have been very meaningful for us to put some more points on the board. Also, I recall a couple of weeks ago when we lost a late lead to the Seahawks you were disturbed because you felt we had become too conservative by trying to grind it out on the ground."

"Well, it seems to me that Russell just doesn't come up with the right strategy at the right time," Cedric B. said. "I know from a talk I had with Randy Dolbermeier that he, too, would like to see us be a lot more innovative on offense, but Russell won't go along with it."

"All I can say, Cedric, is that Bobby is keeping the players on track and working hard despite all the difficulties they've had to deal with. We are getting better, and we'll continue to get better if we just allow him to stay the course."

"Well, I have faith in you, Brant, and I do like Bobby, too. I don't always agree with everything that's taking place, and I'm not going to hesitate to speak up and let you know how I feel. But you guys are in charge. I do wish, however, that Russell would listen more to what Dolbermeier has to offer."

"From what I've observed, Randy keeps offering plenty."

"Yeah, he's a character. That's obvious! But I also notice a lot of the media guys laughing at his antics. They really seem to like interviewing him, too."

"And he enjoys all the attention. Maybe a little bit too much."

"All I know is that I think he is one heckuva coach. I just wish sometimes that our players would get as fired up as I've seen him be when he's out on that practice field."

CHAPTER NINE

No member of the media had better insight into what was happening with the Los Angeles Leopards than Mel Herbert. His sources were the best. He had won the trust of Brant Gilbert, and on rare occasions he knew that he could inquire of Brant about matters that the general manager might be reluctant to discuss with others. Mel knew when to capitalize on this special relationship, and he knew when not to abuse it.

Besides Brant there was his old pal, Joe Skoronski. Joe wasn't "Deep Throat," the bearer of scandalous information, but he was often the provider of a tidbit that made Mel's column the "must read" for serious—and not so serious—football fans.

And then there was Zig Zag Zizzo. It did not take long before Mel's driving partner was welcomed as a buddy by all the Leopards players. If any of them ever needed someone to make them laugh or to go run an errand, Zig Zag was available. He, too, enjoyed passing on to Mel some tales that were designed to either inform, or amuse, or confound.

Zig Zag savored his role, and, when it came to Joe, there may never have been a happier equipment manager in professional football. He was still in L.A. He was still employed by an NFL team. He still shared those occasional nights out on the town with Mel and Zig Zag. His lady friend, Darlene, was happy, and that added even more to Joe's contentment.

"You ain't got no idea, Mel, what my gettin' dis job has done for me and for Darlene," Joe said one day about a month after being hired as the team's equipment manager. "Her whole altitude is better."

"That's great, Joe. How's her work at the museum going?" Mel asked.

"Real good, but dat's not all. She's gone on one a dose real hellty kicks right now. Today she's at dat gymnasium class where dey concentrate on dose abominable muscles, and den she goes wit her pals, Muriel and Gertrude, to da Low Cal Café where she always orders da same ting for lunch. It's dat fruit plate wit da fat free, small turd cottage cheese."

"That's a dish that never really appealed to me," Mel said, "but I'm sure glad that things are working out so well for you and Darlene."

"Yeah, and dey're gonna work out good for dis team, too. I really like dat Bobby Russell guy dat dey brought in as da coach. He's a real organized type a guy. Ya know what else amazes me, too? He knows da names of everybody in da whole organization and what da job is dat dey do."

■

By midway through the season Mel had come to admire Bobby Russell and so many of the players who were responding to Bobby's admonitions to persevere despite their seven lost games. Mel sensed the atmosphere of resolve that permeated the post-game quiet of the locker room following those losses, and he reflected on how he still had not heard any player place blame on anyone else even as victories eluded them. He saw how hard they continued to work at practice sessions, and he saw a group of young men who were getting better as athletes, as teammates, and as representatives of the game itself.

When the second half of the season began, their resilience was rewarded. On the road, in Cincinnati, they upset the Bengals 22–14. Defensive cornerback Kirby "Psychiatric" Ward, in the game as part of the Leopards' prevent-defense package during the Bengals last-gasp drive, sealed the win when he intercepted a pass and raced 82 yards for a touchdown.

Kirby, upon streaking into the end zone, considered treating the fans to a viewing of the celebratory dance that he had choreographed in the event he was ever provided an opportunity and a stage for such a performance, but a glance at his team's bench where he caught a glimpse of Coach Russell, whose disapproval of such an act he knew he would incur, persuaded him to just flip the ball to the nearest game official and then serve as host to the embrace of all those howling teammates who were zooming toward him at NASCAR speed.

■

The flight back to Los Angeles after the game was joy-filled for the players and coaches. Their only other win that season had been at home, and so return trips from road games prior to this one had been somber experiences. Not this time. On three separate occasions the pilot's announcement from the cockpit was a plea for "all passengers to please return to your seats and fasten your seat belts." Part of the turbulence aboard was probably the result of the jubilant, change-of-direction roaming up and down the aisle by 345-pound defensive tackle Marcus "Big Butt" Beamer, who was still aglow over having been the recipient of the game ball awarded to him by his teammates in the locker room after the game.

"B.B.B.," as he was affectionately called by his teammates, had had quite a day. He stuffed a Bengals fourth-and-goal quarterback sneak for no gain in the second quarter. He forced and recovered a fumble in the third quarter, thereby helping to set up one of the two field goals the Leopards scored. Add to that the two quarterback sacks he registered during the course of the contest, the biggest one coming early in the fourth quarter when, with the Leopards trailing 14–13, he tackled Bengals signal caller Bjorn Gustafson in the end zone for a safety and the two points that put the Leopards ahead 15–14.

Up in the first class section of the aircraft, where the coaches and the high echelon front office personnel were sitting, the atmosphere was slightly more subdued. Most of the coaches were pouring over the play-by-play and statistical printouts that Director of Media Relations Bert Scott distributed to them after the game.

When that task was completed, the coaches talked briefly with each other about how good it felt to be riding home on this victory lap, but after a few pleasantries of that nature, they reached into their briefcases and pulled out the preliminary scouting report they had on the Detroit Lions, their next opponent. They devoted the remainder of the flight to scrutinizing those reports and to sipping, with the exception of offensive line coach Dudley "Pudge" Steckhauser, on their diet colas. Pudge went instead with his sugar-saturated regular cola drink to go along with the double chocolate brownie a la mode dessert that was being served on the flight.

On most of their flights, Brant and Bobby sat next to each other, and they were able to discuss a variety of team matters. Personnel usage, personnel needs, reasons for having made a crucial call or decision a few hours earlier in the game from which they were now returning home, injury concerns, information on other teams in the league, yesterday's college results, and individual player performances by players on those college teams were but a few of the topics they discussed. Once they were even overheard talking about the presidential election that was still a year away.

Cedric B. Medill did not make many of the road game trips with the team. He was too busy attending to his movie enterprises. When he did find the time to travel with them, however, seating arrangements aboard the plane were adjusted so that Cedric B. and Brant would be sitting next to each other. The Cincinnati game marked just the second time that season that Cedric B. had come along for the ride.

"I guess you brought us some good luck today, Cedric," Brant said soon after they were airborne.

"Well, I don't know if it was me, but we sure did need a ton of luck to win that one, didn't we?"

"I thought we played very opportunistically, though, and when you do that, a lot of lucky things do happen for you," Brant responded.

"Come on, face it Brant: our offense stunk. What did we get—less than 200 yards total? Q.T. throws 26 times and has just nine completions. He gets sacked four times and throws two interceptions on top of that. How are we going to win games that way?"

"Cedric, we did win the game."

"We didn't win it. They lost it."

"There are a lot of ways to look at it," Brant said while feeling like the jury had already made up its mind. "We intercepted Gustafson *three* times, and came up with four sacks ourselves, one of them for a safety. We returned a kickoff for a touchdown; we blocked a field goal, too. Those kinds of things lead to winning football games."

"That stuff's all okay, but we need some offense, period! I get tired of hearing about all that kicking game and defense crap. We've got to light up that scoreboard with some offensive fireworks, damn it! We go all out in the draft for a quarterback like Q.T., and then we only have him throw the ball 26 times during the whole game. I don't get it."

"Cedric, yes, he did throw it 26 times, but he was sacked four times, and he had to scramble out of there and run with the ball three other times. That adds up to 33 called pass plays. Besides that, we were nursing that one-point lead throughout almost all of the fourth quarter, so Bobby kept it on the ground and tried to eat up the clock. I know he didn't want to have a repeat of what happened last week when we tried to throw the ball in a similar situation."

"That Bobby's always got a reason we should not open it up. When is he going to learn that points win games, I wonder?"

"He's learning, and so are the players on this team," Brant said.

"Well, I still wish he'd listen more—and learn more—from Dolbermeier. I called Randy aside in the locker room after the game and had a great chat with him. He agrees with me that we ought to be playing a more daring style on both offense and defense. He told me that he's mentioned that to Russell several times already, but doesn't seem to be getting through to him."

"Believe me, Cedric, Bobby listens to all of his coaches. When it makes sense, he implements their suggestions, but he doesn't always cave in and do everything they present. He has a sound philosophy, and he adheres to it. Most of the coaches understand that perfectly, and, frankly, I feel Randy is off base in spouting off about it outside the staff meeting rooms. Bobby has even cautioned him about it more than once."

"I don't see anything wrong with him talking to me about things like that," Cedric B. said. "After all, I'm the one he gets his paychecks from, and I like getting those insights from on-the-ball coaches like Dolbermeier."

The discussion continued through the remainder of the flight. Brant felt relieved when the pilot announced that they were about to land in Los Angeles, and, as the plane was touching down, he sought to wind up his conversation with Cedric B. by leaving him with some reasons to be encouraged.

"Cedric, this is still a young team; first year in the league," he said. "It takes some time, and honestly, we are getting better, little by little."

"A *little too little* as far as I see it," Cedric said as he gathered his belongings. Brant took a smidgen of solace from noting that at least Cedric B. chuckled a bit at his own clever play-on-words parting comment.

CHAPTER TEN

The following Sunday, at home against the Detroit Lions, the Leopards winning "streak" ended at one. The Lions, in charge throughout the game, cruised to a 34–16 win. Cedric B. was not happy. The Leopards coaches and players refused to be distracted. When meetings and practice resumed, a posting by Coach Russell on the locker room bulletin board summed up the attitude and approach that would continue to drive their efforts:

ADVERSITY IS JUST AN OPPORTUNITY FOR HEROISM

And the adversity with which they had to deal continued to mount, because their quarterback, Q.T. Pye, while scrambling from the pocket midway through the fourth quarter of the game against the Lions, sustained a severe groin injury. Team doctor Frank Quinello informed them that Q.T. would have to miss the next three games. Thirty-six-year-old Colby Hollister, a career backup quarterback, a veteran of fourteen NFL seasons and an alumnus of five other NFL teams, would be the man under center when the Leopards lined up to play that coming Sunday against the Atlanta Falcons.

What a debut Colby had! He completed 16 of 24 pass attempts, three of them for touchdowns. The Leopards, while forcing the anguished Falcons to cough up two fumbles and to throw two inter-ceptions, suffered no turnovers of their own. When it was all over, the Leopards players danced off the field with a 31–17 upset victory. For the second time that season they had won at home.

The following Sunday's challenge was more formidable. They were back on the road again. This time it included a trip all the way across the continent where they would be meeting the Philadelphia Eagles, whose record was 7–4.

Although it didn't turn out to be as pretty as it had been the week before against the Falcons, it was even more gratifying. The statistics were modest, but the victory was monumental. The final score was Los Angeles: 12, Philadelphia: 10. If those Leopards fans in L.A. thought that their ardent cheers at the conclusion of the previous week's win at home were loud, they should have heard the crescendo of boos that cascaded down onto the Eagles players from the painted faces and other fans in the City of Brotherly Love.

■

Post-game locker room interviews were a lot more fun following a victory. First to the podium was Bobby Russell.

"Coach, will Hollister continue to be your quarterback even after Q.T. gets the green light to go again?" Earl Swanson of the *Coachella Valley Enterprise* asked.

"We'll deal with that at the appropriate time," Bobby answered. "Right now we're just enjoying today's win." Bobby looked quickly around the room hoping to spot another raised hand. "Yes, that gentleman over there."

It was Sterling Silverman of the *Barnaby Business Digest*. "Do you think that these two straight wins will have any effect in helping to stimulate corporate sponsorship sales for next season?" he asked.

"You'd have to ask Ross Branson from our front office about that one. Me? I'm just hoping that it helps to stimulate some more first downs on our part to tell you the truth, heh, heh." Bobby added a hasty smile. A few of the reporters smiled in return, but there were no laughs. There were more questions, however, and after responding with a bevy of predictable answers to the ones that he could have predicted were coming, Bobby concluded his remarks by telling the gathered scribes that he would fill them in on more of the specifics about which they had inquired after he and his staff reviewed the game tapes the next day. That was his getaway line. He smiled again, said, "Thanks guys," waved and then exited the room. It appeared that he had at least acquired a good handle on that part of the drill.

When Hollister's turn to be interviewed came, his efforts to be noncommittal equaled those that he had exerted while trying to decipher the Eagles complex pass coverage schemes during the course of the just completed game.

"Do you think your performances these past two weeks have earned you the right to step into the starting role from this point on?" Robert Santiago of *The Pasadena Post* wanted to know.

"That's not my decision to make. I leave that up to the coaches. All I really care about is doing everything I can to help us win, whatever that takes," Colby answered.

"Then you'd be content to sit on the bench if that's what they decide?" Bella DePaul of *The Huntington Beach Herald* asked.

"Well, no one prefers sitting on the bench," Colby said, "but I'd rather concentrate right now on getting ready for our game against the 49ers next week."

So it went. Several more players underwent the process of extolling the game plan and the play of their teammates. It was the usual ho-hum until Bert Scott responded to requests from several members of the media by ushering defensive coordinator Randy Dolbermeier into the interview room.

"Did we kick ass, or what?" Randy exclaimed even before anyone in the room had a chance to ask him a question. The up-til-now wearying members of the press corps lighted up. Scott, standing behind and off to the left of the speaker, tried hard, and with debatable success, to suppress a grimace.

"Well, coach, you guys didn't put many points up there on the scoreboard. It seems like the offense struggled throughout the whole game," Tom Carmichael of *The Santa Monica Ledger-Star* said.

"Yeah, we did look like a bunch of pussy cats on that side of the ball, I'll admit, but that's not my department," Randy answered while rotating the peak of his baseball cap around so that it now faced backwards. "I'm in charge of defense, and we shut them down pretty damn good, didn't we? Don't forget, they didn't score a single point in the second half. After I made those halftime adjustments, I could see, just by looking at their quarterback's face, that it really frustrated them. That's when they started to press, and then my defense *really* took charge."

The buzz continued. The reporters enjoyed prodding this guy. Randy was enjoying it, too, and he concluded his stint in the spotlight by informing them that, after practice the next day, he would make himself available to elaborate on the intricacies of the "battle plan for victory" (as he called it) that he had devised in preparation for today's "assault on the Eagles' Nest." He looked forward to that even more than he was looking forward to the resumption of practice.

■

When Brant Gilbert placed his usual Monday afternoon telephone call to Cedric B. Medill, he was able to utter barely more than one word before Cedric B. interrupted him.

"Hello, Ced-"

"Hey, Brant, wasn't that some performance by our defense yesterday? That Dolbermeier, I keep telling you, is some whale of a coach. Did you read his comments after the game? He is really a piece of work, isn't he?"

Brant decided that this wasn't the time to get into a back-and-forth with Cedric B. about how inappropriate Brant felt that some of Randy's remarks had been, and so he kept it generic. "Our defense *was* outstanding, Cedric," he said. "Randy does do a good job of teaching on the field, and so does that whole staff. Remember, too, that the system they use is the one that Bobby brought in with him from San Diego."

"I still like the way Dolbermeier gets his players so charged up, though. And you know what else I like? He's got a dandy sense of humor, too. Did he ever tell you the one about the priest, the rabbi, and the Presbyterian minister who all meet for the first time in the checkout line at the supermarket?"

"Yeah, several times."

"That was a good one, wasn't it?"

"I'm still chuckling."

Brant, aware of the good mood that Cedric B. was enjoying, raised no other topics. He let the conversation come to an amicable conclusion, and then he turned his attention to scanning that day's waiver wire. Other than the four players around the league who would be going on injured reserve, there wasn't much else on the list that was meaningful or that inspired any action on his part. Tomorrow it might be different.

CHAPTER ELEVEN

The celebration was over. It was time for the Leopards players and coaches to immerse themselves in preparations for the game that coming weekend against the San Francisco 49ers. It was a week during which their level of concentration was keen. Their execution of assignments was sharp. The rising confidence that resulted from their on-the-field successes in the previous two games was apparent. "Bring them on" was the feeling that the players were experiencing.

It was what Dolbermeier was feeling, too.

"Bring them on!" Randy exclaimed when asked by reporter Maury Zeigler of *The Escondido Examiner* about what the Leopards would have to do in order to defend against the 49ers outstanding offensive personnel and production. "We are in a butt-kicking mood, and we're gonna stay that way."

Butts were indeed kicked on that otherwise pleasant Sunday afternoon in the San Francisco Bay Area, but, as it appeared in Mel Herbert's account of the game on Monday morning: "It was the San Francisco 49ers who applied the foot. The curved protuberance just south of the Los Angeles Leopards posterior beltline was the repeated recipient of the 49ers well-aimed adidas," he wrote. The rest of his column elaborated on the "whys" and on the "ouches."

The final score was: San Francisco: 38, Los Angeles: 7. The longest winning streak in L.A. Leopards history—two straight—had come to an abrupt finish. The season's record was now an unimpressive 4-9. Medill was not happy with Russell. Russell was not happy with Dolbermeier.

Bobby called Randy into his office early Monday afternoon, and he told Randy to knock it off. Randy responded by saying that he meant no harm, and that he was only trying to get his players fired up.

"Leave that to me," Bobby said. "Just teach them how to play.

You do a good job of that, and that's what really counts."

"Okay. Anything else?"

"Nope. That's all. Let's go back to work."

Randy popped out of his chair, pivoted, and strode out of the room closing the door to Bobby's office with just a trifle more force than was necessary.

■

Cedric B. dispensed with the usual cordialities during his post-game talk with Gilbert on the Monday following the game against the 49ers.

"We're four and nine now." Cedric B. said. "We aren't even going to have a break-even season. Even if we win all three of our remaining games, we'll wind up seven and nine. That doesn't cut it."

"Cedric, I know I keep repeating it, but we are an expansion team. It's not realistic to expect a winning record the first year from a team that has to start from scratch like we have."

"Well, I think we ought to set our sights higher than that. We should take an optimistic, aggressive view of things the way I keep hearing Dolbermeier express it."

"He overstepped his grounds last week, Cedric, with all that pre-game ranting, and Bobby has told him so, too, in no uncertain terms."

"He did? That's stupid! What he ought to be doing is talking tough like Dolbermeier does. Maybe it would rub off on his players for a change."

"Please don't forget, Cedric, we've won three out of our last five games."

"All I know is that we've won only four all season. And about that 'expansion team' excuse, Brant, how do you explain the Portland Pioneers? They've got *five* wins. That's not good enough either, but it's better than what we've done."

"They have done an outstanding job up there, in my opinion," Brant answered. "And this isn't an excuse, but if you study it, you'll see that they haven't played near as many teams with winning records as we have. Also, the season isn't over yet. We still may catch them."

"We'll see."

"We are getting better, Cedric, and we're going to continue to get better. Yesterday was bad; it was a setback. But it was against a damn good team. I bet we'll bounce back."

"Hey, no betting allowed in the NFL," Cedric B. said before hanging up. Brant did note, with some sense of relief, that Cedric B. almost always took a light-hearted stab at defusing the tension at the conclusion of any of their conversations that had taken on contentious overtones.

CHAPTER TWELVE

Although the St. Louis Rams were next on the Leopards schedule, the greatest obstacle with which Bobby Russell had to contend leading up to that game was not the opponent they were about to play. It was having to cope with a bugaboo he had been urging his players to avoid since that first day they reported to training camp back in July: "distractions." And nothing is more distracting than "a quarterback controversy."

"Coach, is Q.T. healthy?" Guido Capriano of *The Torrance Tattler* inquired at Tuesday's media session five days prior to the game against the Rams.

"Our doctors have given him the go-ahead to begin practicing again," Bobby said. "We'll see how he handles it tomorrow."

"If he is okay, will he be the starter?"

"We're not ready this early in the week to make any decisions about that yet." As Bobby was finishing his sentence, he silently castigated himself for having just added the fuel necessary to keep the griddle hot all week long. Then he consoled himself as he realized that no matter how he might have responded, the media's "have we got a story here" mentality would result in keeping that kettle boiling. It was their job. He understood, and so, even though he didn't like it, he went with the flow.

"Do you have a specific target day for reaching a decision?" It was the third time that the same reporter, Mike Michaels of *The Redondo Redundant*, directed an inquiry on that subject to Bobby.

"No. Hey, folks, I've got a question of my own. How come no one ever writes about a left guard controversy?" A few smiles, but no laughs.

When it came their turn to be questioned, Q.T. Pye and Colby Hollister also had to wrestle with how to respond courteously and in a manner that wasn't unsettling to teammates and coaches. Problem is, there was no right answer.

∎

Despite the controversy, there was one person in the Leopards organization who had already made up his mind about who the starter should be on Sunday. That was Cedric B. Medill.

"Russell's got to get Q.T. back in there," Cedric B. told Brant.

"This is really a head coach's decision to make, Cedric, and honestly, I haven't pressured him about it. He'll let us know as soon as it shapes up during this week's practices."

"Why in heaven's name would he even think about playing some old has-been like Hollister when he's got the No. 1 pick in the whole damned draft on his team; a guy, by the way, I gave a contract to that's worth more than what I made on our first night's take when my studio released *Dancing On Mars* last month. Have you seen that movie?"

"Not yet. But to answer your first question, Bobby just cares about what gives us the best chance to win a game, and he's the person who's in the best position to determine that. He tells me that he's not confident yet about how ready Q.T will be after missing three weeks of practice or even of how ready he'll be to function physically at full speed. Also, please remember, we've won two of our last three games with Hollister at quarterback."

"Oh boy! More reasons to do the wrong thing."

"I'll be talking with Bobby about it after practice tomorrow and I'll let you know then what his thinking is. Okay?"

"Well, you don't need until tomorrow to know what *my* thinking is, do you?

"Right on!" Brant said, and as he prepared to say goodbye, Cedric B. interrupted.

"Oh, Brant."

"Yes."

"*Dancing On Mars* is showing at the Movie Mecca Complex in the Century City Mall. Go see it. You'll really enjoy it."

"Now that is something that I can handle a lot easier than all that other stuff we've been talking about," Brant said.

■

After practice almost every day during the season, Bobby would stop by Brant's office. Most of the time their meetings were brief. They'd do a fast review of the day's practice, scan the waiver wire together, address any injury and player personnel concerns, and then they'd part so that they could each get back to doing what needed their more individual attention.

On the Wednesday leading up to the game against the Rams, when Bobby walked into the room and before any words were spoken, they both knew what the main topic of discussion was going to be.

"How do you think he looked?" Brant asked even before Bobby finished twisting the cap off his bottle of water.

"From a health standpoint, pretty good. Q.T. moved well. Didn't show any lingering signs of his injury, and his overall conditioning level was really better than what I had been expecting," Bobby said. "That's the good part. It's obvious, though, that he's rusty, and he did struggle a bit when it came to reading coverages and to using the right audibles at the right time. Maybe it'll get better as the week goes along, but, man, we don't have that kind of time. We've got to give the heavy work to whoever it is that's gonna start."

"Which means what?"

"I'm more comfortable with Colby right now. I think he gives us the best chance to win this game. I know, Brant, that in the long run Q.T. is the best bet for the future of this team. Right now though, he's still got a long way to go."

"Well, Bobby, this happens to be a team—if you will allow me to use the old cliché—that is building for the future."

"Sometimes, Brant, I think that's a classic example of an incomplete sentence. Teams with a philosophy like that appear to me to be building for the future—*coach!*"

"Good point. But there is also another important point that I'm sure you are aware of. You know what Cedric B. wants, don't you?"

They continued to discuss the matter, and, when their talk finally concluded, Bobby conceded that this wasn't an issue worthy of his taking an obstinate stand. He, himself, had felt merely inclined— not convinced—to go with Colby Hollister. With either quarterback playing, this current Leopards team would be a considerable under-dog, and for sound reasons, too.

On Sunday afternoon against the Rams, with Q.T. Pye back in the lineup as the starting quarterback, Cedric B. Medill was happy. He was, at least, until the final outcome of the game: Rams: 28, Leopards: 14.

The Leopards were now 4–10 and, with just two weeks remaining in the regular season, the Denver Broncos, sporting the best record in the NFL, were coming to town.

CHAPTER THIRTEEN

Late in the second quarter the Leopards were hanging in there against the Broncos. They trailed Denver by a score of 3–0 and, although the Leopards were playing at an intense level, there were additional factors that contributed to the score being so close. Coming into the game, the Broncos, with a 12–2 record, had already clinched the home field advantage throughout the upcoming playoffs, and so their head coach, Norb "Headstrong" Armstrong, decided that he would not play several of their star players whom he felt needed a break from the season-long pounding and pressures. He wanted them to enter the playoffs rested and healthy.

Broncos starting quarterback Elroy Jonathan was on the sidelines holding a clipboard. His star receiver, Donnell "Rocket" Gibraltar, was standing next to him, leaning in and beaming for the TV camera whenever it was turned in their direction. Also getting a well-deserved day off was the NFL's leading ground gainer and most highly compensated running back, Darius "Paycheck" Danning.

On their final series in the first half, the Leopards put together their first serious offensive drive of the game. They moved from their own 30-yard line into Denver territory, and then Q.T. Pye, on a quarterback scramble, reeled off a gain of 22 yards. The ball was now in field goal position at the Broncos' 21-yard line. Q.T. was also at the 21-yard line, but he was in a remain-on-the-ground position. He had reinjured his groin. He was out for the remainder of this game and for the following week's season finale.

After Q.T. was transported to the locker room on the injury cart, Leopards place kicker, Garland "Uprights" Updyke, booted the three-pointer that tied the game at 3–3 as the first half ended.

When the second half began, Hollister was at quarterback for the Leopards. He was the only second-stringer on the field for L.A.

When it came to playing the backups, however, Denver went all out. In addition to the marquee stars whom they held out in the first half, the Broncos now sat down almost every starter on their roster. Resting them—and getting good game experience for their reserve players who needed it—was their primary objective now.

That was fine with the Leopards. So fine, in fact, that they came away with their fifth win of the season. The final score was: Leopards: 17, Broncos: 10. In the locker rooms after the game, the Leopards were hootin' and hollerin'; the Broncos players and coaches were yawnin'.

■

On that same weekend, the Portland Pioneers were pummeled in their game against the 49ers. Both L.A. and Portland would be entering their final game of the season with identical 5–10 records. The problem for the Leopards was that they'd be facing the Dallas Cowboys in Dallas. It was a victory the Cowboys needed in order to ensure that they would be in the playoffs. The Pioneers were at home against the Carolina Panthers, one of the four teams in the league with a poorer record than either of the two expansion teams.

The Pioneers won their game and finished 6–10. The Leopards lost, leaving them at 5–11. Now it was Medill who was hootin' and hollerin', but it wasn't because he was happy.

"Come on, Brant, tell me straight. Can we be a winning team with Russell as our coach?"

"If we are patient, Cedric, he will get the job done. I have a lot of confidence in Bobby."

"Well, damn it, I'm not patient, don't want to be, and besides that, I don't have much confidence in him, either."

"We've had one draft. We've tried to go with a rookie quarter-back and with a system that's totally new to almost everyone on the team. Bobby has kept these guys focused and playing hard despite all the difficulties they've had to deal with. And, Cedric, we have gotten better. Think about it. During the second half of the season we won half of our games; we went four and four."

"If he wasn't so damned conservative all the time we probably would have won more games," Cedric B. said. "I know I keep harping on it, but if he'd pay a little more attention to what Dolbermeier says, he might start logging a few more wins *and* create a lot more excitement."

"You can't help *but* listen to Randy," Brant said. "He keeps sounding off all the time. Too much, in my opinion."

"I don't agree there," Cedric B. said. "I talk to him almost every week. Sometimes he even calls me, and he makes sense to me, especially about wanting to see us play a more aggressive style."

Brant felt it would be best if he steered the conversation elsewhere. "Speaking of aggressive, Cedric, I see where your *Dancing On Mars* is up for a number of Academy Award nominations."

"It sure is. I know you still haven't gone yet, but just wait until you see that Hattie Sombrero and Gustavo Bacchanalia do their dance routine. She is unbelievable, and so is he. And now I'm going to ask you something one more time. When in the hell are you going to see that movie?"

"Now that our season is over, I'm going to go this week."

"Promise?"

"Promise."

It was a promise that Brant kept. He did enjoy that cinematic extravaganza every bit as much as Cedric B predicted he would. What he had a hard time understanding, however, was all the thump-bang-explode-screech-swerve-leap-spin-din turmoil blasted at the assembled popcorn gobblers in the audience by the coming attractions trailers that didn't afford anyone a clue as to what those movies might be about.

CHAPTER FOURTEEN

Mel Herbert's post-season assessment of Bobby Russell's performance as coach of the Leopards during their first season in the NFL differed from the one being voiced by Cedric B. Medill. Mel hailed it as a commendable example of leadership under daunting circumstances, and he elaborated by specifying all the signs he saw that signaled how the Leopards under Russell's tutelage were heading in the right direction.

To the delight of (or maybe as a result of some instruction from —who knows?) Sports Editor Carroll Blumenthal of the *Los Angeles Guardian*, there was a contrary opinion expressed in a companion column written by Mel's co-worker at the paper, Jordy Nerdmann. Criticism was Jordy's shtick. He was good at it, too.

Beyond his expertise at playing video game football, Jordy's participation as a competitor in the gridiron sport had been confined to one game of choose-up touch football when he was a fifth grader. After that, he decided to retire at an early age, and thereafter he confined his athletic endeavors to playing shuffleboard and checkers.

Although he never played a down of tackle football in his life, Nerdmann prided himself on becoming the self-appointed authority on who wasn't really hard-nosed enough to play in the NFL. He also derived great satisfaction from knowing that there was no one as capable as he was in skewering a coach who didn't have the guts to make a damn decision—*Right Now!*—about who was going to be the starting quarterback.

The essence of his season recap, the one that appeared opposite Mel's, was that the Leopards were destined to never become winners with Russell as their coach. It was so obvious, he contended, what their game strategy and tactics were going to be. "How can a coach always be so predictable? How can his game plan always be so predictable? How can the outcome of his games always be so predictable?" he asked in the first paragraph and then again in the final paragraph of his critique.

When Cedric B. finished reading Nerdmann's column, he placed a call to Brant in order to be certain that Brant had not missed out on a true expert's insights.

"Did you read that sharp, astute analysis of our season in the newspaper by Jordy Nerdmann?" Cedric B. asked

"Yes, I sure did."

"Well, what did you think?"

"I thought it was predictable," Brant said.

■

On Wednesday evening, three days after the Leopards' first season ended, the Three Mustachekateers got together at Trader Vic's restaurant for a pleasant repast and for some reminiscing about note-worthy events that had occurred during the year.

"I read your article, Mel, da one you wrote about Coach Russell," Joe Skoronski said. "I liked it a lot, and, ya know, I really do like dat guy, too. He treats everybody in da whole organization real good; like dey really matter. Da players know, too, dat he's gonna treat 'em real fair, but dat when he says dere are rules dat ya gotta follow, he ain't no patsy if you ain't listenin'."

"I didn't get the impression that he's a big rules and regulations man," Mel said.

"No, no, he ain't one a dose 'My way or da hideaway' types. I dint mean dat. I'm talkin' about when he—and da whole damn team, too, ta tell ya da troot—got fed up wit dat dingbat 'Saggy Pants' Kendall bein' late for practices all da time and gettin' inta fights at dat Hermione and Henrietta's Hangout Lounge place and den drivin' drunk when he smashed inta dat parked police car at tree in da mornin'. Coach dint care if dat he was our number one runnin' back. He cut his ass, and we was a better team for it after dat."

"What I can't understand," Zig Zag said, "is why no other team claimed Kendall on waivers. He's got a career 4.4 average yards per carry. That's third best in the NFC for players in the league five years or more."

"Dat's a mute point," Joe said, "and I'll tell you why. When he keeps comin' up wit all dose fragrant violations of da rules, he finally wears out his welcome mat, and den he leaves a bad taste in everyone's mout."

"And probably a bad smell, too," Mel said.

"Could be," Joe said, "But don't get me wrong. Coach sees ta it dat we got mostly real high characters on dis team."

"I see that all the time," Zig Zag said. "In fact, did you guys know that tomorrow Beau Ralston is going to visit some YMCA in the inner city and give a talk about good behavior to a bunch of kids?"

"Yeah, I know dat," Joe answered. "In fact, I even grabbed Beau aside and gave him some advice. He talks alla da time wit dat real down sout suddern accent, and so I told him dat if he wants dese kids ta be able ta unnerstan' him, he's gonna have ta announciate his words real clear. You know what I mean?"

"Sometimes," Mel said.

■

The season may have been over, but for Brant Gilbert and Bobby Russell it definitely was not vacation time. Player evaluations came first. Each position coach, during a full staff meeting with Brant and Bobby, reviewed the performance of all the players at the position he had coached during the season, summarizing his remarks by assigning a grade to each of those players. The position coach specified also whether that player was on the rise or on the decline.

Answers to some oversimplified sum-it-up questions usually concluded each coach's report: Can he win for us? If he's not a starter, is he a player who provides good depth at the position? Do I question his work ethic? Is he a good run defender but an inadequate third-down pass rusher? Does he look like his father but play like his mother?

The Leopards Director of Player Personnel, Butler Johnson, was also in attendance at that meeting as was the team's chief contract negotiator, Tim Underdorf. So were salary cap administrator Jess

Littleton, and Head Trainer Eddie Carpentierie. Eddie was there to update everyone at the meeting on the physical condition, readiness, and any other medical concerns relative to each player. Tim and Jess were present so that they could prepare to deal with all the financial considerations affecting contract negotiations that the coaches never would be able to (or care to) understand.

When those meetings concluded, Butler Johnson and the assistant coaches, along with the team's talent scouts, were dispatched to destinations around the country to watch practices leading up to the numerous college all-star games that featured that year's top senior draft prospects.

Brant and Bobby would then retire to Brant's office for their own one-on-one review. They needed to answer three questions:

1. Where are we now?
2. Where do we want to go?
3. How are we going to get there?

The agenda was simple. The answers *were* not.

"Brant, right now my biggest concern isn't player personnel," Bobby said.

"I know where you're heading," Brant said.

"I'm glad that you do because I think you'll understand. I'm talking about Randy. Is that what you were thinking?"

"Yep."

"He's been a problem, and he's getting worse."

"I know. You've talked to him several times. How does he respond?"

"He says the right things—sort of, anyway—when just the two of us meet in my office, but I know now he doesn't mean it at all. I'm not the only one who feels this way. He belittles other coaches on the staff, sometimes right in front of the players. He's got a foul mouth, and he uses it around the building too darn much. He's rude to our secretaries, and even some of the players have seen that happen."

"I've noticed," Brant said, "I've even mentioned it to Mr. Medill, but he just waves it off. He likes the guy."

"Well, I'm totally fed up with him, and although I don't like doing something like this after just one year, I want to get him out of here."

"Fire him?"

"Call it whatever you want."

"Bobby, it won't fly. I know. Mr. Medill will never go along, and if you even bring that subject up to him, I'm afraid you'll be making waves that might wash *you* away. Please, see what you can do to try to make it work. Randy does do a good job of teaching fundamentals, at least, doesn't he?"

"Yes, he does," Bobby said. He realized that Brant's cautionings had merit. "Damn. Okay, Brant, I hear you. I'll try, but I'm not going to take any kid gloves approach. Our team deserves better, and Randy is going to hear that from me loud and clear. I appreciate your listening and everything you told me. Thanks again."

"You're welcome. Let's go."

Brant and Bobby zipped up their briefcases and headed for the airport. It was time to join the rest of the coaches and scouts at some of those all-star game practices.

■

Preparation for the draft was in full gear now. So was the monitoring of off-season conditioning workouts for the healthy players and of rehabilitation activities for those who were recovering from injuries they had sustained during the season.

The study of free-agent players from other teams was now a top priority for Brant. Determining how he'd be able to fit any of them in while grappling with the restraints imposed by the team's delicate salary cap situation required him to spend more time with financial gurus Underdorf and Littleton than he did with his wife, Noreen. She told him not to fret, that she understood, and that she would fill her lonely hours by visiting the chic boutiques on Rodeo Drive in Beverly Hills instead. For company she would bring along her dearly beloved MasterCard.

After attending the all-star games and the Indianapolis Combine, where workouts for that year's top-rated draft-eligible players took place, the coaches then turned their attention to changes that they might make in their offensive, defensive, and kicking game playbooks and in their practice procedures. Discussions in those staff meetings often became heated, especially with a name-calling table-pounder like Dolbermeier in the room, and they would be resolved only by some timely—and not always popular—decisions that would have to be made by Russell.

On the last weekend in April the college draft takes place, and for the full month leading up to that over-hyped burlesque show everyone at team headquarters was busy girding for "D-Day." Following the draft came a series of mini-camps—some that included rookies only and some with the full squad participating. And then, once the NFL schedule for the coming fall was made public, the coaching staff needed to devote many intense hours to the study of, and to the preliminary game planning for, the opponents against whom they would be competing once the ball was kicked off for the season opener in September.

The drawing up of precise training camp player meeting agendas and practice routines also took countless hours of fine-tuning by the coaches before finally, in late June, they were paroled for a couple of weeks of vacation. Then, in mid-July, it was time for the coaches to report to training camp to begin again that seven-months-long, seven-days-a-week, 17-hours-a-day quest for the Lombardi Trophy.

CHAPTER FIFTEEN

A welcome getaway from the rigors of the post-season activities for head coaches and for general managers came every year in late March when they and their families were invited to join the team owners and other front office personnel and their families for a four-day weekend at some posh resort where the annual NFL Owners Meetings were being held. Following the L.A. Leopards' initial season in the league, those meetings took place at the elegant Breakers Hotel and Resort in Palm Beach, Florida.

The "break at The Breakers" for Brant and Bobby was a refreshing experience. There were some business meetings that they attended, but those dealt with issues of primary interest to the commissioner, to the owners, and to the few men in the room who were wearing suits and ties.

The meetings that interested Bobby the most, and in which he participated, were those that dealt with proposed rules changes and interpretations. Those sessions plodded on and on. Contrary opinions, convincingly presented, dominated those discussions until finally the only sensible resolution available was reached. The motion would be sent back to committee for further study and refinement.

It wasn't what was being transacted in the meeting rooms, however, that made it so enjoyable and rejuvenating for all the coaches and GMs. There were numerous social events, as well. The chance to mingle with other coaches and GMs, with team owners and front office personnel, and with the members of their families was what they all came to relish. It was here they learned that those folks from all those other teams were human beings, too. They weren't the enemy; they were worthy opponents in a sport, the merits of which, they all conceded, transcended gate receipts.

On their first evening at the Breakers, while attending a poolside cocktail party hosted by the ABC Monday Night Football broadcasting team, Bobby and his wife, Cindy, sat down at the same table where René and Lilly Napoleon, along with Portland Pioneers Head Coach Denzel Jackson and his wife, Vanessa, were enjoying some margaritas and hors d'oeuvres.

"Looks good," Bobby said.

"Are you talking about us or the refreshments?" Denzel asked.

Bobby had started to reach for one of the goodies on the platter at the table, but upon hearing Denzel's query he hesitated. "I think he's going to plead the Fifth Amendment," Cindy said.

"I think he's going to plead for that little cracker with the petite crab cake and avocado moussé on it," Lilly said.

"Now that is the best scouting report I've heard all year," Bobby countered. "No wonder you finished with a better record than we did."

"By one stinking game. Big deal," Denzel said. "All that means is that in this year's draft you get to make your selection one spot ahead of us. You'll probably grab Deuce Smithers, won't you?"

"Yeah, sure. You know darn well he is gone on the first pick as soon as the bell rings to start the draft. I don't know if I've ever seen another defensive lineman like him. He's going to Buffalo unless they do something stupid by going for a quarterback like that Brian Flowers. Even if they do, Carolina will throw them a kiss, and then they'll take Deuce with the second pick in the draft."

"No matter what," Denzel said, "you still get to pick just before we do, and I can just see you grabbing the guy that we'd want most."

"I promise you that we will not take Tyrell Jenkins with our first-round pick," Bobby said.

"Gee, thanks. We've got him on our board as a possible sixth rounder."

"Sacre bleu," René interjected. "Can we, si'l vous plais, steal just a few moments away from talking football so that I can apprise you of the magnificent architectural majesty that will grace the new stadium we are planning for construction in Portland? That's if funding for it, of course, passes a vote of the state legislature?"

"By all means," Bobby said. "You go right ahead. Please excuse me for a minute, though. I've got to use the men's room."

"Me, too," Denzel said.

On their trip back from the restroom, Bobby and Denzel employed their best delay-of-game tactics by stopping to exchange wisdom—and a few good-natured jibes—with many of the other partygoers. By the time they did arrive back at their own table, Lilly, Cindy, and Vanessa were gushing about how the façade on the projected new stadium might prove to be the most startling innovation to hit the game since the introduction of the forward pass.

■

During the days that followed, Bobby and Cindy got to know the Napoleons and the Jacksons quite well. They all clicked. Bobby was already aware of Denzel's well-respected coaching abilities. After all, each of them had been in the league for over a dozen years before they became head coaches for the first time just a year ago. Now Bobby was learning about Denzel's intelligence and about his winning personality. Denzel's impressions of Bobby mirrored those that Bobby had of him.

Cindy and Vanessa hit it off, too. Cindy, intrigued by how Vanessa had learned to communicate in French with Lilly and René, embarked on her own fun-filled four-day crash course *en la langue française* with Vanessa, Lilly, and René as her instructors.

Jackson's grasp of the game was no surprise to Bobby, but he was astounded by how well versed Lilly Napoleon was in understanding how a successful general manager in the NFL should operate. It wasn't just her ability in scouting for good players, picking good coaches, handling finances, goosing up ticket sales, and a long list of additional administrative responsibilities at which she had already proven herself that impressed him. It was her knack for creating a cooperative, high-morale, pride-in-being-a-Pioneer mentality among all the people in the employ of the Portland Pioneers that made her special. Well, that wasn't *all*, Bobby noted. She was a looker, too.

At the various meetings and social functions, and during idle moments in the hotel lobby or at the swimming pool, Bobby gained an appreciation for how eclectic a group that gathering of owners was. Some were all business, concerned only with spreadsheets and the bottom line, while others were enamored by the realization that they were major players in "the game." Some were sourpusses; some were jokesters. Some were friendly, and some were too preoccupied with their cell phones to notice that you were in the area. Some wore ties and polished leather shoes while others wore Hawaiian shirts and flip-flops. Some envisioned themselves as surrogate coaches, and some were none of the above.

The ladies in attendance, mostly wives of owners, coaches, and front office managers, were just as diverse and interesting a group. Bobby and Cindy first became aware of that when, while going through the buffet line at breakfast one morning, they began to chat with Ricky Epstein, son of Baltimore Ravens owner Sheldon Epstein. Ricky invited them to join him and his wife at their table, and they were pleased to do it.

Upon meeting Ricky's wife, who had gone to her seat before the other three went through the line, they were even more pleased. She was bright, witty, mannerly, and totally loveable. They understood why Ricky would have fallen in love with her seven years earlier when the two of them were attending graduate school at the Massachusetts Institute of Technology.

Ricky's journey to M.I.T. required a one-day auto trip north from Baltimore up to Boston. Her ride to the same destination began when she boarded an airplane in her home city for a flight that would take her halfway around the world. Miss Ming Toy Chow was from Shanghai, China. She was now Mrs. Ming Toy Epstein from Baltimore, Maryland.

■

Members of the media were always in attendance at the NFL Owners Meetings. For them, too, it was a semi-vacation. Even the coaches, now relaxed and a few of them fresh from having had their contracts renewed, were approachable and responsive.

Mel Herbert always enjoyed being there, and this year was no exception. At noon on his third day there, while strolling down a hallway leading to the main lobby, Mel was startled when he saw coming toward him none other than "Malaprop Joe" Skoronski.

"What are you doing here? You didn't buy one of these teams, did you?" Mel asked.

"Not unless ya loan me da money," Joe answered. "You know why I'm here."

"I do not. I guess I'll have to read all about it in *The Wall Street Journal*."

"Boy, if dey write a story like dat about me, den I'm gonna go buy me a prescription ta dat paper."

"In the meantime, I still don't know. C'mon, tell me. What's the deal?"

"I taught ya knew. Ya know da lecture dat Dave Rebbick, da Jets aquipment guy, was supposed to give about safe aquipment and da new rules about helmets and lotsa udder stuff? Well Dave, he got real sick at da last minute, and dey had ta put some kinduva stunt inta his coronation artery, and den he couldn't come ta da meetins. I hear he's doin' real good now, dough."

"They asked you to pinch hit for him, is that it?" Mel asked.

"Dat's right. Dey called me, and I caught a plane ride here last night. Dey flew me here first class, too, where ya get all da free wine ya want and a real good movie pitcher show dat comes wit it. And even when dat heavyweight lug sittin' in fronta me moved his seat back inta dat inclining position, da top of it didn't bang me under da chin like it does back dere in da economic section."

"That was nice. When do you give your talk?"

"I just finished wit it, and dat's why I'm headin' now over ta da lunchroom. I'm starvin'."

Mel accompanied Joe to the patio coffee shop where, during their midday meal, they resumed their conversation. "So," Mel asked, "how did it go?"

"Real good. Dey assed me a whole buncha questions, and I tink I came up wit all da right answers. I musta told a coupla jokes, too, cause I heard dem laugh at me a few times. And at da end, dey clapped for me, too."

"Sounds like they treated you real well."

"Dey sure did, and lemme tell ya, somma dem was really interested in how da equipment works, especially dat Ming Toy Pepstein lady. She is really nice. And smart, too. She told me dat she grew up in China, but man, she can talk in American almost good as me."

"That's hard to believe," Mel said.

"Yeah, she really can. Besides dat, dat lady knows alla da little differences between concussions and contusions and alla dose udder confusions."

"Are you sure, or is it just some illusions that bring you to those conclusions?"

"Hey, whatna heck ya tryin' ta do; get me all mixed up or sumpthin'?"

CHAPTER SIXTEEN

When the league meetings were over it was back to the grind because on the last weekend of April the NFL's college draft would take place. Preparation for the draft was intense work, but everyone acknowledged that it was a lot of fun, too. No one enjoyed participating in the process more than Cedric B. Medill.

"We're going after Chase Banks, that wide receiver from LSU I've been hearing so much about, aren't we?" Cedric B. asked Brant, Bobby, and Director of Player Personnel Butler Johnson during a visit one week before the draft.

"We like him," Brant said, "but he's the 12th ranked player on our board. We've got the fifth pick in the first round."

"And Mr. Medill, we really need to strengthen our defense," Bobby added. "I've been keeping my fingers crossed hoping that Junior Hooper, that defensive end from Tennessee, is still there in the fifth slot."

"Oh, please fellas," Cedric B. said. "Are we going to start talking defense again? We need to get some help at the receiver position if we are going to give Q.T. any kind of a chance to realize all that potential we saw in him. And also, if I may add, if we are going to realize any return on the pile of money I invested in order to sign him."

"Actually, sir, we do have some pretty good receivers on the team right now," Johnson said. "Both Pierson and Showalter ran the 40-yard dash in the low 4.4s at the Combine when they came out a few years ago. They've both got good hands, and they run good routes."

"Yeah, sure," Cedric B. said. "We've got Pee Wee Pierson and Peanuts Showalter. Neither one of those guys is as tall as I am, and I'm not even as tall as my wife."

"Our No. 3 wideout, James Fleet, is 6'4"," Bobby said.

"Fleet? If there ever was a person who was misnamed, he's the one," Cedric B. said. "Talk about lacking speed. I'll bet you that Fats Domino can run up Blueberry Hill faster than Fleet runs the 40."

"Honestly, Mr. Medill, the best way for us to help Q.T. right now is to build a defense strong enough so that he isn't always having to play catch up," Bobby said. "That's when the other team knows that we've got to be throwing the ball, and that's when they bring all that pressure."

"I'd rather build an *offense* that makes it necessary for the *other* team to have to be the one playing catch up," Cecil B. countered. "Heck, I even talked to *our* defensive coordinator about it, and when I told him what I was thinking, he told me that he agreed with me wholeheartedly."

"Ouch!" Bobby said to himself when he bit his tongue in order to squelch the response that had welled up inside him. He left the talking to Brant.

"Cedric, you spoke with Randy Dolbermeier about whom we ought to draft?"

"Darn right. He called me, and I'm glad he did. It might help if you fellows conferred with him a bit more on matters like this, too, but I keep getting the impression from him that you sort of tune him out."

■

Draft day arrived. The Buffalo Bills, with the first pick in the first round, selected defensive end Deuce Smithers from Virginia Tech. When ESPN's chief panelist, Clint Fuhrman, who had just received a phone call from an insider at the Bills headquarters, broke the news even before Commissioner Paul Rogers reached the podium to make the announcement, half of the patrons at the Anchor Bar in downtown Buffalo thrust their fists into the air, yelled "Yo Baby!" and then gave vent to a rousing, discordant singing of "The Bills Make Me Want To Shout."

The other half hurled their Bills Backers caps onto the floor and screamed out in disgust over Bills General Manager Will Pulleyam's obvious idiocy in having passed up quarterback Brian Flowers. Both contingents then ordered another round of beer.

The Carolina Panthers passed on Flowers, also. So did the Jacksonville Jaguars. The Arizona Cardinals were now on the clock, and following their pick, it would be the Leopards' turn.

All through that final week leading up to the draft, Brant, Bobby, Butler, and Cedric B. had continued to hassle over whom they should take. Bobby, Butler, and Brant wanted to go for defensive lineman Junior Hooper while Cedric B. remained firm in his conviction that wide receiver Chase Banks was their guy.

The Arizona Cardinals solved part of the problem for them. With the fourth pick in the draft they selected Hooper. Brant flipped his pen into the air, and Butler fumbled it to the floor in his feeble attempt to catch it when gravity brought it down his way. Bobby banged his hand against the desktop. Cedric B. smiled.

"Boy, are they dumb," he said. "I guess we go for Banks now, don't we?"

"Picking him at No. 5 is really a reach," Brant said. Eleven minutes remained of the fifteen that each team was allotted when it was their turn to pick.

"Then let's reach."

Brant did reach. He reached for the telephone and inquired of the teams that picked sixth, seventh, and eighth in the first round about whether they would be willing to give their current first round pick plus some additional compensation later in the draft for the rights to move up to the fifth spot currently held by the Leopards.

There were no takers, but with less than four minutes to go, Brant's phone rang. It was J.A. Jones, general manager of the New York Jets, on the line.

"Brant, I heard from Allen Bruce of the Buccaneers that you might be willing to trade your choice." J.A. said.

"Yeah, that's right. You have No. 10 in this round, I see. We'd be willing to switch places with you depending on what else we'd be able to get."

"What are you looking for?" J.A. asked.

"Well, you've got two picks in the third round: the 10th and the 22nd. We'd want the 10th."

"Sorry. Can't do that. How about we offer you our No. 22 in the third round? That's as high as we're going to be able to go."

"Give me a second to talk it over with Mr. Medill and with Butler and Bobby," Brant said. "Stay on, please."

Brant turned to Cedric B. and explained the terms.

"If we go all the way down to the 10th pick in this round, I'm afraid we'll lose out on Banks," Cedric B. said.

"No one can guarantee anything, Cedric," Brant said, "but I'd wager anything that he'll still be there. We've projected different players and at different positions, too, for the teams that pick sixth, seventh, eighth, and ninth."

"What if the *Jets* go ahead and take him with that pick we're sending to them?" Cedric B. said. "He'd cruise into New York and become Chase 'Manhattan' Banks, and we'd wind up with some dodo who'll steer me one step closer to bankruptcy."

"I'm almost certain that the *Jets* would be moving up so that they can pick Brian Flowers," Brant said. "They need a quarterback." Brant held his breath, hoping that he had not inspired Cedric B. to say that the Leopards should be the ones to grab Brian Flowers first. Cedric B. stayed on target, however.

"Chase Banks is the guy I want. How many times do I have to say it?"

Forty-one seconds to go. "I think we'd get him at the 10th spot, and then we'd get a darn good prospect with that extra pick in the third round, too," Brant said.

"Oooohkay. Go ahead."

Brant put the phone back into action. "J.A., you've got a deal. What do you say?"

"Deal done," J.A. responded.

Eight seconds remained on the clock when the New York Jets selected quarterback Brian Flowers with the fifth pick in the first round. The debate still rages over who was more elated: the Jets fans or Brant Gilbert.

The Portland Pioneers were next, and they went for 6'8" offensive tackle Maurice "House" Zanzibar. ESPN's Del Piper called that one the steal of the draft thus far.

The Detroit Lions, with the seventh pick in the draft, startled everyone when their selection was announced. It was Decibel "Bad Rap" Howling.

"Whoa!" Cedric B. said. "Who is this guy, anyway? I don't even see his name up there on our board."

"He's not on our board for a lot of reasons, Cedric. Look over there on the back wall at our 'Do Not Draft' list. That's where we've got him listed."

"Is he any good? He sure must be if someone wants him that high in the draft."

"Yes, he's got tons of talent. He's also got a history of drug abuse and a million other problems with the law and with his teammates. He may have the size, the speed, and the ability, but I guarantee you that he'll wind up at the police station and in the courtroom more times than he will in the end zone."

"One way or the other I don't really care about Howling," Cedric B. said. "Banks is the guy I want."

Now it was Houston's turn, and they went for 5'8" running back "Wiggly" Wrigley Wiggins from Kansas State.

It was getting close. Cincinnati was next and after that the Leopards would finally get to choose their man. The Bengals dawdled. Five minutes passed. Then 10, 11, 12. Still no decision.

"They know who they want," Cedric B. grumbled. "Why in the hell don't they just announce it already?"

Butler leaned over and whispered to Brant through clenched teeth, "Maybe they're trying to make a trade."

The Leopards Assistant Director of Media Relations, Dino Kladoris, who was in the draft room manning the team's direct telephone connection with NFL draft headquarters in New York City, overheard Butler's comment, and he felt compelled to interrupt.

"Mr. Medill, Mr. Gilbert, Mr. Johnson," he said, "They're telling me that Cincinnati just completed a trade with San Francisco, and that the 49ers are on the way up to the front to turn in their choice."

Cedric B., after recovering from a quick downward snap of his chin, and with his voice level raised a noticeable notch or two, exclaimed, "That is *the* one team you told me really needed a receiver now that Jerry Beans has retired and, damn it, they've moved up ahead of us and they are going to get him!"

Brant did a masterful job of disguising all signs of the panic he was experiencing as he groped within himself for an adequate response to Cedric B.'s logic, but he needed help fast. He got it.

With the ninth pick in the draft, the 49ers selected strong safety Lonnie Mott from USC. Del Piper, in full view of the nationwide television audience, was so astounded that he swished his hand over the top of his head, seriously mussing up the hair-styling artistry that had taken the studio makeup lady half an hour to craft.

"He's ours now," Cedric B. cried out.

Bobby Russell would have preferred that Cedric B. was talking about Shawn Conrad, that stud linebacker from Penn State, but he knew better. Five minutes later, wide receiver Chase Banks from LSU became a future member of the Los Angeles Leopards. Let the negotiations begin.

■

In the second round the Leopards selected defensive end Bill Hanlon from the University of Nebraska. Cedric B. had suggested that they think about zeroing in on the best quarterback still available at that spot. That would provide good competition for Q.T., he said, and, under any circumstance, he added, it would give them a solid backup at the position. Brant, Bobby, and Butler were all so persuasive in extolling Hanlon's high-motor abilities, pointing out that he had earned the designation of "the Kickasska from Nebraska," that Cedric B. deferred to their counsel.

When Cedric B. stepped out into the hallway for a bathroom break a short time later, he found reason to become further content with the choice they had made. He ran into Randy Dolbermeier who told him that Hanlon would be a great addition to their defense if he got the right kind of coaching, and Randy assured him that, with Randy in charge of the defense, Cedric B. could count on that.

There was still one more positive indicator, because even Del Piper, back from a touchup in the makeup room, flashed thumbs up when the selection was announced.

By the time the third round began, there were no high-profile quarterback prospects still available, and so Cedric B. took on more of a listen-and-observe role. It was an exciting round for Brant, Bobby, and Butler, however, because by virtue of the trade executed with the Jets earlier in the day, they had two choices—the fifth and the 22nd —available to them during that round.

They had a hard time believing that defensive cornerback Lamont Dewey hadn't been taken by the time the third round began, and they held their breath hoping he'd still be there for them five choices into the round. Buffalo didn't call out his name, and neither did Carolina. And then, just two picks ahead of theirs, the New Orleans Saints, who had traded up to that slot, plucked Dewey off the board.

The Leopards settled for Odell Nathan, a cornerback from Wisconsin who was their next highest-rated player at the position. Then they played the waiting game again with their eyes this time on linebacker Colin Fitch from Southern Methodist University. Because they had assigned a grade to Fitch that was higher than any accorded by the multitude of draft gurus who were being interviewed on television, they felt confident that he would still be available when their turn came.

Cedric B. was somewhat uneasy about Fitch's inflated grade and about another consideration, also. "Say, we've just made two defensive picks in a row," he said. "Isn't it time we start looking back at the offensive side of the ball?"

This time it was Butler Johnson who stepped out of the huddle and carried the argument.

"Mr. Medill, this guy is really something special," Butler said. "He didn't come close to getting the recognition he deserves because he played on a team that had a lousy record, but there isn't a linebacker in the whole draft that I'd prefer over him."

"How can you say that?" Cedric B. asked. "The other teams in the league do a darn good job of scouting, too, don't they?"

"Absolutely. But it isn't a science. Heck, no one even drafted Johnny Unitas when he came out, and the 49ers, for example, didn't pick Joe Montana until the third round when he was drafted."

"So what is it you see that makes you so high on Fitch?"

"Tough. Smart. Loves the game. Great leadership ability. He's never been hurt. And do you know what else?"

"What else?"

"You know who Jock Fitch is, don't you?"

"Of course I do. He was that great linebacker for the Giants back in the late 60s?"

"That's the one. Hall of Famer Jock Fitch. He's Colin's father. And not only that, Colin's brother, Jeremy, at the University of Texas, is going to be the No. 1 tight end in the draft next year. Pretty good genes, huh?"

"I sure hope you fellows are as good at evaluating talent as you are at arguing your points," Cedric B. said. "Go ahead and take him."

Mel Herbert's newspaper account of the draft's first three rounds that appeared the next morning carried the headline, "LEOPARDS DRAFT A SON OF A FITCH."

CHAPTER SEVENTEEN

After three rounds, the first day of the draft came to a close. There would be four more rounds the following day involving players that most fans knew little about, but some of those second-day picks would eventually turn out to be stars whose accomplishments would far exceed those of many of the early rounders who had been touted as "sure things."

The best way to find those unpolished gems, Bobby Russell had said during the screening interviews that led to his being hired as the team's head coach, was to select only players who possessed what he described as "football temperament." Brant Gilbert and Butler Johnson agreed.

Cedric B. appeared puzzled. "What does that mean?" he asked.

"We want players with a work ethic that tells me not that they're *willing* to work hard, but that they *want* to work hard," Bobby answered. "I want players who are in it primarily, like me, for the love of the game, not just the rewards. I don't care if they are extroverts or introverts, but I do care that they are unselfish. That's what teamwork is all about. I want players who are comfortable allowing their statistics to take a backseat. Team success and teammates ride up front.

"I want players who honor the game, and who do it by playing by the rules and by being good citizens," Bobby continued. "I want players who don't play dumb and who don't play dirty. I want players who every single time they walk off the practice field are able to say to themselves, 'Today I got a little bit better.'"

"Very commendable qualities," Cedric B. said, "but tell me, how do you motivate these guys?"

"Mr. Medill, that's simple. You select only *intrinsically motivated* people. That's where I'd rely so heavily on Brant and on Butler, and on everyone in the scouting department."

"But isn't motivation a big part of a coach's job?"

"Yes, it is, and it works best with players who are hungering for instruction, who want to know how to get better, who aren't all 'me, me,' and who understand that football is truly a team game."

That is the philosophy to which the Leopards continued to adhere as they entered the second day of the draft.

In the fourth round they did go for offense, but it wasn't at a position that excited Cedric B. very much. It was for some big, smart offensive lineman named Glenn Grabowski from the University of New Mexico.

In round No. 5, the New Orleans Saints did it again. They stole the player the Leopards had targeted, free safety Jonas Henry from Illinois, just two picks ahead of when the Leopards were going to take him.

"You know, I never knew much about Walter Louis until the Saints hired him as their GM back in January," Brant said, "but I'm beginning to think that he is one smart dude."

"Tough, too, I'd wager," Butler said. "Did you know that his grandfather was that great former heavyweight boxing champ, Joe Louis?"

"He was! Wow, you could have knocked me for a loop with that one," Brant said.

"Maybe I couldn't, but his grandpa sure could have."

The Leopards brain trust made a quick adjustment, and, since they were talking about tough, they used their fifth-round pick on hard-nosed fullback and special teams ace Gardner Cardwell from Purdue. Less than 60 seconds after that pick was official, Brant Gilbert's phone rang. It was Mike Miller, Brant's friend who was also the general manager of the Detroit Lions.

"You S.O.B.," Miller said. "I bet you knew we were going after Cardwell. You took him just so you could piss me off, didn't you?"

"Not really, Mike, but that sounds like a wonderful by-product. Hang in there, buddy, you'll probably blunder now into getting the biggest sleeper on the board. Good luck. Hey, I gotta go now 'cause we're trying to figure out who you're thinking about taking in the next round. We're planning to grab him, too, before you do."

"You keep doing that and you will have had one hell of a draft. Good luck to you, too. I hope you have the *second best* draft of the year. You'll need it if we're on your schedule this fall."

"Okay. See you at the Super Bowl."

"I hope it's down on the field and not up in the stands. Bye, bye."

■

Round number six was unique because this time it wasn't Cedric B. who was campaigning for them to choose a quarterback. It was Bobby.

"We do need another candidate at the position, Mr. Medill. As I recall, you even pointed that out yourself earlier in the draft."

"That's when there were some big-name prospects still available. This Eggleston fellow that you're pushing now, I don't think anyone other than his parents and his teammates know who he is. Let's wait until next year, and then we'll take the best quarterback on the board with our first pick."

"Mr. Medill, I really believe that Toby Eggleston is the perfect fit for us right now," Bobby said. "He doesn't come in as a threat to Q.T. There won't be any 'controversy,' so Q.T. can concentrate on the job. In the meantime, we'll be developing a very solid young backup who has a tremendous amount of upside."

"If he's that good, why has no one else taken him?"

"I think it's because hardly anyone ever pays attention to some Ivy Leaguer from Dartmouth. They brush off the level of competition. They shouldn't, but they do."

"Butler, Brant, what do you fellows think?" Cedric B. asked.

"Like him a lot, Mr. Medill," Butler answered.

"How about you, Brant?"

"From what I've seen, Cedric, I'm really impressed. He's got a strong arm, a quick release, and he does a great job of reading pass coverages. Also, he has an excellent knack for feeling pressure, and when he runs with the ball he looks better than any of their running backs. And, oh yeah, one more thing. When he took that IQ test at the Indy Combine, he got a score higher even than my blood pressure reading is on game days."

"Okay," Cedric B. said. "It would be nice to have another young quarterback, I guess, and I don't see any other names up there that knock me out, anyway. Even if Eggleston doesn't pan out, we could always draft another quarterback next year. Go ahead."

So, the Leopards drafted Toby "Scrambles" Eggleston from Dartmouth College. It was their third consecutive offensive pick. In the seventh round, they went for defense by selecting a wide-bodied defensive tackle, Sidney "Matzo" Ball from Temple University.

ESPN's Del Piper reeled off the names of 14 other still undrafted prospects whom the Leopards, in an embarrassing display of their inept evaluation skills, he said, had somehow bypassed when they opted to go for Ball.

"How could they look right past that free safety, Kelsey Marco?" Piper asked moderator Clint Fuhrman. "They need a lot of help in the secondary."

"I'll answer that one right after this commercial break," Fuhrman answered. "Stay tuned."

By the time the break was over, four other teams had made their final round picks, and none of them selected Kelsey Marco. Neither did any other team when their turn came. The draft was over.

It was now time for the Leopards chief contract negotiator, Tim Underdorf, to start talking with the players' agents, an ordeal that would last well into training camp in August. Poor guy.

■

The draft may have been completed, but the pursuit of players continued. Every team in the NFL had its own list of about 10 undrafted players whom they would now try to sign as free agents.

The Leopards must have been tuned in and listening to the wisdom being dispensed by Del Piper because they went hard in their efforts to shore up their secondary. They did it by going after free safety Kelsey Marco from the College of William and Mary, and they signed him.

Chalk one up for Del Piper.

■

No one was privy to better information about what was going on inside the Leopards' draft room than Mel Herbert. His sources were the best. During much of the activity that transpired, Joe Skoronski had been sitting in. From Joe, and even from Brant and Bobby during their many visits to the media room, Mel was able to gain insights on how the Leopards arrived at the consensus that resulted in the making of their draft selections.

They didn't mind confiding in Mel. They trusted him, and he applied the type of discretion that led them to feel at ease in giving him the inside story. In Mel's column the morning after the draft, he provided keen insights for his readers. And to wrap it all up he decided that he'd try to amuse them, as well, and so he concluded his analysis with, yet again, one of his signature poems:

THE DRAFT IS DONE

> *The draft is done, and wasn't it fun*
> *Getting Chase Banks with our No. 1.*
> *And then came Hanlon, the Kickasska from Nebraska.*
> *You may have wanted someone else, but no one asked ya.*
> *It was on to Wisconsin where we picked up Odell.*
> *We preferred Scooby Dewey, but what the hell.*
> *Next we drafted Colin, that son of a Fitch.*
> *If he's as good as they say, he's going to get rich.*
> *A lineman, Glenn Grabowski, made us all yawn,*
> *But if you were a quarterback, you'd be singing a song.*
> *Cardwell's a blocker who'll knock 'em on their butts.*

It's a job short on glamour, but it's long on guts.
Then we took that QB from the Ivy League.
When they try to catch "Scrambles," they'll faint from fatigue.
Our seventh-rounder nose tackle may not be tall,
But no one's going to feast on our "Matzo" Ball.
So there you have it; those are our rookies.
Let's hope the men who picked them are real smart cookies.

CHAPTER EIGHTEEN

Season number two for the L.A. Leopards and for the Portland Pioneers arrived. Training camp began, and the pace became swift once again for coaches and players. As hard as they were required to work, their activities could have qualified as a vacation romp when compared with the demands placed on Equipment Manager Joe Skoronski and Head Trainer Eddie Carpentierie.

Every day, Joe and his staff laundered more T-shirts, socks, and undershorts (a.k.a. jock straps) than any mother of 12 children would be required to wash in a week, and they lugged more bags of equipment to and from the practice fields in one day than American Airlines dumped onto the baggage claim conveyors at O'Hare Airport during an entire Labor Day weekend. And Eddie looked at more human feet everyday before practice, as he taped all those players' ankles, than a podiatrist did in a month. Or so it all seemed.

Two weeks into training camp, however, the constant tearing of tape and then applying it so precisely had taken its toll on Eddie, and he was forced to turn all of his ankle taping duties over to his two assistants and to the two young student interns who were so elated over the opportunity they had been afforded to gaze day after day at so many fungus-infested toenails. Joe explained the situation to Mel after practice one day.

"Yeah, it finally caught up wit Eddie," Joe said. "He kept doin' all dat tuggin' and pullin' and wrappin' and now da doc tells him ta lay off for a while 'cause he's got one a dose car pool tunnel syndromes in his hand."

"Well, with the traffic situation like it is here in L.A., I can understand that," Mel said.

"Naw, it ain't dat bad. Da doc says he can still drive around in his own car."

For all the coaches in the NFL, their main objectives prior to the beginning of the regular season extend beyond being able to walk off the field as winners of those preseason exhibition games. Sure, they preferred to be on the long end of the score, but, unlike the games that really count, that is not the primary consideration.

Eighty players come to training camp. Deciding which 53 of them are going to make the final roster is crucial. Those teams with veteran, well-entrenched starters play them just enough to get the off-season rust scraped away. Why expose them to prolonged, unnecessary periods on the field that increase the possibilities for injury in order to try winning a game that doesn't count in the standings?

Having the luxury of resting those veterans also allows the team to do a more thorough job of evaluating all the other players who are vying so hard for one of those 53 roster spots. Who fills the backup positions behind the team's starters is a vital determinant of how successful a team can count on being once the long season begins.

Coaches know that winning depends on more than just avoiding injuries. It depends on overcoming injuries. Injuries are going to occur. Will the team continue to function as a winner when that happens? That depends on who is going to step in, and on how ready he is to play when he does step in.

Other than personnel evaluation, coaches also place a high priority on the teaching of fundamentals and refining the execution of the team's offensive, defensive, and kicking game schemes. Strategy and game planning for specific opponents are put on hold until the whistle blows to signal the start of the regular season games.

Those are the reasons that winning a preseason game isn't the main focus for the coaches or for the players.

■

There is a famous personage (whose identity must remain anonymous) who, upon being caught in violation of accepted procedures, uttered that time-honored sentiment: "There is an exception to every rule."

It was on the basis of that wisdom that the Leopards players —and even a majority of their coaching staff—felt driven to pursue victory-above-all in one of those preseason contests. They were at home facing the Seattle Seahawks, but the opponent had nothing to do with the motivation that drove them.

It was because of Zig Zag Zizzo and his once happy pooch, The Gipper, both of whom had been embraced as buddies by everyone in the Leopards locker room. Earlier in the week, a truck cruising through the team's parking lot ran into Zig Zag's dear tail-wagging companion. Zig Zag rushed his little pal to the veterinarian, but the injuries were so severe that The Gipper had to be put to rest. Zig Zag was devastated, and so were the players on the team.

On Friday night, in their final preseason game prior to their second year of NFL competition, the Leopards played with extra fervor, and they came away with a 31–10 victory over the Seahawks. Clark Stallwell, the Leopards chief security officer, had been told before the game that if the Leopards did come out on top, he was to bring Zig Zag into the locker room immediately after the game. Clark carried out that assignment as instructed.

The awarding of game balls in the locker room following team victories during the regular season is part of an NFL post-game ritual, but no such ceremonies take place after preseason games. Then again,

"There is an exception to every rule."

In the locker room after the victory over the Seahawks, one of those exceptions occurred when the Leopards players and coaches presented the game ball to Zig Zag. It had already been inscribed, in hopeful anticipation of the outcome: "We Won This One For The Gipper." Zig Zag wouldn't have traded that ball for the original painting of the Mona Lisa.

■

The momentum generated by the Leopards' victory in that final preseason game against the Seahawks carried over. They won their regular season opener by defeating the Jacksonville Jaguars, 20–14. For the first time in their short history, the Leopards had a winning record.

They were 1–0.

Two weeks later they were 1–2. In both of those losses the Leopards came close, losing one of them by three points and the other by four. Late in those games, the Leopards had gained possession of the ball, and then failed to get the score they needed. In the first one their drive ended in an interception, and in the following week's game it petered out when they failed to convert a third-and-two situation and then a fourth-and-two. Cedric B. couldn't understand it, and he expressed his frustration to Brant. What else was new?

"We land the premier college quarterback in years, and then we can't teach him how to run a two-minute drill. Why?" Cedric B. asked.

"It is frustrating, Cedric. I know that, but we're coming close, and we are getting better. Sometimes it just takes some patience and learning from what didn't go right."

"You really didn't answer my question, but I'll tell you what I think. I've got some real doubts about that offensive coordinator of ours. His play calling stinks."

"Are you talking about Fred Cantrell? He is an excellent coach, Cedric."

"Yeah, sure. He runs the ball on third and two. No gain. Then he calls a pass on fourth down, and the quarterback gets sacked. Even Homer Runstead, the CEO of Homerun Industries, who was a guest in my box, thinks the play calling was lousy."

"On the third and two, Cedric, the Browns were in a three-man front with the linebackers and defensive backs playing way off the line expecting a pass. Getting a first down and more on a running play should have been a cinch except that Pete Haskins missed his block," Brant said.

"Well, that's Pudge Steckhauser's fault then, isn't it. He's the one who is supposed to be coaching the offensive linemen."

"It's not the coaches' fault, Cedric, they're doing a good job."

"That's not the way I'm seeing it. And it isn't the way Homer sees it, either."

"I respect Mr. Runstead, and although he may be a good fan, I don't think he qualifies as an authority on the fine points of coaching."

"Maybe *he* doesn't, but did you see that scathing account of the game by Jordy Nerdmann in yesterday morning's *Guardian*? Now there is a man who knows what he's talking about! And besides all that, when I spoke with Randy Dolbermeier earlier today, he wasn't too complimentary about Cantrell, or Steckhauser, and a few of the other coaches, either."

Brant was aware that a problem bigger than how to execute a two-minute drill was growing. He knew part of the solution—win! It was the other part—how to deal with Dolbermeier—that was so perplexing. He knew it would be futile to say what he felt like saying about Randy, and so he refrained from commenting on Cedric B.'s revelation.

"I hear you, Cedric," he said. "Now, if we're going to bounce back, I'd better get back to work."

Brant hung up the phone and took a deep breath. Then, with his head still shaking, he stepped over to the fax machine and began checking out that day's waiver wire. There was no one on it who interested him.

CHAPTER NINETEEN

After their two losses, the Leopards didn't just bounce back: they leapt back! They hung on to beat the Green Bay Packers, 21-19, in Green Bay when "Matzo" Ball blocked a late fourth quarter field goal attempt by Packers place kicker, Don "Bootin'" Wooten. And then, at home the following weekend, Q.T. Pye led them on a fourth-quarter rally from a 13-point deficit to pull out a 28–27 victory over the Kansas City Chiefs. The winning score came at the culmination of an 82-yard drive with just eight seconds remaining to be played. Their record, now at 3–2, had them, once again, over the .500 mark.

On Sunday night after the game, they all celebrated, and then it was back to work as they prepared for the following weekend's long trip to upstate New York where they would be facing the Buffalo Bills. During that week of intense practice, Q.T. was the media darling. Even Nerdmann wrote a complimentary sentence about him before cautioning his avid readers not to get too excited about this Hollywood playboy from UCLA.

Joe, at one of his dinner meetings with Mel and Zig Zag late that week, asked Mel what the "Hollywood playboy" zinger was all about.

"I don't pay much attention when Jordy spouts off," Mel told him. "He said something about Q.T. being out at a fancy nightclub late last Sunday night after the game with some real hot number."

"Geez, what's he talkin' about, anyway? Q.T.'s been datin' dis real good lookin' cheerleader, 'Yum Yum' Baklava, ever since way back dere last season. She's a real sweet gal, too. She's nice ta everybody."

"Her name is Yum Yum?" Mel asked.

"Naw, dat's just a nickname, ya know. Her real name is Angela, but last year when she came ta dat Kickoff-Da-Season Banquet at da Beverly Wilshire Hotel wearin' dat gownless evening strap, dey all clapped and whistled, ya know, and den dey gave her dat nickname. She liked it, dey tell me, and so dat's what dey all call her now."

"Gotcha," Mel said. "The guys on this team are a pretty amusing bunch, aren't they?"

Zig Zag interrupted. "They're that and lots more," he said. "I can't believe what they've done since that awful accident happened to The Gipper."

"Dat game ball ta honor da Gipper was really sumpthin', wasn't it?" Joe said.

"Apparently, Joe, you haven't heard what happened today, have you?" Mel asked.

"Like what?"

"Tell him, Zig Zag."

Zig Zag tried to talk, but he kept choking up and drying his eyes with his sleeve.

"You ain't got no allergy goin', have ya?" Joe asked.

Zig Zag still couldn't get it out, so Mel explained on his behalf. "Fonseco Gonzales and Rocco Esposito both gave Zig Zag a little puppy today."

"So now you gotta dog again, huh?" Joe asked.

"No. He has *two* dogs. A cocker spaniel and a springer spaniel. Like I said, they *both* gave him a dog," Mel explained. Zig Zag sniffled.

"Da Fonz and Rocky, dose two great big awnrey O-linemen did sumpthin' sedimental like dat, huh? Da world is really changin'. Whataya gonna call dem, Zig Zag?"

Zig Zag tried to answer, and then, looking down at the floor, he shook his head and pointed at Mel.

"They already named them," Mel said. "Gonzales called his 'Amigo,' and Esposito named the other one 'Paisan.' I guess from now on I'll be getting driven around town with *three* friends in my car."

■

The Saturday flight to Buffalo was smooth and on time. It was the day after the Leopards arrived that their visit began to feel like the proverbial ride over Niagara Falls in a barrel. They weren't at Niagara Falls, however. They were at Ralph C. Wilson Stadium, and so were

70,000 Buffalo Bills fans who were doing a much better job of coping with the early onset of Buffalo football weather than the Leopards players were.

Still, it wasn't the 35-mile-per-hour winds (with gusts of up to 50) or the chaotic mix of horizontal rain, sleet, and occasional snow that was the most unsettling. After all, if those fans could have handled it out in the parking lot during their pre-game tailgating activities in preparation for more serious imbibing after the kickoff, then the hardened, well-conditioned elite members of a professional athletic team should certainly have been able to manage it, as well. At least *almost* as well.

What was making that afternoon so uncomfortable for the Leopards, and especially for Pye, wasn't the weather. It was the Buffalo pass rush. By the time the final gun sounded, Q.T. had been sacked seven times. Rookie defensive end Deuce Smithers had three of them, and all-pro linebacker Benny Cornelius had two. Team captain and outside linebacker Darnell Valley added one sack to go along with an interception, while nose tackle Ted Smirnoff contributed a sack and a forced fumble.

The final score was Buffalo: 27, Los Angeles: 0. That wasn't the worst of it. Early in the fourth quarter, Q.T. came limping off the field with a sprained ankle. Colby Hollister finished the game at quarterback. Later it was determined that Q.T. would probably miss the next three games while recovering from his injury. The plane ride home was not fun.

■

The Leopards were now 3–3. One week later they were 3–4, and one week after that, they lost at home to the Houston Oilers, 30–24. Their record sank to 3–5. Colby Hollister hadn't played badly, but the team had been struck with multiple injuries on both sides of the ball. On the Tuesday after the loss to the Oilers, Bobby Russell was called out of his coaching staff meeting in order to take a phone call from Cedric B. Medill.

"Bobby, have you thought at all about giving that rookie, Eggleston, a shot at playing quarterback until Q.T. is ready to go again?" he asked. "I know how high you were on him back on draft day."

"And I still like him, Mr. Medill, but Colby has a better grasp right now of what we're doing, and I think he definitely gives us the best chance to win this Sunday's game against the Raiders."

"We're 3–5 and not going anywhere." Cedric B. said. "If Eggelston's going to be anywhere near what you hope he'll be, I think right now is our best opportunity to find out. Don't you?"

"My honest answer to that, sir, is that I don't think so. We're banged up. He's still got a lot to learn, and our players have a lot of faith in Colby. They haven't given up. They want to win as badly as you and I do, and they feel, just as I do, that Colby gives us the best shot at winning this one."

"*They* may," Cedric B. said, "but I don't think all the coaches on your staff feel the same way. I talked to Dolbermeier about an hour ago, and he didn't hesitate to express some doubts about a few of the players we've been using. When I told him my feelings about the quarterback situation, he said that made sense to him, too."

"Mr. Medill, our coaches frequently have varying opinions on a lot of the decisions we make, and I encourage them to let me know what those opinions are. I listen, and then it's up to me to make the final call. What they have to say ought to stay inside the coaches' meeting room, however, and I think Randy is way off base saying anything to you about that."

"Oh, he meant no harm," Cedric B. said. "I talk to him all the time. He just tells it like he sees it, and I appreciate that. If it hadn't been for him, for instance, I never would have known about the problem you've been having with that rookie, Bill Hanlon."

"Problem? With Hanlon? He's been super, Mr. Medill. He's tuned in to everything and he's leading all our defensive linemen in tackles and in sacks. What is Randy talking about?"

"He says that Hanlon refuses to take coaching. That he flouts some of the instructions he gets from Randy, and that he gets angry when Randy calls him on it. What did we know about Hanlon's attitude when he was in college? That's what I'd like to know."

"Everything we had on him was top-notch. This really surprises me. Randy hasn't mentioned a word about it to me, but I assure you that I'll be addressing that with him *and* with Bill Hanlon *today*."

"Good. So now, how about that quarterback situation?"

"Mr. Medill, I want our team to win, and I'd be lying if I told you anything other than that our best chance lies with Colby Hollister."

"Bobby, I still have to say that I don't agree with you, but you're the coach. I understand that, and I enjoyed being able to exchange ideas with you. I hope you turn out to be right. Good luck."

"Thank you, Mr. Medill. I truly appreciate what you just said. I'll be talking with Randy and Hanlon as soon as we hang up."

"Okay then, let's hang up."

Bobby, after completing his conversation with Cedric B., peeked out of his office door into the reception area where the coaching staff's two secretaries, the Klock sisters, had their desks.

"Ada," he said, "please tell the coaches—they're in our meeting room—that they can go back to their film review work until I call them back together later, but tell Randy that I'd like to see him here in my office first.

"And Nina, will you call down to the weight training room, please, and ask Dusty to send Bill Hanlon up here. When he gets here please let me know."

Randy arrived first. "What's this you've been telling Mr. Medill about Bill Hanlon refusing to do what he's being coached to do?" Bobby asked.

"That's right. He not only won't do what he's told, but he takes a 'screw you' attitude when you tell him to shape up."

"Why haven't you said anything to me about it, then?"

"I didn't want to make any waves, and I was hoping that I could handle it by myself without bothering you. You've got too many other important things to deal with."

"You didn't mind bothering Mr. Medill with it though, did you?"

"We were just talking and he asked me how our draft choices were doing. I've got to shoot straight with him. He owns the damn team."

"And I'm the head coach of the damn team, and I want to be informed. If Hanlon or any other player is being such a problem, then I want to know about it. He's on his way up here now, and he's going to hear, straight from me, what we expect from our players."

The intercom on Bobby's desk buzzed. It was Nina. "Bill Hanlon is here to see you," she said.

"Good. Tell him to come in." She did. He did.

"Sit down, Bill," Bobby said. Hanlon took the empty chair farthest from the one in which Randy was seated.

"Coach Dolbermeier here tells me that you've been refusing to follow his instructions, and he tells me that you've been very vocal in letting him know that you won't. What's up, Bill?"

"Coach, he keeps trying to get me to play dirty. Many of the things he wants us to do are for the purpose of knocking players on the other team out of the game with an injury. I am not going to do that, and the only reason I do any talking back to Coach Dolbermeier is because, when I tell him I won't use those dirty tricks, he tries to embarrass me in front of the other players by calling me a 'pussy' and by telling me to pull down my skirt and a bunch of other demeaning things like that."

"Randy, is that true?" Bobby asked.

"This is a tough game, and you both know it," Randy answered. "If you don't take the other guy out, he's going to get you. Hell, do we want to win or don't we?"

"I think you both know," Bobby said, "that I want to win as much as anyone else does, but I want it clearly understood that I want to win while playing by the rules. I love winning, but I love this game, too, and I will not condone our doing anything that brings discredit to it or to the people who play it."

"Coach, that's the only reason I've said anything," Hanlon said. "Most of the other players feel the same way, but maybe I've been the most outspoken. I'm sorry if it's been a problem, but I honestly can't do it any other way."

"Just so you hear it straight from me, Bill," Bobby said, "understand that I do not want you or anyone else on our team to be a dirty player or to be a cheater, and I will make that known again to all of our players and coaches. I hope this meeting helps clear the air on that issue. Thanks for coming up. I'm going to let you get back down to the weight room now. We've got the Raiders coming up this Sunday, you know."

"I've heard a rumor to that effect," Bill said. "Thank you, coach. I really do feel better about it now. And Coach Dolbermeier, I want you to know that we all think you do a great job of teaching us fundamentals and techniques. I value that, and I look forward to receiving that kind of coaching from you."

Randy said nothing. He just sat there and glared as Hanlon walked to the door. Only after Bill left the room did Randy speak up.

"You have just undercut me with a player I am supposed to coach," he said. "How can I possibly get him to believe me and to respect me now?"

"By earning it. And if you want the respect of the players and the coaches, you're going to have to show us that you're going to play by the rules."

"There is an even better way to earn respect in this game, and that is by winning."

"Regardless of how?"

"Yes, absolutely, in any way that you can. There are other teams in this league who'll do whatever they have to do, including breaking some rules if they have to, in order to win, and you know it."

"There may be some, but I'll bet you there are very few who would use a scumbag approach like that."

"Now you're calling me a scumbag?"

"You were asking our players to use scumbag tactics, and I want you to stop that immediately. How often have I said to them, 'Don't be dumb and don't be dirty?' Those aren't just cute words. It's what I believe in. It's what we are going to teach. It's how we are going to operate."

"Yeah, well I think there are a lot of times where it's dumb if you *don't* play dirty. The other guys are going to do it to us, damn it, and then we'll be the nice guys who lose the game because of it."

"You've had your say. It appears, unfortunately, that I am not going to convince you, but I am going to tell you something now. No more! Not if you want to keep your job here. Do you understand that, Randy?"

"Yeah. Anything else?"

"Not right now. We've got to get back to work on the Raiders." That ended the pleasantries.

CHAPTER TWENTY

DON'T BE DUMB AND DON'T BE DIRTY.

That was one of the two signs that Bobby Russell posted on the bulletin board in the locker room during the week leading up to the game against the Oakland Raiders. The other sign was a repeat of one he had displayed before:

ADVERSITY IS JUST AN OPPORTUNITY FOR HEROISM

The Leopards, despite all the injuries and all the turmoil afflicting them, played smart, clean football against the Raiders, and in doing so they did overcome adversity—and the Raiders, as well. They ended their three-game losing streak, coming away with a 24–17 victory. Hollister validated the faith that his coach expressed in him during Bobby's earlier-in-the-week exchange of opinions with Cedric B. Two touchdown passes, no interceptions, and, most of all, a win, provided testimony to support that.

Nine games into the season, the Leopards were 4–5 and they were still battling. Now, going into their bye week, several of their injured players were on the mend, and that included Q.T. Pye, whom the team doctors pronounced ready to play. Hollister had performed admirably under difficult circumstances, but still the team had registered just one win and two losses since he entered the lineup. Q.T was back under center when the Leopards resumed play on the road against the Minnesota Vikings.

When the game in Minneapolis ended, L.A.'s record had slipped to 4–6, and in the nation's capital one week later, the Leopards listened too many times to the Washington Redskins fans singing "Hail To The Redskins" following scores by their home team. The record was now a dismal 4–7.

As disheartening as events on the playing field had been, they were even more unsettling in the locker room, and the problem continued to center on Dolbermeier.

Randy had the ear of Cedric B., and when either Bobby Russell or Brant Gilbert sought to advise Cedric about how destructive Randy's pronouncements were, they were rebuffed.

"He is just telling it like it is," Cedric B. said to them at a meeting they had on the Monday after their loss to the Redskins.

"We've got a quarterback here who was talented enough to merit the very first pick in the whole damn draft, and we are so conservative in what we are asking him to do that he's not coming close to living up to his potential. Can't those offensive coaches see that? Randy knows it, and he's got the guts to say it."

Bobby and Brant were at a loss as to how they could convince Cedric B. that Randy was purposely seeking to create trouble. They knew from previous attempts that any criticism they voiced relative to Randy served only to irritate Cedric B. even further.

After the meeting that Bobby, Randy, and Bill Hanlon had in Bobby's office three weeks earlier, Randy had become more of a problem than ever. He seemed to seek confrontations with other coaches on the staff. He was gruff with the secretaries and with all the people who worked in the locker room.

Bobby spoke with Randy about these actions, but they didn't cease. They escalated. Bobby expressed his mounting concerns to Brant Gilbert.

"Brant, I don't think this is a situation that's going to improve."

"It doesn't look that way to me, either, but what can we do about it now?"

"That is a tough one. Firing him now, I think, might solve one problem and create a lot of other complications, I'm afraid."

"I agree, and I also think it would really rock the boat with Mr. Medill. You know that, don't you?"

"Sure I do. And I don't want to divert our team's attention from getting ready for the Chiefs game this Sunday. I will tell you this, though. As soon as this season is over I want him gone."

"After the season is the best time to deal with that. Knowing the way that Mr. Medill feels, it is going to be a delicate situation, so let's wait until then."

■

While Randy may have been a grouch with his co-workers, there was another group at the stadium and at their practices with whom he was most affable. It was with those good old guys and gals from the media. He was always available. He was capable of being outrageous. He knew when to leak a story ("Don't tell anyone it was me that you heard this from.") to Jordy Nerdmann or to any other pull-no-punches journalist. And he led the league in the use of two pronouns, "I" and "me."

Mel Herbert was not one of Randy's confidantes, but he probably knew more than any of his fellow sports writers about the unrest for which Randy was responsible. Joe Skoronski kept Mel abreast of that.

Not all of Mel's dinners out with Joe and Zig Zag were for the men only. During the week following their game in Washington, they brought the ladies along, too. Mel and Frannie were there, and so were Joe and Darlene. They were all on hand to greet, for the first time, the woman in charge of the Inglewood PETA animal shelter with whom Zig Zag had connected when he visited there one Monday evening in order to get some immunization shots for Amigo and Paisan.

Seeing to it that such loving care was provided for his newly acquired puppies had called for an admirable sacrifice on Zig Zag's part since for the first time in 17 years, he was required to forego watching the Monday Night Football telecast in order to bring his pups in on the only night of the week that such a service was provided.

Frannie, Mel, Joe, and Darlene arrived at the Chez Claude Restaurant on La Cienega Boulevard early so they could all be there when Zig Zag and his date arrived.

"Hi, everyone," Zig Zag cried out upon seeing them there with champagne glasses raised. "This is my wonderful new friend, Zelda."

"To Zelda," they all cheered before sipping—in Joe's case, make that gulping—from their glasses. "Welcome."

"She is really some lady," Zig Zag said as Zelda blushed. "You should see how great she treats those cats and dogs and all those other little animals. And not only that, wait until you hear this. Her Pop grew up back there in Cicero, right outside of Chi town, and this gal is a real big Chicago Cubs fan. How do you top that?"

No one tried to, but before the evening was over they all agreed that Zelda Zaftig was someone they were really going to like. In fact, they already did.

At one point during the evening, while the women were talking among themselves about eyeliner, Joe commented about the difficulties that the Leopards were enduring.

"We've lost five outta our last six games," he said, "and dat Coach Dolbermeier makes it all da worse by walkin' around da locker room blamin' everyone else 'cept himself. I tried ta tell him we're gettin' helltier every day and maybe tings'll start ta look up, and he just gives me a dirty look, and den he calls me some names I ain't gonna repeat wit all dese nice ladies sittin' here."

"How have the players reacted?" Mel asked.

"A lotta dem know dat he's just a buncha hot air, but dere is a few who seem like dey're fallin' for dat crap. He tinks dey all really go for all his BS, but I'll tell ya, dat's just a fragment of his imagination."

"Wow, he must have some huge imagination," Mel said.

"It's even bigger den dat, and most a dose players ain't listenin' ta him. And dere ain't nunna dem who is gonna quit eadder. Somma dem told me dat Coach Russell really laid it on da line when he talked ta dem in yesterday's meetin'. He's da guy dey listens to."

"I heard about coach's talk," Mel said. "I spoke with Glenn Grabowski after the players came out of the meeting, and he told me all about it."

"Glenn's da one ta talk ta, I'm tellin' ya. He's dat real intellectual type a guy we drafted just dis year. You won't believe dis, but on da airplane trips when all da udder guys is playin' around wit video games and stuff like dat, he just sits dere in his seat and reads. And besides dat, it's a real book dat he's readin'."

"I believe that," Mel said. "When I talked with Glenn, he was excited because he said that Coach Russell, in seeking some words of inspiration, had actually adapted some quotes from Charles Dickens. Glenn even repeated some of it for me. Do you want to hear what he said?"

"Course I do," Joe said.

"Me, too," Zig Zag chimed in.

"Okay, as I remember, it was something like this: 'Is it the best of times, or is it the worst of times? Is it the season of darkness, or is it the season of light? Is it the winter of despair, or is it the spring of hope? We have everything before us.'"

"Wow!" Zig Zag said. "Boy, that Dickens guy really knew what he was talking about. Tell me again, though, I keep forgetting, what team was it that he used to coach?"

"His story is really *A Tale of Two Cities*," Mel said.

"I seem to recall that," Zig Zag said. "Was one of them Green Bay?"

"I'll fill you in on that later. Right now we are neglecting these fine ladies. Darlene, I couldn't help eavesdropping when I heard you telling Frannie and Zelda that you got Joe to take you to that Big Band Extravaganza at the American Legion Hall last month. Is that right?"

"Yes, it is. It took some real coaxing on my part, but once he got there, you should have seen him. I never knew he could dance like that."

"Well, dey started right off wit dat all-time great Glenn Miller number, 'In Da Nude,' and dat really got me goin'," Joe explained.

"I can understand," Mel said. "All of us would have loved to have seen that."

"Depends," Frannie whispered.

It was time to order dessert, and so Joe changed the subject. They were all grateful.

CHAPTER TWENTY-ONE

Following Q.T. Pye's return to his starting role after their bye week, the Leopards lost their next two games. The same call-in show addicts who blasted Coach Russell for playing Colby Hollister when the Leopards suffered through a two-game losing streak with Colby at the helm a few weeks earlier, were now clamoring for Russell to replace Q.T.

Bobby stared up at the framed quotation that he had fastened to his office wall on the first day he came to work for the Leopards: "If a coach starts listening to the fans, he's going to wind up sitting next to them." Bobby heeded that advice. At the team's Tuesday media session, he announced that Pye would be the starting quarterback for that coming Sunday's game against the Kansas City Chiefs.

"How seriously did you consider the possibility of making a change?" Jordy Nerdmann asked.

"Q.T. is our starting quarterback, and as long as he is healthy, I plan to have him continue to play and to continue his development process," Bobby answered.

Jordy's column the next morning was a diatribe about a coach who is so out of it that he lent no thought and no time to trying to solve the quarterback dilemma that is plaguing the Leopards. "If he had given it the attention and thought that I and so many of our insightful fans have invested in studying the situation," Jordy wrote, "there is no doubt that he would have made a bold change at that position. But no, not 'Bobby the Conservative'. "

■

When the Kansas City Chiefs arrived in Los Angeles for their game against the Leopards, it turned out that Pye was not in the starting lineup. The reason wasn't that Coach Russell had succumbed to media and fan pressure. It was that Q.T. had succumbed to a mean-spirited flu bug, and the team doctors prescribed that he be closely monitored while remaining home in bed.

Hollister started the game at quarterback, and he played well. So did his teammates. Injured players were back in the lineup. The kicking teams excelled. The Leopards never trailed. They played conservatively and didn't lose any fumbles or throw any interceptions. They ran the ball and ate up the clock. They were in control throughout the game, and won 20–7.

Nerdmann's lead line in his game account the next morning was, "I told you so."

Cedric B. Medill's lead line when talking with Brant Gilbert after the game was, "Did you see how Dolbermeier's defense dominated that game despite our boring, grind-it-out, put-you-to-sleep offensive game plan?"

On Monday, Q.T. was feeling better. On Tuesday, he was given permission by the team doctors to begin practicing again. On Wednesday, he showed up for practice, and he looked sharp. On Thursday, Russell announced that Q.T. would be the starting quarterback that coming Sunday when the Leopards would be playing host to the St. Louis Rams. On Friday and Saturday, the call-in radio show hotlines had backups of several hundred irate fans who trumpeted their doubts about whether Bobby (one caller, with a chuckle, called him "Booby") Russell ever took the time to review the keen advice available to him in those columns written by Nerdmann.

On Sunday the Leopards defeated the Rams, 31–17. Pye threw for over 300 yards and three touchdowns. Two of them went to rookie wide receiver Chase Banks.

Medill was pleased, but Nerdmann was perplexed. "How come," Jordy asked his readers, "the Leopards coaching staff has not been able to get such sterling production from this talented young athlete in all of his previous games? It is apparent that they just did not prepare him sufficiently, that's why."

With just three games remaining in the regular season, the Leopards had improved their record to 6–7. Then, in their final home game of the season, they squeezed out a 24–21 victory over the favored Baltimore Ravens.

Q.T. Pye was the hero in that one as he led the team 68 yards down the field in the game's dying seconds, putting place kicker Garland Updyke in position to boot the winning field goal on the last play of the game. They were now 7–7. Win the final two games and they'd not only have a winning season, but they'd also have a shot at being one of the wild card playoff teams.

■

If Charles Dickens had delivered his "Is it the best of times or is it the worst of times?" inquiry at Three Rivers Stadium in Pittsburgh, Pennsylvania, the following Sunday, the responses he received might have confused him. The Pittsburgh Steelers, 30-10 winners in that game, would avow that it was the best of times, while the humbled Leopards would express a contrary opinion.

It was no contest right from the beginning. Q.T. Pye was sacked the first two times he dropped back to pass. On his next attempt, he was intercepted. The Steelers, on both of their first two possessions, marched through swirling snow on long, time-consuming touchdown drives. Chase Banks left the game with a pulled hamstring midway through the second quarter. Then, early in the fourth quarter, Pye, upon being sacked for the fourth time that afternoon, aggravated the injury to his ankle, and he had to be taken from the field to the locker room. He was done for the season.

Hollister took over at quarterback, but no late-game heroics ensued. It was obvious that the Leopards, if they harbored any hopes of catching up, were in a have-to-pass-the-ball situation. The Leopards knew it. The Steelers knew it. Fantasy football fans knew it. Yes, even Nerdmann knew it.

During those final 12 minutes when Colby was the quarterback, he was sacked twice, and he threw two interceptions. He completed just four of his 14 pass attempts. It was the worst performance of his career.

The Steelers, to the ecstatic approval of their "terrible towel" waving fans, clinched their division title, and they were heading for the playoffs. The Leopards were heading home, and, after one more meaningless game, they would be heading for the sofas in front of their TV sets from where they'd watch *other* teams engage in the exciting post-season quest for the NFL championship.

To most fans and observers from outside the team's locker room, their one remaining game may have seemed meaningless, but that was not how the Leopards players and coaches saw it. They would be on the road again, and their opponent would be the Portland Pioneers.

The Leopards and the Pioneers, expansion teams just one year earlier, had exceeded most experts' expectations. They both came into that final contest of the year with 7–8 records. Avoiding a losing season, especially for these newcomer teams on the rise, would bring gratification, and it would also provide momentum for swift improvement the following year. That was how the players and coaches viewed it. Cedric B. Medill saw it differently.

"I can't understand how we can play so well one week, and then so poorly in a game where we've got so much on the line," he said when meeting with Brant and Bobby in the team offices the day after they returned from Pittsburgh.

"Mr. Medill," Bobby responded, "I'm as upset as you are. We can play better, and I do take responsibility for how badly we played. Pittsburgh is a darned good team, though. They're 12–3 right now, and once we had to start playing catch up against them, it all went downhill fast from there. All I can do about it now is get our team ready for the Pioneers. That would be a really big one for us to win right now."

"It *could have* been a big one, but even if we do win it, we're still 8–8. Big deal. We've just lost our chance to have a winning season, and maybe even to get into the playoffs."

"Cedric," Brant said, "We've won three of our last four games. We've battled back from 4–7 with an opportunity now to finish with a .500 record. That's pretty darn good for a team that's only in its second year in the NFL."

"You fellows seem a little too ready to settle for a mediocre outcome. We've got to start setting our sights higher than that."

"The best way to do that, Mr. Medill, is for us to win this Sunday," Bobby said. "I want our players to get that lift in confidence that comes when your hard work pays off."

"Speaking of confidence, I sure don't have any confidence in Hollister. Isn't this a good time to get a look at that rookie, Eggleston?"

"Mr. Medill, we've won the last two games when Colby was our starter. We really had no chance to pull it out last Sunday by the time he took over in the fourth quarter. And now that Q.T. is out, Colby gives us by far our best chance of bouncing back. To plunge Eggleston in there now would be an injustice not only to our players who want so badly to win this one, but it would be an injustice to Toby, as well."

"Dolbermeier tells me this kid has tons of talent, and Randy's surprised that you haven't gotten him into the lineup."

Bobby's instincts told him not to make Dolbermeier the issue. He'd deal with that matter—one that he had put on hold until after the season ended—next Monday.

"Toby is a great young prospect," Bobby said. "After a full season of learning like he's had now, he will be much more ready to play going into his second season, especially after that second year of training camp next summer. But our best chance to win this game is with Colby, and I feel that that should be our top priority."

"Maybe if the game meant getting into the playoffs," Cedric B. said, "but it's a game that means nothing."

Brant felt it was time to come to Bobby's aid.

"Cedric," he said, "if we win this game it would mean that we will have won four of our last five, two of them without our starting quarterback in the lineup. It would mean no losing season, and that's real progress for a team in its second year. It would give us a terrific running start on next season, and—I know you'll like this one—it would be a big factor in helping to boost next year's season ticket sales."

"At last, some convincing logic," Cedric B. said. "Why is it that I always seem to lose my debates with you two?"

"Not true," Brant said. "As I recall, you are the man who insisted that we take Chase Banks with our first pick in last April's draft. He's looking pretty darn good so far."

"And Pye the year before," Bobby added.

"See, you ought to do exactly as I tell you," a smiling Cedric B. said.

"What a coincidence," Bobby said. "Those are the very same words I hear from my wife, Cindy, whenever she and I disagree about anything."

CHAPTER TWENTY-TWO

Shortly after the Leopards and the Portland Pioneers came out of their locker rooms for their pre-game warm-ups, Bobby Russell and Denzel Jackson met at midfield.

"Denzel, you've done a great job with these guys," Bobby told him.

"Like you haven't? At least our quarterback has stayed healthy all year, and he is a good one."

"Tell me about it. I've used up my complete supply of Maalox trying to figure out how we're going to defend against him. You got any I can borrow?"

"Sorry, we are not allowed to aid and abet the enemy."

"I thought I was your friend."

"As soon as the game is over, you are once again."

"And you're mine, too," Bobby said. "Win or lose."

"Win or lose, that's right."

They shook hands, and then they each moved to the end zones where their teams had begun stretching exercises.

The game was a thriller, played at high intensity. The Leopards were leading, 30–22, when the Pioneers forced them to punt with just a minute and 20 seconds left to play. Then Pioneers quarterback Kelly James completed six straight passes on a drive that covered 62 yards and culminated with a 14-yard touchdown pass to his speedy wide receiver, Dan Beady.

It was now 30–28, with a mere three seconds of regulation time on the clock, and Las Vegas was laying a trillion to one odds that the Pioneers would attempt a two-point conversion. As usual, Vegas called it right. The Pioneers did it right, too. They connected, Kelly James to Jimmy Loftus, and the score was tied. The game went into overtime.

There are 200 or more instant decisions that must be made during the course of an NFL game. The coaches and the quarterbacks bear responsibility for most of them, but on that late December afternoon in Portland it was an obscure offensive lineman who made the most meaningful choice of the day.

Offensive tackle Wolfe Wilfred of the Leopards was one of the team's captains, and when referee Gerry Sharpsite flipped the coin into the air, it was Wolfe who made the split-second decision to blurt out the word "Tails." The coin landed, nestled in the grass, and it was, indeed, tails side up. The Leopards elected to receive the overtime kickoff. At least they wouldn't be putting the ball immediately back into the hands of Kelly James.

As it turned out, James never did get the ball back in his hands. Colby Hollister capped off his own outstanding performance in that game by engineering a drive to the Pioneers 29. From there, Updyke nailed his fourth successful field goal attempt of the day. The Leopards won, 33–30.

The post-game handshake between opposing coaches is always an awkward moment. The coach of the winning team does not want to reflect a rub-it-in demeanor, and, as joyful as he feels over his team's success, he knows the anguish his opponent is experiencing. After all, he has stood in those shoes himself.

For the coach whose team has come out on the short end, his main concern is to be gracious and dignified. He prefers hearing no words of solace. Both coaches want the ritual to be brief.

"Congratulations, Bobby," Denzel said. "You guys earned it."

"Thank you. But you know, we're *both* getting better," Bobby responded. "Let's keep heading that way. I'll see you down at the Senior Bowl Game practices. Good luck, Denzel."

"See you there. Good luck to you, too."

With that, they both trotted off to their own team's locker room.

Laughs, banter, giddiness, and practical jokes dominated the post-game scene in the Leopards locker room. In the Pioneers locker room, all one could hear was the tearing off of tape from ankles and wrists and the hiss of splashing water from the shower room.

The season was over. The Leopards had finished strong. Great! Now let's start getting ready for next year.

CHAPTER TWENTY-THREE

On the flight home from Portland after the game, both Bobby Russell and Brant Gilbert were in the mood to mellow out and savor the victory.

"We'll talk business tomorrow." Brant said. "I'm feeling too good right now to think about anything other than what that pretty flight attendant up there is serving for dinner. What are you going to have, the chicken cordon bleu or the halibut with risotto and snap peas?"

"I hereby appoint you as my culinary coordinator. What do you suggest?"

"I suggest that you make up your own mind."

"That's what I was going to do, anyway, but I was trying to be nice. Beginning tomorrow I'll start being a hard ass again."

"That'll make two of us. I'm going for the halibut. Made up your mind yet?

"There's still 15 seconds left on the play clock, so please don't rush me."

They dined, watched the in-flight movie for a while, dozed off, and relaxed. It was serene. Beginning the next day, however, matters would heat up even more intensely than they could have imagined.

■

At eight o'clock the next morning, Bobby walked into Brant's office. They had arranged to meet so they could prepare for the meeting later that day that Cedric B. had set up for the three of them.

"I think you ought to know, Bobby," Brant said, "the top item on Mr. Medill's list is going to be for you to replace Fred Cantrell with a new offensive coordinator. He's been hammering on that one for weeks now, but I didn't want to bother you about it while the season was still in progress."

"I'm aware," Bobby said. "He's made his feelings about Fred known to me many times, and it's just not fair. Fred does an excellent job, and if we replace him, all we're going to do is set ourselves back. A new system, new terminology, a new playbook. We'd forfeit 90% of what we've worked so hard to install and develop over the past two years. *And* we'd be dumping all over a good coach and a good man who doesn't deserve to be treated that way."

"I'm just telling you now, beforehand, Bobby, so that you'll know what to expect when we meet this afternoon."

"Why is he so down on Fred?"

"Thinks he's way too conservative, and—hang on—Randy Dolbermeier has convinced Mr. Medill that Fred is a lousy coach. I can't wait to hear what you have to say about that one."

"Randy has to be the one who goes, Brant. I've already made up my mind about that. I have waited out the season as we agreed, but now it's over. Randy keeps getting worse. He is going to destroy the morale and the fiber of this team unless we get him out of here. I can't dance around it any longer, and I intend to make that point without any waffling when we meet with Mr. Medill."

"Be careful, Bobby, you'll be going into dangerous territory with that approach."

"I know that, but I won't like myself if I wimp out of doing the right thing."

It was the day after a big win for the Leopards, but Cedric B. Medill wasn't smiling when he looked up from the papers on his desk at Bobby and Brant.

"Come on in, gentlemen," he said. "There are a few things we all need to discuss. There is one thing, though, that I want you both to know, and that is that although it's nice to make money, my main concern is that we develop this team into a real NFL powerhouse," he continued.

"That sounds like fun to me, too," Brant said, "but I'm sure the financial aspect of it is important to you, also. You'll be pleased to know that we did real well at the gate, and Ross Branson in our front office did an outstanding job of selling suites and sponsorships."

"I am aware of all that, but, as I said a moment ago, if money was my top motivator, I could have sold this franchise already for almost double what I paid for it two years ago."

"Who'd pay that?" Brant asked.

"That crazy Marc Galapagos. He already owns the top soccer team in Greece, and they tell me he's got a bid in for an NHL hockey team up in Canada."

"Is that all?" Brant asked.

"Probably not, but I'll let him wrestle with all that stuff. I'm here to talk about us, and so I'm going to start it out with a question of my own. Bobby, are you happy with the way our coaching staff has performed?"

I know where this is heading, Bobby thought.

"For the most part, I'm very pleased with them," he answered. "There is one exception, though, and I'm glad we have this opportunity to talk about it now."

"Well, me, too. You know from what I've been telling you all season that I think that offensive coordinator of ours is a real dud. Not only that, some of the other coaches on your staff tell me that he is a difficult person to get along with."

"Mr. Medill, I have a feeling you've heard that from only one coach, and that would be Randy."

"Yes, Randy is the one who told me, but he also said that a lot of the other men on the staff agree with him."

"He's not telling you the truth."

"Come on, Bobby. Randy's a straight-shooter, and he doesn't mince any words."

"Mr. Medill, he is a liar, a cheater, and a troublemaker. I've waited until now to say this, but I guess the time has come because there is no way that I can, in good conscience, keep a man like Randy Dolbermeier on as a member of my coaching staff."

"What!" Cedric B. exclaimed. And then he just sat there, stern-faced, silent, and contemplative for a few moments, before speaking again.

"Bobby, I'm going to ask you to step out into the waiting room for a few minutes," he said. "There is something I want to discuss privately with Brant. We'll get back to you."

■

Thirty minutes later, Brant opened the office door and beckoned Bobby to come back inside. Cedric B. was no longer there. Apparently, he had exited through the door at the other side of the room.

"Bobby, I can't believe this," Brant said. He gulped, raised a fist to his mouth, and bit down on the knuckle of his thumb.

"That bad?" Bobby said.

"As bad as it gets. How do I tell you this? He said he was going to replace you as coach of the team. I pleaded with him, but he was unbending."

"I guess I should be surprised," Bobby said, "but when he asked me to leave the meeting, I could feel that this was coming."

"There wasn't anything I said that made him want to recon-sider," Brant said. "I just don't understand it. He told me that he'd like to talk with you personally in the conference room across the hall after you and I are finished in here. *And then*, while he was stalking out of the room, he turned and told me that he wants Dolbermeier to be his new coach."

"Maybe he just wanted Randy all along," Bobby said. "Isn't this something? After all these years in the league hoping that some day I might get a head coaching job, I wind up getting canned after just two seasons. And, Brant, I feel even worse knowing that I've put you in such an uncomfortable position."

"It's not your fault, Bobby. I'll tell you something else, though. I don't think I want to stay under these circumstances, either."

"Oh, no. Please, Brant, it would just magnify my misery if what I did winds up costing you your job, too. You can make it work somehow. I'll get a coaching job somewhere. I know that. You? You've got two young daughters in high school here. This is where all their friends are. This is their life. And this is your family's livelihood. You stay and keep plugging. Please! I'll get over it."

"I don't know if *I'll* get over it, though," Brant said. "I learn more every day about why I wanted you as our coach. Right now, I'm just hoping that something good happens when you go over and meet with Cedric. I've got my fingers crossed."

■

Brant crossed his fingers, and Bobby crossed the hall, but neither action helped achieve the desired result.

Cedric B. gestured towards a seat at the conference room table, and he waited until Bobby settled in before breaking the silence.

"Bobby, I am sorry that it had to come to this."

"Mr. Medill, are you really that unhappy with the job I've done coaching this team?"

"No, of course not. You teach well, you have the respect of the players, and I can see that we have made progress. It's just that you and I seem to constantly disagree about matters that I feel are so vital if we are going to become a championship level team."

"Mr. Medill, I thought you wanted me to make tough coaching decisions, ones that I believed gave us the best chance to succeed. I've always listened to your opinions, and there are times when I was swayed because you did make a valid point. There are times, too, where maybe I didn't agree but still felt that the issue wasn't big enough for me to be bullheaded about it. But whenever I have been so convinced about a decision that needed to be made or about an action that should be taken, I felt that I would be doing you, the team, the fans, and myself, too, a disservice if I weaseled out of doing what I believed was truly the right thing to do."

"I understand that you feel that way, Bobby. I admire your honesty, and I like you as a person, but I still am aware that your coaching beliefs just don't jibe with my outlook on what we need to do in order to reach the top."

"We showed tremendous improvement this year."

"We improved, but with the sentiments you expressed about some of our assistant coaches, I can't see us getting to where I want to go. We have completely contrasting views on Cantrell and Dolbermeier, for instance. I'm right about that, am I not?"

"Yes, sir, you are, and I'd be glad once again to tell you why I feel as I do about each of them."

"No need for that. I've heard it all already. Is there any chance you would change your mind? That means Cantrell goes and Randy stays."

"I can't do that, Mr. Medill, without hating myself."

"I know that, Bobby, and that's why I have to stick with the decision I've made. It hasn't been an easy one. You do have a year left on your contract, and we will, of course, see to it that you are paid in full unless you are coaching elsewhere in the NFL this coming year."

"I appreciate your mentioning that, Mr. Medill. I guess there's nothing more I can say right now except to thank you for having given me this opportunity. Goodbye."

Two hours later, after cleaning out his office and his locker, the first coach ever hired by the Los Angeles Leopards walked out of the team's administration building. For the first time in two years, Bobby Russell would not be returning to work there the next day.

■

It was early that same Monday evening when Mel Herbert's phone rang. He was busy writing his season wrap up story for Tuesday morning's paper, and so he debated about whether to answer it. Then he remembered that his youngest daughter, Pamela, was close to the expected delivery date for her first baby. He grabbed the phone.

"Hi, is this you, Frannie? Any news?"

"Naw, dis ain't Frances, but I got some news for ya anyways."

"Joe, can I call you back in about an hour? I've got a deadline on this story I'm doing right now."

"You don't wanna wait for no hour ta hear what I gotta tell ya. You ain't gonna believe dis, but dey just fired Bobby Russell."

"Come on! Where did you hear that, Joe? Really, I haven't got time right now for any silly jokes."

"I wish it *was* some silly joke like you said, but it ain't. Bobby was just here in da locker room, pickin' up all his stuff, and he told me dat it just happened. I dint know what ta say."

"Are you sure?"

"All I know is what he told me, but he was lookin' like he really meant it. And he ain't da kinda guy dat goes around jokin' about sumpthin' like dat."

"Okay, Joe. Thanks for letting me know. I'm going to hang up now. I've got to do some more checking on this one. I sure hope I find out that what you told me isn't true."

"Boy, ya know, Mel, you and me, we got ESPN. Dat's exactly what I was hopin'."

"I'll be back in touch," Mel said. He hung up his phone. Then he picked it up again and dialed Brant Gilbert's number. Brant answered.

"Hello."

"Brant, this is Mel Herbert. Tell me it isn't true."

"No comment. Does that answer your question?"

"Wait. I want to be certain we're talking about the same thing because it seems so damn illogical. I'm calling about Bobby Russell. Has he been fired?"

"That's what my 'no comment' was about, Mel. I can't go any further than that right now. Media Relations is getting information out in the next half hour or so that we are having a press conference first thing tomorrow morning. I can say nothing official until that press conference takes place."

"I can't sit on this, Brant, but I don't want to cause a stupid problem by writing some speculative garbage that's totally unfounded, either."

"I think you know that I wouldn't let you do that, Mel, and you have to know, also, from my response so far, where this thing is heading. After the press conference tomorrow, I'll fill you in on a lot of the background information on this whole crazy situation. I know I can trust you to use it with good judgment."

"I understand," Mel said. "What I don't understand is how or why this is happening."

"Once again, no comment. At least until after tomorrow's press conference."

"I'm not very happy about this, Brant."

"Join the club. Don't print that."

"I won't. And thanks for the little bit of light you shed. Talk to you tomorrow."

"You and a thousand others, I'm afraid."

That was all they had to say to each other on that solemn Monday evening in Los Angeles. Had only 24 hours gone by since the Leopards victory celebration in Portland? It couldn't be so. But it was.

CHAPTER TWENTY-FOUR

Tension was in the air at the Leopards media headquarters on Tuesday morning where the assembled members of the press tried to remain straight-faced as Director of Media Relations Bert Scott stepped to the podium.

They all knew what the essence of Bert's announcement was going to be because Mel Herbert (how in the hell did he get the story and not me, they all brooded) had written in the morning *Guardian* that Bobby Russell was about to be fired, but they found it hard to believe.

Why? What happened? Tell me! Let's hear it! Man, have I got some questions for you.

"Gentlemen—*and* ladies," Bert added as he smiled, raised his eyebrows, and tilted his head towards Bella DePaul of the *Huntington Beach Herald* and Cassandra Dalrymple of *The Long Beach Monitor.* "I would like to read a statement from Mr. Cedric B. Medill. It is as follows: 'As the Los Angeles Leopards begin preparations for our third season in the National Football League, I have made the difficult decision that a change at our head coaching position needs to be made. While I retain high regard for Bobby Russell, and while I appreciate everything he has contributed to our team and to the community, I have found that we have sharp philosophical differences about what it will require for our team to take that next big step forward. We wish Bobby well.'

"That is the full statement from Mr. Medill," Bert said. "I'll turn the microphone over now to General Manager Brant Gilbert for the question and answer session," Bert said as he stepped aside. Brant took his place.

"What philosophical differences?" Jack Cass of *The Venice Voyeur* asked.

"I do not want to speak for Mr. Medill on an issue such as that," Brant answered in response to Cass's inquiry. "He did ask me to stress, however, that what has motivated him to take this action is that—and these are his words—he feels it is time for us to go in a different direction."

An anonymous voice from out of the throng crooned, "It seems to me I've heard that song before."

"Are those your feelings, too?" Ira Denkoff from the *Associated Press* asked.

"I did express to Mr. Medill my feelings that Coach Russell has done a good job. Mr. Medill agreed, but he has spelled out, in the statement that Bert Scott just presented to you, why he has determined to take this action."

"Then it was his decision, not yours. Is that correct?" Denkoff asked.

"I do not believe that it is fitting for me to comment on the give-and-take details of discussions which we hold in private."

Denkoff rolled his eyes, sending a signal that he knew what the hard, direct answer to his question really was, and that if Gilbert wasn't going to deliver it, then you'd better believe that Denkoff would. He passed the hand microphone over to Gabriel Frye of *The Thousand Oaks Traveller*, who asked the obvious.

"What are your plans regarding the selection of a new coach?"

"Mr. Medill and I are in discussions about that now."

"Have you contacted anyone as yet?"

"Once again, all I can say is that we are taking all the proper steps, and I do not anticipate that it will be very long before we will be ready to announce who the new coach will be."

Brant was aware that while he was busy deflecting these questions from the media, Cedric B. and Randy Dolbermeier were meeting elsewhere. Cedric B. had already made up his mind that Randy—and no one else—was his man. The two of them were engaged in a jovial conversation, one that included the presentation to Randy of some attractive contract terms. Randy accepted, and they agreed that the announcement of his promotion would be made the following morning.

Meanwhile, the Tuesday morning press conference continued to grind along with very little insight being provided relative to what had caused this startling turn of events. Many of the journalists in attendance preferred it that way, since it allowed them the leeway to call upon their own creative expertise in explaining and dissecting the "real story" for the benefit of their perplexed readers.

Some of the writers were stunned. Many were critical. A few professed that they had seen it coming. Jordy Nerdmann informed his readers that he'd be telling them why in a series of special columns that he planned to write over the next several days.

During the press conference, several members of the Leopards administrative staff drifted into the room and sat in the back listening. One of them was Joe Skoronski. When the session ended and the writers scrambled to their laptops, Joe crossed the room and grabbed Mel Herbert by the sleeve.

"Man, dere sure was some tough questions gettin' assed, wasn't dere."

"It's only the beginning, Joe. I'm still in shock."

"Ya sure ain't da only one. Lotsa da players came by da locker room, and dey don't like it one bit. I dint know what ta tell 'em. Ya know, I really felt bad just now, too, for Brant up dere at da platform. He was really gettin' hit on hard by dat Irate Dumbkopf guy from da 'Sociated Press."

"Ira Denkoff?"

"Yeah, dat's da one."

CHAPTER TWENTY-FIVE

Throughout the football season that just ended, Cedric B. had constantly railed that his team's approach was "too damn conservative." He rid himself, and anyone else who might have concurred, of that impression in a hurry. As astonished as the players, media, and fans had been over the Tuesday announcement that Bobby Russell had been fired, no one was prepared for the bombshell that Cedric B. dropped on Wednesday.

Again, it was press conference time. Cedric B., Brant, and Randy Dolbermeier were there. Randy was wearing a Leopards cap, a Leopards necktie, and a mile-wide smile.

Bert Scott introduced Brant, who, after some brief words of welcome, segued into his presentation of Cedric B.

"Hello, everyone," Cedric B. beamed. "I'm here to proudly announce that the new head coach of the Los Angeles Leopards is sitting here on this platform with me. Randy Dolbermeier will be taking over that responsibility. This begins a new era for the Leopards, one about which I am confident and excited. Are there any questions?"

There were plenty.

"Mr. Medill, apparently you didn't interview any other people besides Coach Dolbermeier for the job," Dorothy "Dot" Kahm of the *Marina Del Rey Seafarer* said. "Is that true, and, if so, how come?"

"I have been extremely impressed by Randy's coaching abilities and by his coaching style," Cedric B. answered. "Why look around all over the place when you have the right man, right here?"

"Had this been your intent even before the season ended?" Abby Westminster of *The Malibu Mermaid* asked.

"It is our policy to wait until the end of a season in order to evaluate and to review all such matters," Cedric B. answered. "That is what we did on Monday, and as our discussions progressed I reached the conclusion that this was the *new direction* in which I wanted our team to be going."

"Then it actually wasn't until Monday that you decided to replace Coach Russell?"

"Please, we dealt with all of that yesterday. I do not want to continue to dwell on the past. We are primed now to move forward, and I am excited about what lies ahead."

More of the same followed, until Bert Scott, with his acute sense of timing, interceded, thereby satisfying both the writers who were becoming restless waiting to hear from Dolbermeier, and Cedric B. who felt he had fulfilled his mission and who was on the brink of exhausting his supply of evasive responses.

"I'm sure you'd all like to hear now from Randy," Bert said. He was right. Randy kicked off with the wind at his back.

"I am honored and grateful to Mr. Medill, and I want all of you to know that I am going to do everything it takes to reward him for the confidence he has shown in me."

"What *will* it take?" Westminster asked.

"Win! Win! Win! That's what."

"What's the formula for that?"

"Anything it takes. We aren't going to sit back and hope good things happen. We're going to damn well make them happen."

The next question was from Stubby Whitmore of *The Culver City Courier.* "Can we expect any changes in the team's style of offense and defense?"

"Hey, Stubby, can I expect you to change your socks and underwear every day? My answer is the same as yours, buddy—I hope." Cedric B., still sitting on the platform, slapped his hands onto his knees, smiled, closed his eyes, and then shook his head slowly from side to side.

"You are going to see changes, big time," Randy continued.

"Like what?" Stubby asked.

"I'll tell you like what," Randy said. "We're going after 'em. We're going to air it out. I want the fans to send in diagrams of trick plays. Each week we'll select one of them and then find a way to use it during the game. That'll be fun, won't it? Fourth and one? Look out. Punting is for sissies. We're going for it, baby. On defense, we're coming. We're going after their quarterback's ass. I want players who will do whatever it takes to win, and I'll damn well show them what that is. I told all of this to Mr. Medill already, and he was so fired up that I thought about using him on our kickoff coverage team, but he wanted too big of a contract."

"What are your plans at quarterback?" Olivia Oberlin of *The Orange County Oracle* asked.

"Q.T. Pye is my guy. We'll continue to develop Toby Eggleston as his backup. He's a promising young player. Colby Hollister is getting older, and so we'll bring a fourth quarterback to camp to compete with him. There, does that sound as if I'm willing to make some hard decisions, or what?"

"What if Q.T. flops?"

"He won't. I'll see to that."

Randy kept them revved up, *and* he kept them laughing. Some laughed with him, and some *at* him. Many of the writers were charmed and fascinated by this brazen new personality at the helm. Jordy Nerdmann was one of them. Several of the writers were turned off by what they felt was Randy's overbearing self-centeredness. Mel Herbert was one of them.

Despite the negative impressions that Mel was harboring, he restrained himself from being one of those types that comes out hammering even before a man has been on the job for one full day. Time and events will guide me, Mel felt. In his column the next day he directed some comments, instead, to a matter that was being pushed aside as a result of the frenzied interest inspired by Dolbermeier's arrival as the new head coach of the Leopards.

What about Bobby Russell, Mel pondered. Had he been the victim of a raw deal? Mel summed up his reflections on that subject by concluding his account of the unfolding drama with some of his signature verse:

Is Bobby Russell one of those fools
Who paid the price for living by the rules?
He was honest, hard working, and easy to approach.
He loved the game and was a real good coach.
His teams held their own against odds that were long,
And I really can't see that he did anything wrong.
His players were eager and prepared for the tussle.
They learned from and responded to Coach Bobby Russell.
His teams fought hard; they were in every game,
But one morning he was fired, and it's really a shame.
We asked them why, and heard that old deflection
That it's time for us to go in a different direction.
Bobby is a man whom I'll venture to say
That someday they'll regret that they sent him away.

Nerdmann's view did not concur with Mel's. His column, extolling the brilliant move by Medill, was captioned "New and Improved." It appeared in the sports section right next to an unrelated advertisement that trumpeted a "new and improved" laxative available at your local pharmacy.

Jordy's article highlighted the contrast that he discerned between Russell and Dolbermeier. "Randy has style, and, let's face it, the Leopards have just rid themselves of a coach who was overrated," he wrote.

At his own farewell meeting with the press later that week, Bobby Russell was asked if he had read or heard about Jordy's derogatory assertion.

"I can understand why Jordy might lash out so strongly whenever he feels someone is being *overrated*." Bobby said in a voice dripping with compassion. "After all, when he hears all those comments being made about his knowledge of the game, he can't help but get the feeling that he is being grossly *underrated*."

CHAPTER TWENTY-SIX

Although many of the sportswriters, Mel included, were not happy to see Bobby Russell depart, they had to admit, at least, that Dolbermeier gave them much to write about. He started out by replacing all but four of the 11 assistant coaches who had served on Russell's staff. That included Fred Cantrell, who was informed of his dismissal as offensive coordinator less than 15 minutes after Randy exited from the press conference at which his appointment to the head coaching position was announced.

The firing of Cantrell made several people happy. Cedric B. was delighted. Dolbermeier took pleasure in being able to show so quickly that he was a man of action. Nerdmann welcomed the opportunity to knock, once again, "the timorous, ultra-conservative, tip-toeing style of offense that has caused this upheaval and that the Leopards are now so aggressively taking the necessary steps to remedy." His head-nodding believers grunted their approval.

A few days later those fans had even more reason to celebrate when the news broke that that crazy Dolbermeier had hired, as his new offensive coordinator, none other than Moe "Longball" Marks, the architect of the wide open "Fun and Shout" offensive system that had shattered all existing professional football passing records in the process of propelling the Düsseldorf Dragons to the NFL Europe championship two years in a row.

Even Fred Cantrell was happy. He did not want to work under Dolbermeier, and getting fired, rather than walking away as he would have felt compelled to do, meant that he would be getting paid for the remaining year on his contract. That glad feeling must have extended to some of the other teams in the NFL, as well, because before the week was over, three of them came clamoring after Cantrell seeking to hire him as their new offensive coordinator. He signed on, in that capacity, with the Denver Broncos.

Winners exult. Losers grieve. On Sunday evening, Bobby Russell had been all smiles and wisecracks. By Monday evening he was shattered. By Tuesday his anguish accelerated as he realized how devastated his wife, Cindy, and his three children were by the news of his dismissal. By Wednesday, with the announcement that Randy Dolbermeier would be taking over a team that Bobby himself had primed for impending success, he was downright angry. On Thursday he tried to calm down a bit, but he didn't succeed.

On Friday morning Bobby met Brant Gilbert for breakfast at their favorite coffee shop.

"How's Cindy doing?" Brant inquired.

"About like I am."

"That makes three of us."

"Sounds like you're having fun already," Bobby said.

"First thing yesterday morning, Randy was in my office wanting to trade Bill Hanlon. I told him it would be a huge mistake for us to do anything like that, but he kept insisting, saying that Bill wasn't a team player. I know better."

"How'd it finally work out?"

"Work out? It didn't. We left it there, but I know this issue is far from dead. And Bobby, just so you know, I've still got a lot of soul-searching to do about this job."

"Please, Brant, don't do anything foolish."

"I hear you. I won't be hasty. Anyway, the only thing I'm going to do right now is eat my pancakes and give you this envelope. Mel Herbert asked me to pass it along to you."

"What's in it?"

"Don't know. Why don't we finish eating? You can open it later."

Diving into breakfast sounded good to Bobby. Just being with his friend, Brant, despite the nature of their conversation thus far, served to lift some of the darkness that had descended since his firing. For the first time all week he found that his appetite had returned.

Bobby put the envelope into the pocket of his jacket, and then reached for the bottle of Tabasco sauce on the ledge next to the booth where they were sitting. They didn't speak again until after he shook a liberal amount of the bottle's contents onto his three-egg veggie and cheese omelet and then slathered a thick coat of jelly onto his unbuttered whole-wheat toast.

By the time their meal ended, Brant was feeling somewhat gratified by the belief that he had helped Bobby set out on his road to recovery.

"You told me, Bobby, that you'd get another coaching job. I know you will. And so does everyone else."

"We'll see," Bobby said, but deep down he realized that that was what he wanted, and now that Brant had ignited in him a spark of confidence, that is what he foresaw happening.

After Bobby returned home, he realized that they had been so engrossed in talking that he had forgotten about that envelope from Mel Herbert. He returned to the closet, retrieved the envelope from his jacket pocket, took it to his den, sat down at his desk, and sliced it open.

Inside he found a poem. It was not one of Mel's creations, however. In a note that Mel attached, he explained that the author was an unknown 16th century Scottish warrior. "He is no longer with us," Mel wrote, "but his words live on. Take heart from them."
It took Bobby less than 15 seconds to read it.

SIR ANDREW

"Fight on, my men," Sir Andrew said.
"A little I'm hurt, but not yet slain.
I'll just lie down and bleed awhile,
And then I'll rise and fight again."

After reading it, Bobby sat at his desk for a few minutes and let his mind roam. Yes, when you lose, I guess it is okay to lament, he mused, but only true losers continue to lie there in the fetal position and whimper. Thanks to Sir Andrew (and to Mel Herbert) he knew it was time to rise and fight again. He walked into the kitchen, found his wife, Cindy, and surprised her with a hug and a kiss. They shared a romantic evening out and then at home together. The next morning he awoke eager for the days ahead.

CHAPTER TWENTY-SEVEN

For coaches, the immediate post-season was no longer a time when loss of games was a concern. This was the period when loss of jobs—and loss of dreams, too—took place. You could ask Bobby about that. In the few weeks that followed his ordeal, the jobs of four other head coaches and dozens of assistant coaches in the league were terminated. Some of the changes were warranted; some made no sense at all. And then there were those that resulted from the coach being made the scapegoat for the dysfunction of others involved in the team's operation. Whatever it was, the fired coach was out of a job. At least for the time being.

For Mel Herbert and his fellow sportswriters, all of this "fire the coach" activity provided abundant opportunities for them to weigh in with strong opinion pieces. Jordy Nerdmann was assigned to write a column titled: "Five Reasons The Leopards Should Have Fired Bobby Russell." Mel prepared a companion article bearing the title: "Five Reasons The Leopards Should Not Have Fired Bobby Russell."

FIVE REASONS WHY THE LEOPARDS SHOULD HAVE FIRED BOBBY RUSSELL

By Jordy Nerdmann

1. He's too conservative.
2. He's too predictable.
3. He lacks an offensive background.
4. He doesn't deliver high-pitched pep talks at halftime.
5. Mediocre production. Two years in a row his team failed to make the playoffs.

FIVE REASONS WHY THE LEOPARDS SHOULD NOT HAVE FIRED BOBBY RUSSELL

By Mel Herbert

1. He teaches and he reaches. He teaches fundamentals and he reaches his players. They buy in.
2. He is level headed. He keeps his cool in tough situations.
3. He handles adversity and gets his players back on track when setbacks occur.
4. He teaches clean play. He honors the game.
5. His teams exceeded expectations for an expansion franchise, and he had them on track for continuing improvement.

When readers of the *Guardian* responded by submitting letters that included more than 200 additional reasons (about evenly divided between "should have" and "should not have"), Sports Editor Carroll Blumenthal rendered a pat on the back to three people—one to Jordy, one to Mel, and a big one to himself.

■

When coaches are fired, vacancies occur, and so the brighter side of all that churning is that opportunities for advancement and for renewal are prevalent. The interest shown in Bobby Russell by several other NFL teams who wanted him as their defensive coordinator was testimony to that.

The most attractive of all the overtures he received, however, came from one of the four teams that were looking for a new head coach. They flew Bobby back East for an interview with the team's owner, Ronald Frump, a go-getter type of man whose manner—not his hair-do—Bobby admired. The meeting was cordial, and Bobby returned to Los Angeles encouraged and thinking that he might soon be hearing those uplifting words, "You're hired!"

Not so fast! Four days later the announcement came that one of the other candidates for that opening had been awarded the job. Bobby was surprised, but not as surprised as he was when he picked up his ringing telephone just four hours after experiencing this latest disappointment.

"Is this Coach Russell?" Bobby recognized the voice. It was Denzel Jackson's.

"No, this is *former* Coach Russell."

"How'd you like to be plain ol' Coach Russell again?"

"I thought I was going to be, Denzel, but they just announced that they've hired Don Connelly."

"I know that, Bobby. I heard, but I'll bet you don't know that Frosty Figueroa is going to be taking a head coach's job, too."

"Your defensive coordinator?"

"Yep. His alma mater came calling. Ike Witt is retiring, and Frosty's going to be the new head coach at Texas Tech. He'll be a darn good one, too, except that leaves me without a defensive coordinator. Anybody out there you might recommend?"

Bobby hesitated briefly, and then he said, "I know one guy."

"So do I," Denzel said. "In fact I know *only one guy*. And I'm talking to him right now. Are you interested?"

It all clicked for Bobby, but he wanted to see first how Cindy felt about it. "I'm not only interested, Denzel, but I'm complimented, as well. Can I call you back in an hour?"

"I'm not going anywhere. Let me know."

As Bobby suspected, Cindy was as warm to the offer as he was. Forty-five minutes later he dialed Denzel's number.

"Hello, Coach Jackson speaking."

"And this is *Coach* Russell calling. My answer is 'you betcha.'"

"Now that's the kind of decision making I like to see from the coaches on our staff," Denzel said. "Welcome to Portland."

They worked out the contractual details, and one week later the Bekins Van Lines truck pulled out of the driveway at Cindy and Bobby Russell's house in Westwood and headed north to their new home in Portland.

The night before Bobby and Cindy departed for Portland they attended a farewell party held on their behalf at Brant Gilbert's house. With the exception of Randy Dolbermeier, all the men who had been on Bobby's coaching staff, along with their wives, were there. So were Joe Skoronski, his lady friend, Darlene, and head trainer, Eddie Carpentierie, accompanied by his wife, Katie. Many of the front office employees and their spouses were in attendance, as well. As special guests, although they were not in the employ of the Los Angeles Leopards, Brant also invited Mel and Frances Herbert.

When Joe learned from Brant that the Herberts were going to be at the party, it made him wonder whether that might open the door for a couple of additional invitees.

"Say, Brant," Joe said, "dis is really great dat you're givin' dis goodbye party for Bobby, and dat you invited Mel and Mrs. Herbert ta come, too. But if Mel is gonna be dere, does dat mean dat Zig Zag will be comin', too?"

"Sure, by all means let's include him," Brant said.

"Den how about Zelda, dat nice lady from da Human Society dat he's been goin' aroun' wit? She's da one, ya know, dat works at dat Peter Animal Shelter."

"Of course, we want her there, too."

It was because of Zelda's presence that Mel learned how mean-ingful his earlier poetic attempt to buoy Bobby's spirits had been. As Mel sat there swirling the contents in his glass of Merlot, he tuned in on the conversation that his wife, Frannie, was having with Cindy Russell and Zelda.

"Cindy, how's your new puppy doing?" Zelda asked. Before Cindy could respond, Frannie jumped in with a question of her own.

"I didn't know you and Bobby had a dog," Frannie said. She was telling a lie. She did know. "When did that happen?"

"Zelda told us that someone brought an abandoned little Labrador into the shelter, and it just broke my heart when she told me all about it," Cindy said. "I pleaded with Bobby for us to go take a look at it, and once he got there, that did it. We adopted the cute little thing and brought him home just the day before yesterday. He's so much fun."

Frannie pretended that she wanted to know more. "Have you given him a name yet?"

"Bobby has," Cindy answered.

"What is it?" Frannie asked while checking to make certain that Mel was still listening.

"Sir Andrew," Cindy said.

Mel's eyes widened. Then he smiled. The three lady conspirators smiled back at him.

CHAPTER TWENTY-EIGHT

Two weeks later, and the scene at the Leopards office and practice facility was considerably changed. Bobby and Cindy (and Sir Andrew) had moved to Portland. Randy Dolbermeier had moved into the head coach's office. Former assistant coaches had been going out the door while new ones were coming in at a dizzying pace. Coaching secretaries Ada and Nina Klock, after a week of being badgered by Randy, decided that they'd rather retire than continue working in such an atmosphere, and the strained relationship between Randy and Brant had become apparent to several people in the building.

"I gotta tell ya, Mel, dere is a lotta infightin' goin' on awreddy between da coach and Brant," Joe said over the pizza they were sharing one evening. Zig Zag wasn't sitting with them. He had retired to the bar area where the TV sets were tuned in to the L.A. Lakers vs. Chicago Bulls basketball game.

"I'm not surprised they're bumping heads," Mel said, "but how do you know about it?"

"Well, just da udder day, for instance, I saw dem talkin' togedder outside a Randy's office, and den when dey broke it off, needer one a dem seemed happy at all. Den dat Randy winds up givin' me a funny look and jerks his tumb down da hall in da direction dat Brant is walkin'. When I don't do nuttin' back, he sorta acts like he's up dere on a big peddle stool. He just stares at me like, hey, why ain't cha agreein' wit me."

"Well, I hope they figure out some way to work together," Mel said. "This team is right on the brink of being a strong contender next year."

"Yeah, I know dat. We even coulda done lots better dis last season if we only coulda stayed more injury prone."

"Injury *free*," Mel said.

"Darn right. Ooh baby, dese jalapeño peppers is hot. I gotta get me anudder one a dose Heinekens ta cool off my mout."

■

Time flew by. The past season was history, and the next one was fast approaching. The draft, contract renewals, holdouts, a few player brushes with the law, stadium renovations, minicamps, and an occasional player trade all filled the interest gap for media and fans until the whistle would blow in September for the opening kickoff of the new season.

Most of those activities were routine, but occasionally there was a shocker, and one of those took place on the first day of the draft when the Portland Pioneers traded their first round draft choice. It went to the Leopards who, in exchange, sent defensive end Bill Hanlon and the rights to their sixth-round draft pick to the Pioneers.

"Brilliant move," wrote Jordy Nerdmann the next day. "By clever maneuvering, the Leopards, with *two* first-round draft choices, were able to add explosive elements to their offensive arsenal when they selected skilled position players like running back Darryl 'Gunner' Gaines from Minnesota and speedy wide receiver Burton 'Sticky Fingers' Lavell from Florida State. All they gave up to accomplish this coup was some defensive lineman. How many touchdowns did he ever score? They threw in a bottom-of-the-draft sixth-rounder (so what?) in order to ice the deal. Bye-bye to practically nothing. Hello to points on the board."

Mel Herbert's treatment of the trade differed from Jordy's. "Defensive linemen like Bill Hanlon do not come along often," he noted. "With 12 sacks during the year, he set a rookie record. He led all defensive linemen in number of tackles. He's got a motor that never runs out of gas. He's smart. He's prepared. He's unselfish. He's liked and respected by his teammates. Sure, he won't gain any yards carrying the ball, and he won't tally a bunch of pass receiving yards either, but he's as good as they come in keeping the other team from succeeding in their efforts to do all of that. He will be missed."

The trade that sent Hanlon to Portland had repercussions that went beyond a mere exchange of players and draft choices. The ongoing disagreement between Gilbert and Dolbermeier about the status of Hanlon had been gaining momentum since the first time Randy informed Brant of his desire to send "the Kickasska from Nebraska" elsewhere. The friction spilled over into other aspects of their relationship, and soon the coolness turned into a freeze.

Whenever he was able to do it, Randy sought to bypass Brant, choosing instead to communicate directly with Cedric. B. Medill on policy and personnel matters.

During the week prior to the draft, Randy initiated calls to General Managers around the league advising them that the Leopards would consider trading Hanlon. Several teams expressed interest, but they balked when Randy informed them that the Leopards were looking for a first-round pick in exchange.

Randy decided to wait until the morning of the draft, hoping that some team might step up at the last moment with an offer of a first-rounder. He received no further inquiries, however, but Brant Gilbert did.

On draft day morning Brant received a call from Lilly Napoleon.

"I hear that you are open to trading Bill Hanlon," she said after their brief exchange of pleasantries.

"Who told you that?" Brant asked. He wasn't surprised by her answer.

"Randy Dolbermeier. I told him that I hadn't heard anything about it from you, and then he said that you had given him the okay to go ahead and make a deal. We *are* interested, but I wanted to check with you before we go any further."

Brant guessed that Lilly was harboring some suspicions. She was, and his response served to increase the validity of her doubts.

"Lilly, I'll get back to you in just a little while. I want to speak first with Randy and with Mr. Medill."

While Brant, Randy, and Cedric B. were meeting in Los Angeles, there was another trio—Lilly Napoleon, Denzel Jackson, and newly appointed Defensive Coordinator Bobby Russell—meeting in Portland.

"Everything I've seen in Hanlon has been great," Denzel said, "but, Bobby, is there something wrong with him that we don't know about? If he's that good, why in the world would they be looking to trade him?"

"He won't play dirty, and that's it. Period," Bobby said. "That's what got him into Randy's doghouse, and I'm sure that's why Randy's campaigning to get him out of there now. Believe me, he's worth giving up a first-round choice if that's what it's going to take. At least, that's my opinion."

"And that's why we're talking to you, Bobby," Lilly said. "We want your opinion. No one knows him better than you do."

"Well, there is one person who knows him as well as I do," Bobby said, "and that's Brant Gilbert. I can't believe that he'd be going along with this."

"I'm wondering about that, too," Lilly said. "It really seems strange to me. Let's see what he says when he calls. He said he'd be back in touch just as soon as he meets with Randy and Mr. Medill."

Brant did meet with Randy and Cedric B., but it wasn't Brant who called back. It was Cedric B. on the phone for Lilly.

"Hello, Lilly, this is Cedric B. Medill. I'm right here with our coach, Randy Dolbermeier. Brant Gilbert is tied up for the moment, but I just wanted you to know that we are willing, if the price is right, to trade Bill Hanlon. Randy can handle all the negotiating from our end, and so I'm going to turn the phone over to him. I hope it all works out."

Fifteen minutes later the deal was done.

CHAPTER TWENTY-NINE

When Cedric B. Medill telephoned Lilly Napoleon, it was not because Brant Gilbert was busy with other matters. It was because the nature of the conversation that transpired when Brant, Cedric B., and Randy met resulted in Brant's reluctance—or was it his refusal?—to convey a message that violated principles in which he believed.

When the three of them moved into a private room next to the main draft headquarters at their facility to talk, Brant set all preliminaries aside.

"Why are you telling general managers from other teams that I gave you the green light to inquire about making a trade for Bill Hanlon?" he demanded, staring directly into Randy's eyes.

"Oh, c'mon. You've known all along that I wanted to get that jerk out of here. I've told you a thousand times how I feel about him."

"That's not the point. Why are *you* calling them? And without my knowing about it first."

"Because if I waited for you to keep diddling around we'd never get anything done. How's that?"

"Hold it. Hold it," Cedric B. said. "Let's calm down and get civil. Let's stick to the point. The issue is whether or not we should go ahead and try to make this trade. I know Randy has spoken to you, Brant, about trading Hanlon. He's mentioned it to me, too, several times. I kept hoping you two could work it out without me butting in, but maybe it is time to include me. I'm glad you asked for this meeting."

"I asked for the meeting, Cedric, because Randy has consistently sought to bypass me, and this is just one more blatant example of that. Besides, it would be a huge mistake for us to part with Bill Hanlon, and Randy's reasons for wanting to do so are despicable."

"Well, he tells me that Hanlon is not a team player."

"Not true," Brant responded. "He simply won't employ some dirty tactics that Randy wants him to use. If that's not being a team player, then neither am I."

"Maybe you're not," Randy said. "You sure aren't willing to do something now that is going to make us a better team."

Before a seething Brant could respond, Cedric B. jumped in again. "This is getting way too personal. I want that to stop right now. It's apparent that each of you is adamant about whether we should or shouldn't trade Hanlon. From my perspective, Brant,—I know you don't want to hear this—but I have to say that it makes sense to me for us to trade him if we get a first-round pick by doing so. Randy has told me that we could really juice up our offense with that choice, and I'm all for that."

Brant closed his eyes and remained silent for several seconds before speaking. "There is more to this, Cedric, than whether or not we make this trade," he said, "and that is why I wanted the three of us to meet and iron it out."

"We will deal with that, but, please, let's wait until after the draft. I know you told Lilly Napoleon you'd be calling her back, Brant, so I'm going to ask that you do go forward with the trade negotiations when you speak with her."

"Cedric, may I ask, please, that you not put me in the position of having to be the spokesman for something that is so contrary to all that I believe in? Could you, or Randy if you so choose, please make that call to Lilly?"

"I understand. What you just suggested makes sense. Randy and I will take care of it."

The trade was made. Not long afterwards, running back Darryl "Gunner" Gaines and wide receiver Burton "Sticky Fingers" Lavell, wearing Leopards caps, were interviewed by ESPN's Tiffany Diamond at draft headquarters in New York City. Gaines's agent, Drew "Mouse" Ratigan, was at his side.

"Are you surprised that you went this high in the draft?" Tiffany asked Gunner.

Mouse Ratigan jumped in and answered on Gunner's behalf. "We're surprised he didn't go higher," he said, "but we're delighted that he will be joining the Los Angeles Leopards. With that Fun and Shout offense I hear they are going to use, Darryl is really going to light up their scoreboard. I'm looking forward to completing all contract arrangements before the beginning of training camp, and if Darryl gets the deal that I truly believe he deserves, we may be able to change his name to Darryl 'Corporate' Gaines."

"And you," Tiffany asked as she turned to Sticky Fingers Lavell, "what role do you see for yourself with the Leopards?"

"They already told me I could wear my number 85 jersey, the same number that I wore in college, and if they just throw me the ball enough times, that's the number of touchdowns I plan on scoring for them," he chuckled.

"Well, good luck and thank you both," Tiffany said. "Now back to Clint Fuhrman and all the guys at our anchor desk at ESPN headquarters."

For the media, it was interview heaven on that first day of the draft. When the fourth round began on the second day, the number of interviews tailed off sharply, and by the sixth round, when the Portland Pioneers, using the pick they had procured in the previous day's trade with the Leopards, selected wide receiver Reed Andreas from Kutztown State College in Pennsylvania, the only person who requested an interview with Reed was a cub reporter from the *Kutztown Kibitzer.*

CHAPTER THIRTY

The day after the draft, Brant Gilbert entered Cedric B. Medill's office. Brant had full confidence that the issue he was there to address deserved immediate attention, but he had no confidence that the resolution would be the one he most desired.

"I appreciate this opportunity to meet with you, Cedric. I know how busy you are, so I'll get right to the point. Simply, I cannot work with Randy Dolbermeier. I don't even think I need to go into all the reasons because you've seen for yourself how badly we get along."

"Yes, I have, Brant, and it really pains me. I believe in you both, but unless you two can learn to work together we are not going to be successful."

"I've tried, but I don't think he has, or even wants to," Brant said.

"What is the answer, then?"

"Cedric, I don't say this to be confrontational, but I honestly feel that one or the other of us has to go."

"Brant, Randy Dolbermeier is the coach I want for this team. I'm not sending him packing. You know that."

"I didn't think you would, but I had to let you know that it just will not work out with both Randy and me here. I wouldn't like myself very much if I pretended any differently. Therefore, I guess that I don't have any other choice except to submit my resignation."

"Oh, no. I don't accept it. You stay on."

"Cedric, I can't. This has been brewing for quite a while now, and it really isn't in anyone's best interest to have it continue. If at any time you might want some input or information from me, please don't hesitate to ask. I'll give you as straight an answer as I can."

"Well then, Brant, I am going to ask you something right now. How in the world are we going to be able to replace you, particularly at this late date, with a general manager who can handle all the things that need to be done?"

"Why don't you just make Randy the Director of Football Operations? That really is what he's elbowed his way into doing, anyway. I'm not saying he's going to be any good at it, but he isn't the man I'd want as our coach, either. I know you feel differently about that. You can turn all the administrative and business-related items that a GM normally deals with over to Ross Branson and Tim Underdorf. I'm sure both of them would do an excellent job for you."

They continued to talk. Cedric B. tried again to get Brant to reconsider, but to no avail.

■

At the press conference three days later when Brant was asked why he was resigning, he came up with the time-honored standard, "I want to spend more time with my family."

There was an abundance of media speculation regarding what had led to this turn of events, but Mel Herbert was the only one who knew the real story. Brant confided in Mel, but when he did, he emphasized that what had occurred was not the result of any contentious relationship that existed between himself and Cedric B.

Besides Mel and the members of Brant's family, there was only one other person to whom Brant divulged all the details about what led to his departure from his job with the Leopards. That person was Bobby Russell, and Bobby was distressed when he learned that Brant's career, too, had been derailed by Randy Dolbermeier.

"How unfair can this get?" Bobby blared into the telephone after hearing the story from Brant. "Now what, Brant? I know how much you and the girls all want to stay there in L.A. And you just walked away. You don't even have a job."

Strangely, it wasn't Brant who needed consoling. It was Bobby, and Brant was the person who provided it for him.

"Our family *will* be staying here in L.A., Bobby. I got a call already from Ted Noren at Fox Sports. They want me as a game day studio analyst on their NFL programming. The pay is pretty darn good, and I can continue living right here where we are now. It'll all work out great, I'm sure. Not only that, I won't have to be seeing Randy Dolbermeier at work every day, either. And you better look out, pal, because if the Pioneers lose any games next year, I'm going to blame it all on their defensive coordinator."

Bobby did feel better. "Well, that's just fine with me." he said, "because we certainly aren't going to lose any games. But please don't quote me."

CHAPTER THIRTY-ONE

Four games into the season that fall it seemed as if Bobby Russell's bold declaration that the Portland Pioneers wouldn't be losing any games might turn out to be the most clairvoyant assessment of events to come since Nostradamus in 1559 asserted that some day a human being would set foot on the moon. The Pioneers were 4–0.

There were exciting things happening for the Los Angeles Leopards, too. After four games, their Fun and Shout offense was leading the NFL in total yards from scrimmage. They were leading in pass attempts and in pass completions, and they were second in the league in points scored. On opening day they mesmerized the football world by streaking down the field for touchdowns on their first three possessions in the process of registering a 45–34 victory over the favored New York Giants. That was the good news, but it wasn't all good.

Their record was 1–3. They led the league in interceptions thrown and fumbles lost. They had allowed three kick returns for touchdowns, and two of their punts had been blocked. On three occasions near midfield, in fourth-down situations, they had disdained punting, electing to "go for it, baby," instead. Twice they failed to make the first down, and both times their opponent cashed in on the gift of favorable field position by scoring a touchdown after taking possession.

There was one other shoot-from-the-hip gamble that turned into a shoot-*yourself*-in-the-hip experience for rookie coach Randy Dolbermeier. In their fourth game, with three minutes remaining until the final gun, the Leopards were leading the Arizona Cardinals 33–31. It was the Leopards' ball, fourth-and-goal on the Cardinals' eight-yard

line. Randy sent his field goal team onto the field.   Kicker Garland
"Uprights" Updyke had converted all four of the field goals he had
attempted earlier in the game, all from distances longer than this one.

Updyke was not destined to boot his fifth successful field goal
on the ensuing play, however. It wasn't because his kick went awry.
It was because Dolbermeier had sent in a *fake* field goal play.

Holder Toby Eggleston feigned setting the ball in place for the
kick, and then, when he rolled out instead and drilled a pass directly
at tight end Cody Benjamin, who was wide open in the end zone,
Cardinals linebacker Paul Whitney threw his hand into the air just as
the ball was released and deflected it to the ground.

The Cardinals took possession, then marched through the
Leopards porous defense, driving deep into L.A. territory, and with
just 15 seconds remaining to be played, they lined up for a field goal
attempt. They didn't fake it. They kicked it. The kick was good.
Arizona won the game, 34–33.

For the third week in a row, the Leopards, after their auspicious
start, had frittered away an opportunity for a victory.

During the post-game rehash, Dolbermeier defended his decision to call for the fake field goal.

"We scouted them, and they were vulnerable to it. All 11 of
their guys were on the line of scrimmage. No one was covering a pass.
They got plain lucky when that stupid linebacker of theirs, who was
fooled on the play anyway, just stuck up his hand and it got in the way.
If we score what looks like a sure touchdown, we'd have gone up by
nine points. Then they'd have to score twice in less than three minutes in order to beat us. But if we kick another one of those damn 'Oh,
I better play it safe' field goals, they could still beat us by scoring a
touchdown. The hell with that."

"If you had it to do over again, would you make the same call?"
Aaron Knittout of *The Whittier Whistleblower* asked.

"You can bet your boxer shorts I would," Randy answered. "I'm
not going to always be playing it safe like my predecessor did. I'm not
going to be one of those hand-wringing sissies who's afraid to take

some chances. We're shooting for big things, and if our fans are looking for exciting times ahead, then I'm the man who can provide it for them."

■

One week later, the Portland Pioneers suffered their first loss of the season. It hurt, but their pain wasn't as intense as that being endured by the Leopards, who went down to their fourth consecutive defeat.

It got even worse for the Leopards on the following Sunday when their losing streak was extended to five. The Pioneers fared better. They won. With that victory, the Pioneers, sporting a 5–1 record, moved into sole possession of first place in their division. One week later, after defeating the Indianapolis Colts, they made it 6–1, while the forlorn Leopards fell to 1–6 by virtue of their loss to the Green Bay Packers.

Denzel Jackson of the Pioneers was already being touted as a candidate for the NFL's Coach of the Year Award, and General Manager Lilly Napoleon appeared to be the front-runner for Executive of the Year. Why not? The deal she engineered on draft day had provided the foundation for the swift rise in fortunes that the Pioneers were enjoying.

The play of defensive end Bill Hanlon exceeded all they had hoped to gain at that position when they traded for him. By giving up their first-round draft choice in order to bring Hanlon aboard, they knew that they would be foregoing the opportunity to select one of the draft's premier running backs, all of whom would be off the board by the time the first round was completed. They acknowledged that they did need an outstanding running back, but they made the tough decision anyway. As a result, they now had reasons for celebration that went well beyond just having acquired the Kickasska from Nebraska.

During that memorable day at the draft in April, Lilly, Denzel, and all the Pioneers assistant coaches had lounged around waiting for the first round to be over with. With no choice available to them in that round, it was thumb-twiddling time.

Not so for Director of Player Personnel Charlie Navey, however. He was pacing around the room and perspiring as six running backs were gobbled up by other teams in the league.

In the second round, when it was announced that the Minnesota Vikings, picking one spot ahead of the Pioneers, selected running back Jared "Tootsie" Rolle from Ohio State University, Charlie exploded out of his seat and executed the poorest example of a jubilant, arms raised, airborne pirouette ever witnessed. Fortunately, two of the assistant coaches who were standing next to Charlie were able to grab him as he descended into what otherwise would have been a nasty crash landing. He didn't care.

"We've got him!" Charlie yelled.

"Got who?" Lilly asked.

"Tommy."

"Who's Tommy?" Denzel asked.

"Thomas Thurber. That running back from Oklahoma State. He's the best one in the whole damn draft."

"No he's not," Lilly said. "There's a red dot next to his name. That means that he's a medical reject. That's why everyone's gone right past him."

"He's fine," Charlie said. "I really checked it out. The doctors down there say he's almost 100% ready to go. I knew all about it, but I clammed up until now. I wasn't going to take any chances that it might leak out."

"You sure?" Lilly asked.

"Mmmm, yes!"

Lilly glanced at Denzel. "How do you feel about it, Denzel?"

"If you're willing to take the gamble, so am I."

"Okay. Charlie, if you promise not to jump in the air again," Lilly said, "we're taking him right now." And that's what they did.

Seven games into the season, Tommy Thurber had rushed for more yards than any of the seven rookie running backs drafted ahead of him. He had more pass receptions and more receiving yards gained than any of them, as well.

Because of the trade that resulted in bringing Hanlon and Thurber onto the Portland roster, Lilly was being hailed as the reigning genius among NFL front office wheeler-dealers. But it wasn't only because Hanlon and Thurber were now wearing those Pioneers uniforms.

Remember that throw-in sixth-round pick that they received from the Leopards as part of the deal? The one they used to pick some wide receiver from Kutztown State named Reed Andreas? Who? From where?

Andreas, seven games into the season, was second in the NFL in pass receptions. He had scored nine touchdowns, and he was averaging more than 15 yards per catch. Everyone was impressed except for Jordy Nerdmann.

"Remember," Jordy wrote in his weekly column titled *Nerdmann's Fearless Lowdown On The National Football League* (otherwise known as *NFL On The NFL*), "this team would be undefeated if Andreas, in their one loss to Dallas earlier this season, had not dropped what would have been the winning touchdown pass in the fourth quarter. Don't be too quick to make this guy the next Jerry Beans. The jury is still out."

■

In games played on the eighth Sunday of the season, some funny things happened. They were funny enough to keep L.A. Leopards Coach Randy Dolbermeier laughing all the way on the plane trip home after their game in Chicago. The Leopards broke their six-game losing streak by defeating the Chicago Bears, while the Portland Pioneers lost an overtime heartbreaker to the Tennessee Titans. The Leopards record improved to 2–6. The Pioneers slipped to 6–2.

On all of the Leopards trips, a limited number of seats on the team plane were reserved for selected members of the media, and Mel

Herbert was one of the privileged few who was included in that group. Equipment Manager Joe Skoronski, employing his earnest negotiating talents, convinced Director of Media Relations Bert Scott to arrange seating so that Mel would sit next to Joe on those flights.

"We sure got some big breaks today, and dey got some lousy bad ones, dint dey," Joe said once they were airborne. "Dat backup quarterback a dere's, dat Morgan guy, he got all dat stuff in his eyes, and den he hadda leave da game when dey was awreddy witout Carmody, dere startin' QB. And den dat rookie guy, dat Jason Treenowt, comes in, and he couldn't do nuttin', could he?"

"He didn't have a chance," Mel said. "They just brought the kid up onto their active roster from the practice squad this week when they put Carmody on injured reserve. All Treenowt did all week was run opponents' plays for the scout team. They told me after the game that in order to get Morgan ready, he had to take all of the game plan reps at practice, and then, bang! He's out of there. Poor Jason had to go in and wind up being the goat."

"Didja ever find out what it was dat was bodderin' dat Morgan guy?"

"Not yet. There was some kind of irritating substance that got into his eyes on that play when he got sacked by Ronnie Tubbs. It had to be excruciating, they told us. It took until after the game was over, but they finally got it all flushed out. They still don't know what caused it, but they'll be checking it out. Count on that."

"Tubbs hadda good game, ya know. I saw Coach congratulatin' him big time in da locker room after da game. He slapped him on da back, and den, he gave him some kinduva envelope and dat linebacker, Buster Stones, was laughin' and sorta winkin' at him and pumpin' his fist at him, too. Dey weren't all laughin', dough. Colin Fitch and Big Butt Beamer and Sammy Kurtask and lotsa da udder guys had like real teed-off looks on dere faces."

"What was in the envelope? Do you know?" Mel asked.

"I assed him about dat later, and he told me it was a coupla tickets ta da ballet. I taught dat was real funny, but den he reached in and pulled dem outta da envelope and showed dem ta me. He told me dat he was gonna give dem ta Molly Kuehl, dat gal dat works in da ticket office, so dat she and her sister Dolly could go see it. Dere was more stuff in dat envelope, too, but he didn't show dat part ta me.

"Tickets to the ballet? What was that all about?" Mel asked.

"I dunno. Ya know what I mean?"

Mel didn't, so he changed the subject. "It was good to get back here again for a few days in Sweet Home Chicago, wasn't it? You do anything exciting while you were here?

"You bet. Last night I took Eddie Carpentierie ta dat Pilsen parta town, and we went ta Augie's Old Europe Cafe dere. Dey got bratwurst and kielbasa in dat place dat you could die from."

"You could die *for*, you mean."

"Eaderr way."

CHAPTER THIRTY-TWO

By winning that game in Chicago, the Leopards broke their losing streak. And then they won again. And again. And again. Their record improved to 5-6. They were rolling now. But then, on a chilly, overcast late November afternoon in Pittsburgh, they faltered. And how they did was weird.

With 29 seconds remaining in their game against the Pittsburgh Steelers, the Leopards were leading 28–21. They had the ball, first down on Pittsburgh's three-yard line, and the Steelers were out of timeouts. All the Leopards needed to do to wrap up their sixth victory of the year was have quarterback Q.T. Pye take the snap from center and kneel down. The final few seconds would then tick off the clock, the game would be over, and the Leopards would have evened their record at 6–6.

Entering this 12th week of competition, however, only one AFC team, the San Diego Chargers, led the Leopards in points scored, and the margin of difference was a mere four points. Randy Dolbermeier was jealous. He wanted not just victory, but big numbers, as well.

Damn it, we're going to put seven more on the scoreboard right now, he determined. He sent in instructions to run a power off-tackle play to the right. It was stopped at the one-yard line. Instead of allowing the time on the clock to expire, Randy called a timeout.

"Run that same play to the left," he told Pye as they conferred on the Leopards sideline. "And this time let's get the damn ball into the end zone."

Q.T. followed Randy's instructions. Sort of.

He did call the play to the left, and he did get the ball into the end zone. Problem was that it was the wrong end zone.

Q.T. stumbled as he pivoted away from his center towards running back Gunner Gaines. The ball squirted out of his hands and trickled back in the direction of his own distant goal line. The Steelers all-pro cornerback, Pancho DeLeon, scooped it up at the 10-yard line and sprinted 90 yards to a touchdown. The noise in the stadium was so loud that even trainer Eddie Carpentierie, standing next to Dolbermeier on the sidelines, was unable to distinguish the exact expletives that Randy was screeching out.

Pittsburgh added the point after touchdown, and the score was tied, 28–28. The game went into overtime.

Pittsburgh won the coin toss. They elected to receive. The Leopards chose to defend the west goal, and with a strong wind at his back, Garland Updyke boomed his kickoff deep into the Steelers end zone. Their kick return specialist, Shorty Spandex, fielded it there, and, despite Pittsburgh Coach Gil Bauer's frantic gestures directing him to just kneel and hand the ball to the official, Shorty came roaring out.

He didn't let go of the ball until he spiked it over his left shoulder in the opposite end zone 107 yards later. The Steelers won the game, 34–28.

After the game, Dolbermeier sought to explain his decision to go for the touchdown.

"If there is a tie for a playoff spot at the end of the season," he said, "number of points scored is one of the tie-breakers that helps to determine which team gets to go."

Many members of the media scoffed at that one, but team owner Cedric B. Medill came out strong in support of Randy's daring ways.

"That's the kind of a coach I want for this team," he said. "His blood-and-guts approach is why this team has bounced back so well from our rocky start. And let me tell you something else. It's going to be the reason why we rally from this disappointment, too. You just wait and see."

■

Four weeks later, Cedric B. could have summed it all up with a simple "I told you so, didn't I?" The Leopards won all four of the games that remained on their schedule following their loss to the Steelers. Three of those victories came at home, and they even won one on the road against the Carolina Panthers.

What a great second half of the season it had been. After a horrendous 1–6 start, the Leopards came back to win eight of their final nine games. They finished with an overall record of 9–7. Still, they were one victory shy of the 10-6 mark that would have qualified them for the playoffs.

Neither Randy nor Cedric B. reminded anyone that had Q.T. Pye been instructed to take a knee in the waning moments of their game against the Steelers four weeks earlier, rather than going for cosmetic points, the Leopards would have attained that coveted goal. Perhaps, in the excitement surrounding the Leopards whirlwind finish, they forgot about that bleak day at Three Rivers Stadium. And perhaps they just wanted to forget about it.

Mel Herbert remained aware of how that debacle impacted the Leopards playoff aspirations, but, given how successfully they had performed since that time, he felt it would be too persnickety of him to spotlight something that negative. Instead, he devoted himself to a sportswriter's favorite topic: *The Quarterback Controversy.*

Dolbermeier had inadvertently created one of those for himself. Unlike most coaches, he was enjoying it.

After Q.T. Pye's fumble in the waning seconds of the Leopards loss to the Steelers, Randy was stewing. It was time for him, he felt, to show his players who in the hell is in charge around here, and he did that by making Q.T. the subject of some stern discipline. He decreed that backup quarterback Toby Eggleston would take the first snap in their game against the Miami Dolphins the following week.

Q.T.'s contract called for a hefty bonus if he started every game during the season, and so, since Eggleston was technically the starter in that game, Q.T. suffered not only embarrassment but a sizeable financial hit, as well. Discipline—Dolberman style—had been exacted.

After the first series, Q.T. was back in the game at quarterback. He wasn't happy, but he sure kept it exciting after entering the game. Before the final gun sounded he connected on three touchdown passes, and he made it even more exciting by also throwing three interceptions. The Leopards escaped with a 37–31 victory.

The following week, against the Cleveland Browns, Q.T. came out playing more cautiously. He held on to the ball longer, and, as a result, he was sacked three times during the first half. The Leopards left the field after two quarters nursing a 7–3 lead.

"Loosen up," Randy told him in the locker room at half time. Q.T. did, but maybe he shouldn't have. Q.T.'s first two passes after halftime were intercepted. The Browns returned one of them for a touchdown while the second one set up a Cleveland field goal. With five minutes remaining in the third quarter the Browns moved into a 13-7 lead even though they were struggling badly on offense without their starting quarterback, Graham Mottowe, who had come down with food poisoning after the team's pre-game meal earlier that day.

An exasperated Dolbermeier sent Eggleston into the game. Brilliant move. In the final 20 minutes, Toby led the team on two scoring drives. One of them culminated when he connected on a 30-yard touchdown pass to Chase Banks, and on the second one he took the ball into the end zone himself by dashing 18 yards after being chased out of the passing pocket.

The Browns offense continued to fizzle, and the Leopards won, 21–13. With just two games remaining in the regular season they had evened their record at 7–7.

The Leopards must have loved that scenario because they came close to replicating it on the following Sunday when they met the Carolina Panthers. Despite his shaky performance from the previous week, Q.T. Pye was back in his starting role at quarterback. Once again he struggled, and once again Dolbermeier yanked him.

Eggleston entered the game early in the second quarter, and he turned in another sterling performance. The Leopards won again. They were now 8–7.

Randy had seen enough. For the season's finale against the New York Jets he benched Pye. Toby was the starter. He played well, but the Leopards defense was atrocious. Early in the fourth quarter, with the Jets leading, 34–21, matters seemed to grow even worse for the Leopards because Toby, after scrambling for a 15-yard gain on a third-and-eight situation, came down hard on his right shoulder. He was helped off the field, and Pye came in to replace him.

Yesterday's villain became this day's hero. Q.T. took over. He led the Leopards to a touchdown. They still trailed, 34–28, and the Leopards defense was unable to stop the Jets as the clock ticked down while the New Yorkers ground out a long drive.

With just a minute and 20 seconds left to play and with the Jets in possession of the ball at the Leopards' 19-yard line, their backup running back, Omar Goodness, fumbled. Omar had been filling in for Leonard "First" Downes, the Jets starter at that position. By some strange twist of fate, Downes, like Cleveland's quarterback two weeks earlier, had come down with a case of food poisoning shortly after having eaten his pre-game meal.

The Leopards recovered the fumble, and in the final seconds of the game, Q.T. moved his team 81 yards in seven plays for the crucial touchdown.

The Leopards pulled it out, 35–34. They finished with a winning record, and they, like about 25 other teams in the league, now had a quarterback controversy brewing. To hear Dolbermeier tell it, he didn't care.

"Ours is because we have two *good* quarterbacks. That's the kind I don't mind having," he said on his weekly call-in show. It was one of the few statements from Coach Dolbermeier that made sense even to Joe Skoronski.

■

Joe continued to be a prime source of information for Mel Herbert.

"Which one of the quarterbacks do the other players seem to prefer?" Mel asked one evening when Joe joined him and Zig Zag on Mel's ride home from work.

"Dey likes 'em both, but I'll tell ya, dat Scrambled Eggs guy, he looks ta me like he's gonna be da one."

Zig Zag disagreed. "Q.T.'s got way more experience against top competition, and he's got a better arm, too," he said.

"Yeah, but he's turned into a sorta wild guy. He's always runnin' aroun' late at night ta nightclubs and sometimes not payin' attention ta da udder important tings. I tink coach woulda got him outta dere by now awreddy cept dat we all know dat Mr. Medill really likes Q.T."

"Maybe they ought to send Q.T. to one of those psychologists and get him straightened out," Ziz Zag said.

"Nah. Anyone dat's willin' ta go see one a dose psycho guys like dat, oughta have his head examined in my pinion," Joe said. "Speakin' a QBs, Mel, did dey ever figger out what it was dat got inta da eyes a dat Bears quarterback, Morgan, when we played dem a few weeks ago?"

"That's a strange one, Joe. They found nothing on the turf or the field markings that could have caused it. I spoke with Mitch Fredericks from the *Chicago Tribune*, and he said he heard the Bears coaches are speculating that when Ronnie Tubbs got that sack against them, he rubbed something into Morgan's eyes."

"Oh, da Bears dint say dat, did dey?"

"No, they're not commenting about it publicly, but I think that's because they haven't been able to nail down any concrete evidence."

"Hey, maybe dat's why dat big, heavy guy, dat Herschel 'Ice Cream' Cohen, from da league security office was in here a coupla days ago askin' me and Eddie in da trainin' room about a buncha stuff."

"Like what?" Mel asked.

"Lotions and salves and pre-game meals and tings like dat."

"Did you say 'pre-game meals'?"

"Yeah. You heard me right. Dere you go, tinkin about food again. How come?"

"It's because Mitch told me that he also heard some rumbles that the Cleveland Browns and the New York Jets have been comparing notes regarding some players who came down with food poisoning on the day of their games against us."

"Yeah, I read about dat happenin'. Dat's freaky stuff when ya lose yer top QB and yer star runnin' back like dat. I can see why people're lookin' inta dat. Dat 'Ice Cream' Cohen fella, he did some talkin' ta Ronnie Tubbs, too, I noticed. If it keeps up like dis, pretty soon dey're gonna call in dat Federal Bureau of Instigation, it seems like."

"They spoke with Ronnie Tubbs, did they?" Mel asked. "I remember you told me that in the locker room after the Bears game you saw Dolbermeier hand that envelope to Ronnie, the one that Ronnie said contained two tickets to the ballet?"

"Yeah, dat's right. He did."

"Will you guys hold down the noise a little," Zig Zag pleaded. "'The Sally and Simon Football Highlights Hour' is coming on WOOF with predictions for this week's playoff games. I've got to hear Sally. That gal's been right on 72.4% of her picks so far this season. She really knows what she's talking about."

"Who's she pickin' in dat playoff game between da Pioneers and da Redskins?" Joe inquired. "Wit Coach Russell up dere now on dat staff in Portland, I'm pullin' for dose guys ta win it."

"So am I," Zig Zag said. "But be quiet, will you? As soon as this commercial for that high blood pressure medicine is over Sally's coming on. Let's listen to what she says. Please."

Mel reflected on all that he had heard, not only from Mitch Fredericks but from Joe, as well. He'd continue to look into this situation, but he knew that right now there wasn't enough to justify his sprinting over to his computer to start banging out a big story. At least, not yet.

CHAPTER THIRTY-THREE

If the 9-7 record registered by the Leopards in just their third season of existence was commendable, then how about those Portland Pioneers? They finished 12–4, winning six of their last seven games. They were division champions with a first-round bye in the playoffs and with a sold-out home game when they did take the field one week later for what would be the first playoff appearance in the team's brief history.

The Pioneers had a "quarterback situation," too, but it was the best kind. Kelly James was their starter. No doubt about it. Sometimes he had a few bad snaps and, on rare occasion, a not up-to-par full game performance. Coach Denzel Jackson kept him in there at quarterback, however, and Kelly always seemed to recover better than the Dow Jones on a good day.

Right behind Kelly James on the depth chart was Hank Wright. The loving mother of a bride-to-be never could have prepared any more thoroughly for her only daughter's wedding than Hank Wright did for every game. He didn't get to play often, but when he did, he was ready.

One of Hank's best moments came 10 games into the schedule when the Pioneers were on the road in Atlanta playing the Falcons. In the previous two weeks the Pioneers had lost for the second and then for the third time in what had appeared to be such a promising season. Their record at that point was 6–3.

Early in the game against the Falcons, Kelly James, just as he released the ball on a completed pass to Reed Andreas, was drilled in the ribs by Falcons defensive end Beacon Sloanes. Kelly came up hurting, but he gutted it out and stayed in the game.

By late in the third quarter it was obvious that Kelly was still suffering. So was his level of performance, and, as a result, the Pioneers were trailing the Falcons, 20–10. Between winces, Kelly sought to convince Coach Jackson that he could keep going, but Denzel made the tough—and the wise—decision. He sent Hank Wright into the game, and Hank came through. He led the Pioneers to a 27–20 comeback victory.

James was still not ready to play when the Pioneers took the field the following week for their game against the Minnesota Vikings. As a result, Wright got his first starting assignment of the year. The Pioneers stayed on the winning trail by defeating the Vikings, 24–6, and, in the locker room after it was all over, the Pioneers players and coaches awarded the game ball—accompanied by some discordant cheers—to the man whose performance had been so instrumental in helping them gain that victory. It went to Hank Wright.

Some of the media and some of the fans in Portland began to wonder if maybe Hank ought to remain the starter. Jackson heard them, but he didn't heed them. Kelly James was healthy again the next time the Pioneers played, and he was back in there as the starting quarterback for that game and for all the rest of the games that remained on the schedule.

The Pioneers had two solid quarterbacks, but they didn't have a quarterback controversy to distract them from their pursuit of excellence. James was their starter, and Wright was the best there was in the league when it came to handling the difficult task of holding the fort when the situation turned most dire.

Fox Sports Net analyst Brant Gilbert marveled at the chemistry that existed not only between those two quarterbacks, but that was also such a signature characteristic of the entire Pioneers organization. He had to admit that he envied them, but he also delighted in pointing out during his weekly televised segment, "BG's BS on the NFL," that quarterbacks alone are not the sole determinants of whether a team will succeed or fail.

"What fingers are to a master painter," Brant commented, "so can we equate the role that a quarterback plays in putting the exact final touches on a work of art that is far more complex than even the most keenly committed viewer could ever imagine.

"When Van Gogh and Picasso crafted their masterpieces it was not just their fingers—vital as they were—that made it all happen. It was their minds, their hearts, their vision, their resolve, their persistence, their patience, their unique gifts of talent, and so much more that made it all come together in such unmatchable fashion.

"And for the Portland Pioneers, it is not *just* Kelly James and Hank Wright that make it happen. It is also that superb cast of high-character teammates that surround Kelly and Hank. Some of their names you know well, and some you may never have heard of. It is also General Manager Lilly Napoleon, the person who has put it all together.

"It is Coach Denzel Jackson and the outstanding coaching staff that he has assembled, an example of that being defensive coordinator Bobby Russell whose unit led the NFL in takeaways and in allowing the league's fewest points scored by opponents during this just completed regular season. And it is considerably more than all of that, but by now, I think you can see the picture that *I* am painting."

Mel Herbert, Joe Skoronski, and Zig Zag Zizzo were sitting at a table in Bianca's Blue Horizon Bar where they had just finished watching Brant Gilbert's presentation. Mel was trying to figure out how to retrieve a message from the new cell phone that his newspaper had provided for its writers. Joe was putting the finishing touches (make that finishing *lips*) on a glass of brew, and Zig Zag was reviewing the notes he had scribbled during Brant's commentary.

"I really miss dat Brant Gilbert bein' wit da team." Joe said.

"Everybody I talk with around there does, too," Zig Zag said, "but he says some real smart things on TV. I always learn a lot when I listen to him."

Mel sensed this was an opportunity that could serve to relieve him from his faltering tussle with technology. He waved his hand in disgust at his recalcitrant cell phone, snapped it shut, stuffed it into his pocket, and joined the conversation.

"I'd wager that it won't be too long before someone comes after him with an offer," Mel said. "A lot of people in this league know about Brant Gilbert, and it's all good."

"Yeah, but I keep hearin' dat he don't wanta leave L.A.," Joe said. "I wish dere was some way he could come back here ta our team again."

"Not likely, but you never know," Mel said.

"Man, what Brant said just now on TV about quarterbacks is really interesting," Zig Zag said. "Mel, you've been around this game a long time, so you tell me, who'd you rather have at quarterback, Kelly James and Hank Wright or those Picasso and Van Gogh guys he was talking about?"

"Well," Mel said, "that's a tough one, especially since Brant neglected to include that Johnny Unitas/Norman Rockwell combo. They'd have to be in the mix, too. Let me think about it for a couple of days."

Joe changed the subject. "Hey, Bianca," he called out, "could you or Genevieve up dere bring me anudder one a dese flagoons fulla beer? And dis time fill it up, willya? Dat last one was more den at least a full inch from da top. Okay?"

"You got it, Joe-Joe," Bianca said, closing one eye and jangling her array of bracelets as she thrust a bobbing forefinger back in his direction.

■

Although Brant Gilbert didn't get to hear any of the compliments being directed his way by the Three Mustachekateers, there was a pleasant message awaiting him on his answering machine when he returned home after work that night.

"Hello, Mr. Gilbert." Brant recognized Bobby Russell's voice. "This call is from an admirer of yours. I watched your program earlier today, and I appreciate the nice things you said about me. Your insights about this game are truly astounding. Have you ever thought about being a general manager? I think you'd be a good one. Could I have your autograph?"

CHAPTER THIRTY-FOUR

One week later, reporter Mel Herbert, television personality Brant Gilbert, and 72,000 fans (at least 50% of whom were not inebriated) were among those present at Portland's Bekins Van Lines U-Haul Stadium to witness the first NFL playoff game ever to take place in that city. It was the Portland Pioneers vs. the Washington Redskins.

A little more than three hours later, when the game ended, the home team fans (at least 20% of whom were still not inebriated) streamed into the parking lots for their tailgate parties or on to the nearby bars for their post-game celebrations. Their beloved Pioneers had defeated the Redskins, 24–10. Next week it would be on to New Orleans for the NFC Championship game against the New Orleans Saints. The winner of that one would be going to the Super Bowl. Oh, my gosh!

■

For the fans, the game was over, but for Mel and Brant the main part of their assignments came after the game. In their reporting roles they needed to convey the facts, of course, but what about the drama, the excitement, the insights, the critique of strategy and tactics?

When their tasks were completed late that night, they headed for the airport to catch their redeye flight back to Los Angeles. Once aboard, seated next to each other, they talked about whatever came to mind. Today's game. Next week's game. Cedric B. Medill's latest movie spectacular, *When the Mountain Comes over the Moon.* The hairdo on the lady two rows up. Stinking poetry that doesn't rhyme. When are they going to turn off the seat belt sign so that we can use the john? Madonna. Barbara Walters. Joe DiMaggio. Today's music. Irving Berlin. Portobello mushrooms. You name it.

Twenty minutes before their plane touched down at L.A. International Airport, Brant raised a new topic. "I hear a rumor that the league has been questioning Ronnie Tubbs about that incident earlier in the season when the Bears quarterback had to come out of the game because of that eye problem."

"Where did you hear that?" Mel asked.

"Two of the Leopards players that I know real well told me. I can't tell you who they are, Mel, because I promised them I wouldn't divulge their names."

"Well, I can't tell you who told me, but I've heard from a reliable source that the league is looking into it. What do you think it's all about?"

"The way I hear it, Randy pulled a few players aside and offered a rather attractive bounty to any of them who could get the hit that would put the Bears quarterback out of the game."

"Really? And you know, having to go without their top two quarterbacks probably did cost the Bears the game."

"Just like Cleveland's losing Mottowe and the Jets having to go without Downes cost both of them," Brant said.

"Oh! Oh! You've heard something there, too. Right?"

"Sounds like you have, too."

"Are we the only ones?"

"I don't know, but I do know that it is weird when the star players on two different teams that the Leopards were about to play come down with food poisoning right after eating a pre-game meal."

"This one is scary," Mel said, "but really, there's still not enough there to nail it down, and it would be terrible if a story comes out based on these rumors if it then turns out that they aren't true."

"I know that, and that's why I'm not saying anything more right now. But I have my suspicions, so stay tuned."

"You can count on that," Mel said.

CHAPTER THIRTY-FIVE

It was Friday night in New Orleans. In fewer than 48 hours the Portland Pioneers and the New Orleans Saints would be meeting in the Louisiana Superdome for the NFC championship, but on this evening, just a few blocks away from that venue, Mel Herbert was sitting in Antoine's Restaurant in the heart of the French Quarter gazing across the table at a woman with whom he had fallen in love.

It was his wife, Frannie. It was more than 45 years ago since he first found himself falling in love with her, but he was still falling.

"And to think, dear girl, that I didn't even want you to come on this trip," Mel said as they clinked glasses prior to sipping their Cabernet Sauvignon.

"That's because you are always so intense about your work. I'm glad I convinced you that you can have some fun, too, and because of that, you'll probably do an even better job than you would have done by just being a grump."

"Me? A grump? Unheard of," Mel said. "It's just that you'll be missing a whole week at the workout studio, and you know how important exercise and a healthy lifestyle is."

"Are you back on exercise and proper diet again?"

"No. That's not it. With all these tight deadlines that I keep facing, there is something else that I'm even more concerned about. You know what that is, don't you?"

"Oh, you're not going to start bugging me again about always having to be on time are you?"

"No, my darling, I can recognize a lost cause when I see one."

"That's not fair," Frannie said. "Remember, you were so fretful, because I was coming along on this trip, that we were going to be late in catching our flight, and then we wound up getting to the airport with 45 minutes to spare before it even took off. Relax, Melvin."

"Frances, that was because our plane was an hour and 15 minutes late in departing, for heaven's sake."

"Oh, don't be so technical."

"Okay. I won't, and that's because I really am glad that you did come. How you've been able to set up so many enjoyable things for us to do since we got here is remarkable. But, then again, so are you. I'll never be able to figure out how you succeeded in wheedling a reservation at Antoine's on such short notice and on such a crowded night. They get booked weeks in advance."

"If I told you how, I think you might get angry."

"When in the bleepity-bleep do I ever get angry?" Mel asked with a feigned scowl. "C'mon, tell me, how did you pull it off?"

"Okay, if you promise to be nice. The first day we were here I ran into Cindy Russell in our hotel lobby, and we had a wonderful visit. When I told her how impossible a time I was having trying to get dinner reservations here at Antoine's, she must really have been sympathizing because later that day I got a call in our room from Lilly Napoleon. Lilly told me that Cindy had spoken to her about the conversation that Cindy and I had earlier. And then Lilly stunned me when she said that she made a call on our behalf, and that we were all set for this evening here."

"With all she's got on her mind, with the biggest game of her life to concentrate on, you bothered her with making dinner reservations?"

"I didn't. It was Cindy who asked her, and besides, Lilly was so nice. She said she really enjoyed doing it, and then she told me that what really swung the deal wasn't just her General Manager's clout. It was because she was able to carry out the whole conversation with Antoine in French, she said. And she loved that. Apparently, Antoine did, too."

"Frannie, my darling girl, you never cease to amaze me. See, I didn't get angry, did I?"

The next morning at breakfast Mel, after cautioning Frannie to not eat all of her hash brown potatoes and receiving a rebuking stare in response, reached into a folder he had brought with him. From it
he took out a sheet of paper, reached across the table, and handed it to Frannie.

It was another poem, one he composed earlier that morning while Frannie was in the shower and while he reflected on the delightful dinner date that she had arranged for the two of them the previous evening. Frannie took it, set aside her utensils, and glanced down at this unexpected intrusion. She saw the title, said, "Aw," removed the napkin that was tucked into the top of her blouse, snatched Mel's reading glasses from the table top, and immersed herself in reading it.

TO FRANNIE, MY HONEYHEART

You are so beautiful, and you are so wise,
And so I don't care if you don't exercise.
And always being late isn't a crime,
So I'll be more tolerant when you're not on time.
I love you just the way you are,
Even when you put makeup on in the car.
And even if you decide to eat red meat,
You're still gorgeous, and loving, and oh, so sweet.
When you're not near there is one thing I miss.
That's holding you close and getting a kiss.
So just be yourself, and I won't keep score,
I'll just tell you again, you're the one I adore.
So what if you drive me clean out of my mind;
There's no one like you I'd ever find.
Darling, you and I, we fit like a glove,
And that's why we'll always be so much in love.

Frannie, while failing to stifle a sniffle or two, jumped up out her chair, sidestepped some exiting customers, some nearby chairs and a waiter bearing a loaded tray as she manipulated her way around the table towards Mel. Frannie took his cheeks between her hands, bent over, and bestowed a tender kiss on the lips of the man she so loved.

The ripple of applause from other diners in the room became more intense when Mel responded by turning his smiling, lipstick-smudged face towards the audience while waving his hand in acknowledgment of their accolades.

■

On the Friday leading up to the NFC Championship Game, Mel devoted his column to an examination of the brilliant work done by Lilly Napoleon and the Saints' Walter Louis in helping to guide their teams in their quests for the NFC championship.

"What unlikely leaders of professional football teams these two people are," Mel wrote. "Two years ago, both these franchises were struggling to win just a few games a season. Now, the only woman ever to hold a general manager's role and the grandson of a former heavyweight boxing champion will lead their teams into the Louisiana Superdome on Sunday. The winner is going to the Super Bowl."

For the Saturday edition of the paper, the *Guardian's* Sports Editor, Carroll Blumenthal, knowing he could spark some desired controversy by doing so, assigned Jordy Nerdmann to give his views regarding the performance of those two general managers.

"The only reason Lilly Napoleon is serving as general manager of the Portland Pioneers," Jordy wrote, "is because her father-in-law owns the team. They have progressed to where they are now against a patsy of a schedule. Anyone who blunders by hiring Bobby Russell as a member of the coaching staff can't know what he (oops—she) is doing. Here is a team that was in the lower half of the league in number of passes attempted during this past season, and yet they've lucked themselves into the playoffs.

"I can't say that I know a lot about the New Orleans General Manager, Walter Louis, but at least somewhere in his background there is a family history of participating in sports.

"And so, here is my prediction: *On Sunday, Napoleon will meet her Walter Lou!*"

Jordy was prepared, in the event the Pioneers won the game, to explain the unique circumstances that led to what he would then present as such an amusingly unlikely outcome, but he was spared that bit of broken-field running. The Saints won, 20–14.

The Saints players and coaches spent the next 24 hours in celebration, and then went back to work in preparation for their Super Bowl matchup against the Denver Broncos just two weeks hence. Priority No. 1: How do you stop the Denver offense led by quarterback Elroy Jonathan when he has weapons like wide receiver Rocket Gibraltar and running back Paycheck Danning, and when their game plan is crafted by football's newly anointed "genius," offensive coordinator Fred Cantrell, formerly of the L.A. Leopards?

For the Portland Pioneers, their season was over. For them it was time to mourn, and then to begin to heal, to find a way to recover, to get ready for the next season, and to attack it with vigor and persistence. Simple! But not easy.

CHAPTER THIRTY-SIX

Clarence Corcoran was whistling the tune "It's A Lovely Day Today" as he finished buttoning his overcoat and stepped out the door of NFL headquarters and onto the sidewalk at 280 Park Avenue. He was headed to the law offices of Corcoran, Darragh, Madden, and Yates.

The clamor of midtown Manhattan didn't bother him. His briefcase seemed lighter than usual, and so, upon reaching the corner at 49th Street, he ignored the blinking "Don't Walk" sign, quickened his pace, and with almost a yard to spare, beat the taxi that was zipping around the corner even though the yellow light had just turned red. That marked the second time that afternoon that Corcoran had come away a winner.

As he continued striding up Park Avenue he shoved the earplug from his cell phone into his ear and dialed a number.

"Yo," a voice on the other end answered.

"Coach Dolbermeier," Corcoran said, "I'm calling with some good news."

"I hope it's what I think it is."

"Yes, it is. I just finished my meeting with Commissioner Rogers and with Mr. Cohen. I showed them the affidavit from a Miss Molly Kuehl in which she affirmed, just as Ronnie Tubbs told them, that he gave her the two tickets to the ballet that he received in recognition for your naming him as defensive player of the game against the Chicago Bears."

"That's all it was, Mr. Corcoran. I don't know why they're making such a big fuss about it."

"When Ronnie and I were there meeting with the Commissioner and Mr. Cohen, they asked him numerous questions about that play where the Bears quarterback had to leave the game after Ronnie tackled him. It was obvious, of course, that they were probing to see if any skullduggery on his part was involved."

"They know damn well that players get hurt all the time in this game. To call a player all the way into the league offices just because someone saw me give him a pat on the back and that award envelope after the game is pure bullshit. That's why I wanted him to have legal representation when they called him back there to be questioned."

"Right. And after Ronnie left and went back to his hotel, I did convey that same general sentiment—using slightly different terminology, I might add—to the people in the NFL office. When I left there a few minutes ago, it was my impression that they are not going to continue belaboring the issue any further. At least for now."

"Mr. Corcoran, I was told by a former player in this league whom you once represented that you were the man I should contact, and he was right on the money. It's great to have you on our team."

"Not so fast, Coach. You're talking to a lifetime New York Giants fan. But I am pleased that I could be of service, anyway. Right now, before I get back to my office, I'm going to stop at the Waldorf Astoria to visit with Ronnie. I'll tell him the good news."

■

Corcoran conveyed not only the glad tidings to Ronnie Tubbs, but he also favored him with some pro bono counsel. "This turned out very much to your benefit, Ronnie, but my best advice to you right now is that you never do anything to put yourself in this position again."

"I haven't said that I did anything wrong this time, Mr. Corcoran."

"And I'm not going to push you for any more details, either. But I sincerely hope for your sake and for the sake of your team that you understand fully what I've just said to you."

"We're just trying to win games."

"There is a right way and there is a dubious way to do that, young man."

"Well, Coach Dolbemeier is always getting us fired up about what it takes to win in this league, and if we don't buy in he really gets on our butts. In fact, there are a few guys now who are in his dog-house because they object to some of the things he wants us to do."

"Yeah. Well remember, you're better off in the doghouse than you'd be in the outhouse."

"Hey, I like that one," Ronnie said, "and I do appreciate what you did for me today."

"The best thing I did for you today, Ronnie, is give you the advice I just offered. Please remember it and, more importantly, follow it."

"I do get your message, Mr. Corcoran, and I owe you a lot."

"Ronnie, you owe yourself, your teammates, and the game. That's who you owe."

"Yes, sir, and I promise that I'll try to follow what you've been telling me."

"No, don't tell me that you'll *try*. Tell me that you *will*."

"Yes, sir, I will."

CHAPTER THIRTY-SEVEN

Other than the investigation that went nowhere, it was a quiet off-season unless you were one of the 68 players from various teams in the NFL who had surgical repairs done on knees, hips, shoulders, and elbows. Mel Herbert shared in their fun. He had knee replacement surgery.

When Joe Skoronski and Zig Zag came to visit Mel during his recovery period in the hospital, Joe brought along a sizeable order of goodies that he had picked up at Kentucky Fried Chicken on his way there. Mel thanked him for his thoughtfulness, and then watched as Joe consumed 90% of the bag's contents.

"Ya really oughta try one a dese chicken legs," Joe said, chomping into the last one available. "Dey is really good."

"Thanks, Joe, but I don't want to overeat," Mel said as he snatched the single remaining French fry off the paper napkin on the cart next to his bed. "Anything new with the team?"

"Not a whole lot. Dey're just doin' some reparations on da locker rooms out at da stadium."

"Reparations?"

Zig Zag chimed in. "He means renovations."

"Yeah, dat's it," Joe said. "Dis time I gotta give some credit ta Coach Dolbermeier."

"Why?"

"He felt real bad, he said, dat da visitor's locker room wasn't in da shape it oughta be in. I gotta tellya, wit all due lacka respect, ya know, dat dat's da first time I ever seen him care at all about da udder team's guys. He's really inta it, too. He's spent a lotta time dere, too, makin' sure dat da guys doin' da work do it good."

"Interesting," Mel said, and then he turned to Zig Zag. "And what are you doing with all your spare time now that you don't have to drive me around for a few days?"

"I'm keeping busy. Zelda's brother, Zeke, came in from Chicago to visit, and I've been showing him all the sights he's heard about out here in L.A. It's amazing, though. Zelda loves sports, but Zeke isn't interested in them at all. He's all wrapped up into playing the fiddle. Then again, Mel, I've got to realize, like you always say, no one's *perfect*."

■

It was like most other off-seasons. The players, coaches, and front office people prepared, while members of the media analyzed and predicted. They predicted that the Denver Broncos, victors over the New Orleans Saints in last season's Super Bowl Game, would repeat as champions. They predicted that both the Los Angeles Leopards and the Portland Pioneers would be strong contenders for playoff spots. At season's end they would be able to take pride in having been right on two out of three of those assertions.

The competition began with all three of those teams winning their opening game. Denver, because of their status as reigning Super Bowl champions, had to wait until the nationally televised Monday night game to get back on pace with the Leopards and Pioneers, both of whom started strong on that first Sunday of the new season.

The Broncos won their game, 31-10. The Pioneers, on the road against the Arizona Cardinals, dominated on defense, and came away with a 24–7 victory, and the Leopards, at home against the Jacksonville Jaguars, emerged as the winners in what turned out to be the most exciting game of the day.

The Jaguars were trailing 21–20 when they took possession of the ball at their own 22-yard line with 50 seconds left in the game. Hurry-up time. They got moving, and so did the game clock. Only 20 seconds remained when they crossed midfield and raced up to the line of scrimmage at the Leopards' 44-yard line.

That's when the Jaguars quarterback, Ace Knoll, turned frantically toward his sideline and jabbed repeatedly with the middle finger on each hand towards the ear holes on the sides of his helmet.

The clock ticked down: 19, 18, 17, 16. At 15, the exasperated quarterback called his team's final timeout.

"What in the hell is that all about," Coach Les Chuckster screamed as Knoll approached the sideline. The coach's red face came close to matching the color of his disheveled hair.

"The damn headset went all static again. I couldn't hear the play you were telling me to run, and I couldn't even read your lips because of the play card you were holding in front of your mouth."

"I'll be damned. All right, here's the play: Trips right, 585 swing. Look for Rooster Crowe on the out route, and tell him to get his ass out of bounds. We've got to stop the clock, and we just used up our last timeout for crying out loud."

Knoll called the play, and then he drilled a pass that Crowe caught near the sideline at the Leopards' 25. Defensive cornerback Odell Nathan was covering Crowe, and when Odell leapt at the airborne ball and missed, he went tumbling to the ground. That's when Crowe made an instantaneous decision, and it seemed so right at the time.

Why step out of bounds and put our team at risk of missing a 43-yard field goal attempt when there is nothing between me and the winning touchdown, he reasoned. He didn't step out of bounds. Instead, he sprinted for the end zone.

From across the field, so did Leopards safety Kelsey Marco. At the five-yard line, Kelsey dove at Crowe's heels and sent him spinning to the ground two yards shy of the goal line. There were four seconds left on the clock when the whistle blew ending the play, but they evaporated before the Jaguars players could sprint into position for a quick spike-the-ball, kill-the-clock play.

The game was over. The Leopards won.

∎

It was the kind of post-game press conference that Les Chuckster detested.

"Coach Chuckster, what was your thinking in using your last timeout when you did?" Terry Yockey of *The Orlando Observer* asked.

"Had to. Ace's helmet mike wasn't working right, and he couldn't get the play that I wanted. And you know, it was fourth down, and so he couldn't spike the ball."

"Why didn't Crowe get out of bounds and stop the clock?"

"That's what we expected him to do, but then when the man covering him fell down, it looked like clear sailing for him to score the winning touchdown. If we hadn't had to use up that darn timeout we could have called it after he got tackled. Then we'd have been in position to kick a field goal. A chip shot. What really tees me off is that was the third time during the game that Ace couldn't get our call from the sideline, and that's what cost us the damn game."

"Were the Leopards having the same kind of communication problems?" Pandora Boxer of *The Jacksonville Jubilee* asked.

"I don't know. It didn't seem like it. You'll have to ask them."

■

It was the kind of post-game press conference that Randy Dolbermeier relished.

As was often his practice after games the Leopards won, he didn't wait for any questions.

"Welcome to VJ Day everyone," he shouted as he bounded onto the platform. "Victory over Jacksonville! Who's next? The Eagles. Okay, it's time for us to start getting ready for VE Day."

"Do you feel fortunate—or even lucky—to come away with this one?" Avery Higginbotham of *The Beverly Hills Patrician* asked.

"Hell, no. We earned it. We came through when we needed to. We did what it takes to win."

"Yes, but if they hadn't had to use their last timeout when they did, they would have had a chance to kick a game-winning field goal."

"That's their problem. I didn't call their timeout. They did."

"Did you and your quarterbacks have any trouble with your headset communications during the game?" Rhett Torricle of *The Anaheim Arrow* asked.

"No. Why do you ask me that?"

"Because the Jaguars sure did. You know that, don't you?"

"Not until you just told me," Randy said. "I'm too busy concentrating on what we've got to do on our side of the field. Hey, things happen fast during a game, and in order to win, you've got be ready to handle them. That's what we did, and that's why we won."

CHAPTER THIRTY-EIGHT

Week number two was just as successful for both the Leopards and the Pioneers. It was, that is, until *after* the game when Pioneers Coach Denzel Jackson was driving home from the Portland airport following his team's return from their win over the Chargers in San Diego.

Denzel was cruising along the freeway and listening to the late evening radio commentary that dissected how the Pioneers defense, for the second week in a row, had held their opponents to just one touchdown. Pleasant. Then it happened.

Driving in the lane next to the shoulder on the expressway, Denzel was following a 16-wheeler. Both of them were traveling at slightly under the speed limit, but there was another truck trailing Denzel's car, and it was obvious from the repeated honking of that vehicle's horn how impatient its driver was for them to speed up.

They didn't, and that's when the trucker gunned it and swerved into the passing lane with the intention of hurrying on by. In his haste he turned directly in front of a car whose driver was barreling along with the same intention. The panicked car driver responded by twisting his steering wheel, sending his vehicle hurtling into the lane to his right, thereby avoiding a collision. For a split-second, that is.

He didn't collide with the truck. Instead, he slammed into the left rear fender of Denzel's Mitsubishi and sent it spinning. It spun into the side of the truck that had initiated the mayhem, bounced off, and then rolled down the embankment along the side of the highway into the brush below.

Denzel's car was badly damaged. But not as badly as he was.

It was after midnight when Bobby Russell hurried into the waiting room at the hospital. Denzel's wife, Vanessa, was already there. So were Lilly and René Napoleon and several members of the coaching staff. Vanessa was sobbing. René was sitting on the bench next to her with his arm around her shoulder, seeking to console her, and so Bobby turned his questioning gaze towards Lilly.

"Not good," she managed to say. "He's still unconscious. The doctor told us that his condition is critical. He's in intensive care, and the next 24 hours are going to be crucial." Lilly shook her head and stopped talking. She put her hand over her mouth, and she, too, found herself unable to stop the flow of tears that overcame her.

Bobby asked tight ends coach Larry Donald for more information. He didn't like what he heard.

"Bobby, he's really in bad shape," Larry said. "Worst is that he has a broken vertebra in his neck. They did get immediate treatment going, and they say there is some minimal movement in his extremities. It's going to be a while though, they said, before they can determine if any permanent disability might occur. Besides that, we're really sweating it out waiting to find out how serious his head injuries are."

They sat, mostly in silence, waiting to learn more.

Although Denzel Jackson lay comatose in his hospital bed, the games would go on. For most of the teams in the NFL it would be business as usual, but not for the Portland Pioneers.

They'd be traveling to Tampa to face the 2–0 Buccaneers just one week after that awful Sunday. Despite the grief and turmoil that engulfed Denzel's family, his players and coaching staff, and all of the team's fans, the Pioneers had to show up ready to play. What to do?

At 3 o'clock Monday morning Lilly Napoleon broke the

silence that had settled on those who still remained in the hospital waiting room.

"Bobby," she said, "you are going to have to take over Denzel's responsibilities until he is able, I pray, to come back and handle them again himself."

"I understand," Bobby said, and then, after a pause, he added, "I can't imagine a situation that would leave me less exhilarated about why I'd be a head coach again than this one. And, just like you, Lilly, I pray that it only has to be for a little while."

An hour later, Bobby was home in bed. He awoke at 6 a.m. and was in the office by 6:45. He had to meet with the coaching staff and find some way to get them all reoriented. Reviewing the tapes from yesterday's game was next. *Was it only yesterday?* Grade the players, make corrections, plan the agenda for the team meeting this afternoon, meet with the media (this one will be a doozy), and begin this evening to work on the game plan and practice schedule for the week leading up to next Sunday's game against the Buccaneers.

How about meals? I'll eat at my desk or while I'm in the film room. Sleep? What's that? Go to the toilet? I'll find the time somehow. Find time for my own personal workout? Are you kidding?

It was a week like no other. No jokes. No wisecracks. No cute antics. It was all business, interrupted only by everyone's eagerness to hear updates on Jackson's condition.

There was a trickle of encouraging news Tuesday afternoon. Denzel's breathing and heartbeat had begun to stabilize, but he remained in the intensive care unit. The doctors expressed optimism that the quick treatment provided for the head trauma that Denzel had suffered would help to protect him from permanent brain damage. Recovery from the spinal injury was another story. Denzel was not moving his arms or legs, and by late in the week he was still unable to communicate verbally. Family and friends were informed that his condition would continue to be monitored, but that the length of the recovery process and the extent of recovery itself were questions for which they were unable to provide answers. Continue to hope. Continue to pray.

CHAPTER THIRTY-NINE

Sunday arrived, and the Pioneers, in their first game under the direction of Coach Bobby Russell, went down to their first defeat of the young season. It was the Tampa Bay Buccaneers who remained undefeated, winning, 13–10.

Jordy Nerdmann, in his column the next morning, knew where to place the blame. "Here we go again," he wrote, "Bobby 'Mr. Defense' Russell has done it again. His team held its opponent to just one touchdown, just 13 points, but guess who won the game. Yep. You're right. He forgot about offense again, and in doing so he held *his own* team to a stinking *10* points. The Buccaneers are undefeated while the *formerly undefeated* Pioneers are now heading in the wrong direction with this proven failure of a coach at their helm."

Other writers, such as Boyd Prohaska of *The Portland Panorama*, saw it differently. "As much as the Pioneers have suffered during this past week in the wake of the devastating accident that struck down Coach Denzel Jackson," he wrote, "they displayed the type of effort and dedication in yesterday's game against the Buccaneers that would have made him proud. True, they weren't rewarded with a victory on the playing field, but they exhibited qualities that make this writer believe they will rebound and rally around the leadership of interim head coach Bobby Russell, who has had to step into the breach on short notice and under daunting circumstances. Time will tell."

On that same Sunday, a different scenario unfolded 820 miles to the south in La La Land where the Fun and Shout offensive fireworks provided by the Los Angeles Leopards propelled them to a 38–17 romp over the visiting Philadelphia Eagles.

When the game ended, Randy Dolbermeier walked to the middle of the field where he responded to Eagles Coach Brighton Early's words of congratulations with a grunt and a tepid wave of his hand. Then he pivoted and sprinted to the locker room, slowing down only briefly to answer a question from CBS sideline reporter Phyllis Steen who, while grasping a microphone in one hand and using the other to hold her beret in place, was bustling along matching him stride for stride.

"Coach, how important was this win?" she asked.

"How important? C'mon. We just beat the Eagles, and I'm heading into the locker room right now for one heck of a celebration. See you later. At the Super Bowl, I hope."

"Okay. Thank you, coach. Now, back to our gang up in the booth."

■

Other than Cedric B. Medill, no one was more pleased with the success the Leopards were enjoying than Jordy Nerdmann. He had called it, hadn't he? Replace that dum-dum Bobby Russell with a gunslinger like Randy Dolbermeier and watch the big yards *and the big wins* continue to come our way, he trumpeted. The wins continued, and 10 games into the season the Leopards were 8–2. Jordy kept his fans informed about how his keen foresight had alerted them that this would occur.

There was another big story taking place in the NFL, but Jordy paid scant attention to it. The Pioneers, with an identical 8–2 record, didn't seem to present a topic that held much interest for him. Others can waste their time on those guys, was his attitude. He'd keep his focus on the home team.

Mel Herbert, too, was following the home team closely, and it was at home that the Leopards had been invincible. They were 5-0 in games played in L.A., and in every one of those contests they had outscored their opponents in the second half. Were their coaching staff's halftime adjustments always that superior to those of their opponents, Mel wondered. His curiosity prompted him to seek input from the most reliable source available to him.

"Joe," he asked one evening as he, Joe, and Zig Zag were dining together at Harry's Hamburger Heaven, "you're in the locker room at halftime when the coaches go over their instructions with the players, aren't you?"

Joe's bulging cheeks provided evidence that it would be too difficult for him to respond verbally, and so he nodded his head as he speeded up the chewing process.

"Has the routine been any different this year from what you've normally observed?" Mel asked.

Joe brought the fist of one hand up to shoulder level, forefinger extended towards the ceiling, as a signal that as soon as he finished masticating the remnants of the humongous bite out of the burger he had taken, he would have something meaningful to say.

"Nine, eight, seven, six," Zig Zag counted down. His timing was superb. Just as he hit "two, one, bingo!" Joe swallowed. After a gulp from his soda, followed by a deep sigh, he answered.

"Sorta," he said.

"How?"

"Well, two a dose coaches, Denny Koontz and Milo Becker, dey don't meet wit dere players hardly at all. Dey go off into dat little dark room dat no one else ever uses behind da door offa da aquipment room, and den dey stay dere til it's almost time ta go back out for da second half a da game."

"Why? What's that all about?" Mel asked.

"I dunno. Da real funny ting is dat when dey do come back outta dere dey got like dis little tape recorder type machine wit dem dat dey gives ta Coach Dolbermeier, and den him and da two coordinator coaches, dey go off in da corner and dey listen ta it."

"Do they do this at every game?"

"Yeah. Well, not always. It seems like dey do it only at da home games, now dat I tink about it."

"Maybe they're just trying to catch up on the scores of the other games going on around the league," Zig Zag offered.

"I doubt it," Mel said.

"Well, then what do you think it is?" Zig Zag asked.

"I hope it *isn't* what I think it could be," Mel answered.

"Whadaya tink dat is?" Joe asked.

"For now, Joe, I'd prefer not to say, but I won't promise that it's always going to be that way."

"Dere ya go again, Mel. Ya really know how ta keep a guy in suspenders, I'll tell ya dat."

■

As Boyd Prohaska had written in *The Portland Panorama* seven weeks earlier: "Time will tell." And as those weeks passed, the story being told by the Pioneers on the noisy fields of play was an exciting one. In the quiet isolation of Denzel Jackson's hospital room, however, an even more exciting saga was unfolding.

It was on a Wednesday—10 days after Denzel's accident—that Vanessa came rushing out of the intensive care unit into the waiting room where Lilly Napoleon and Cindy Russell had come to keep her company and to offer support. Vanessa was gasping, and tears were streaming down her face, but through it all there was a look of joy that came shining through.

"Oh, my God. My dear God," she managed to say. Neither Lilly nor Cindy could come up with the right way to ask the question that they were both so eager to have answered. They didn't need to.

"He moved his lips," Vanessa said. And then she froze in place, the moisture on her cheeks glistening like jewels as she gazed upwards with an open-mouthed reverence that revealed the euphoria she was experiencing.

"He looked over at me, and then he whispered it," Vanessa said.

"Whispered what?" Lilly and Cindy asked simultaneously.

Vanessa's look turned shy. "Love you," she said.

"He did? Aw," Vanessa heard one of them say.

"And then he whispered it again," she told them.

Denzel Jackson had taken his first step on the long road back. Would he ever be able to take a much bigger first step, the one that would allow him, feet on the floor, to step away from the bed where he now lay almost motionless?

Only time would tell.

CHAPTER FORTY

While both the Leopards and the Pioneers, in packed stadiums and on national television before millions of enchanted NFL fans, seemed to be getting better at an accelerating pace, Denzel Jackson continued his heroic battle in the quiet of his hospital room. The speed of his progress came nowhere near matching that of those more fortunate on-the-field competitors who could go out frolicking after games and practices, and who could return to their homes at night and enjoy the company of family and loved ones, but that did not keep Denzel, his medical team, nor his loved ones from persisting in their far more important endeavors.

After Denzel first moved his lips, another week filled with a mixture of anxiety and hope marched slowly by. At the conclusion of that week, the doctors reported that Denzel was exhibiting increased movement in his hands and feet. Also, the doctors now placed over Denzel's head a monstrous neck brace. It was uncomfortable as hell, but it did enable him to roll slightly towards the side of his bed and look at his visitors.

Two more weeks, comprised of excruciatingly long days, eked on by.

And then one day, Vanessa walked into the room, and there he was—propped up in his bed. His eyes were still droopy, but a flicker of a smile adorned his face.

"Darling, you're up!" she gushed.

"Uh, huh, I yam," he responded. To Vanessa, that semi-grunt was pure eloquence.

A few minutes later Vanessa was delighted by another utterance. This one came not from Denzel, but from Dr. John Marzaccino who entered the room, his face aglow in anticipation of delivering to her some encouraging information.

"Vanessa," he said, "Denzel has regained enough movement in his hands, feet, and legs so that we can now begin some daily rehabilitation sessions for him. If he keeps progressing over the next several weeks as we hope he will, it would then be feasible for him to return home. He'd still have to come in daily for those rehab appointments, but at least he'd be back home the rest of the time."

At first Vanessa couldn't speak. She cried instead. Dr. Marzaccino understood, and it pleased him to see that although Vanessa was crying, Denzel was beaming. Finally, Vanessa regained some control. "How about his neck brace, doctor? How long will he have to wear it?"

"For quite a while yet. We need to be very cautious about the spinal trauma he suffered, but if his condition continues to progress, we will eventually be able to remove it. We'll keep you up to date, but I don't want to set up any hypothetical time frame until we see the right kind of progress taking place. On a brighter note, Denzel is continuing to regain more movement in his extremities, and I am hopeful that in a month or so we might be able to initiate some walking exercises for him."

Vanessa conveyed the great news to Lilly, Bobby, and all the others. There was joy throughout the Pioneers organization. That next Sunday they defeated the San Francisco 49ers, 27–14. In the locker room after the game, team captain and offensive center Elliott "Hulk" Kent, on behalf of all the grateful Pioneers players and coaches, presented the game ball to Dr. John Andrew Marzaccino.

■

By the time week No. 11 of the season arrived, Denzel's condition had advanced to the point where he was able to return home. The goalpost-like brace that extended from his shoulders over the crown of his head allowed him to sit in his favorite living room chair, and from there he stared stiffly at the television set as his Pioneers played host to the Kansas City Chiefs. They entertained him by coming away with the victory that improved their record to 9–2. On that same Sunday afternoon, the Los Angeles Leopards, on the road in Indianapolis, suffered their third loss of the season. They were now 8–3.

That one-game disparity in their records didn't last long because on the following Sunday the Leopards, at home against the defending NFC champion New Orleans Saints, rallied from a 13-point halftime deficit to pull out a thrilling comeback victory.

For the Pioneers, the results were different. They limped home after suffering a heartbreaking 28–27 defeat at the hands of the Baltimore Ravens.

Both the Leopards and the Pioneers, at 9–3, were leading their respective divisions, and, barring a disastrous four-game losing streak in their remaining regular season games, they were heading for the playoffs. For each of them, one more win would probably assure a playoff berth, but they wanted more than that. The team with the best record in each conference would have home field advantage throughout the playoffs, and achieving that objective provided a huge boost for a team in its quest to make it all the way to the Super Bowl.

Nothing was assured, however, and the road ahead would be difficult to predict and even more difficult to travel.

■

The Leopards' next two games were on the road, and they lost them both, leaving them sputtering with a 9–5 record. All five of their losses had come on the road. In away games they were 3–5. At home they were 6–0. Things were getting scary, but at least their final two games would be back in L.A. where they had enjoyed so much success. If they wanted to make the playoffs, they'd better win at least one of those last two contests.

In week No. 15, the Leopards won at home. A playoff spot was now a certainty, but as far as home field advantage was concerned, things didn't look so rosy. That was because even though both the Leopards and the defending AFC and Super Bowl Champion Denver Broncos came into the final week of the season with matching 10–5 records, the Broncos, by virtue of having won the game they played against each other in Denver earlier that year, held the top seed in the AFC playoffs.

For the Leopards to ascend to that envied home-field-advantage spot, they'd have to win their season's home finale on Sunday against the Minnesota Vikings, while hoping that the Broncos, who would also be playing at home in the final Monday Night Football game of the NFL season, would go down to defeat.

The Leopards did their part. For the eighth consecutive time on their home turf, they emerged as winners. Now it was time to sweat it out and wait to see how the Broncos fared on Monday night.

■

An intriguingly similar scenario was unfolding in the NFC where both the Portland Pioneers and the NFC defending champion New Orleans Saints—the team that had won their conference title game matchup one year earlier—came into week No. 16 riding high with 12–3 records. The league's intricate tie-breaking formula decreed that if they finished with the same won/lost records, the nod for home field advantage would go to the Pioneers.

On the regular season's concluding Sunday, the Saints kept on marching in. They defeated the Miami Dolphins, improving to 13–3. That left it up to the Pioneers to do something about it. Simple, but not easy.

The "simple" part meant that all they had to do was win their game. The "not easy" part meant that they had to do it on the road in Denver, on Monday night, against the previous year's Super Bowl champions.

CHAPTER FORTY-ONE

Late Monday morning, at the hotel in Denver where the Pioneers were staying, the players and coaches assembled for the last team meeting they would hold during that long week of preparation for their game against the Broncos.

Bobby Russell's agenda for those sessions included a review of key elements in the game plan, substitution procedures, and any pertinent reminders regarding how this particular opponent might be different from the norm. Those were the usual subjects that he addressed.

Pep talks were out. After a long week of preparation, pep talks were just noise to most players, and they usually resulted more in distracting them than in motivating them.

The time to provide motivation, Bobby believed, came at the beginning of the week, and that was when he directed his inspirational efforts towards convincing his players how intensely they needed to prepare for the upcoming opponent.

Was there ever an exception to that "early in the week only" approach? Yes. And at the conclusion of the Monday morning meeting at the hotel in Denver, Bobby instituted one of those exceptions.

"That's about it, fellas," Bobby said. He was standing at the podium at the front of the room, and he had covered all the technical matters that he had planned to discuss.

"But there is just one more item that I think you'd all be interested in seeing and hearing," he continued. Bobby then pointed a finger and nodded his head at the team's Director of Video Operations, Henry Debbie, who was hovering over video equipment at the back of the room.

The lights dimmed and the videotape began to roll. At the outset, the picture on the screen showed nothing more than the empty living room of what was apparently a private residence. The doorway from the hallway into that room was unlighted, but a few moments later the viewers could detect the form of a stiffly erect figure maneuvering some contraption through that dimly lit entrance towards the more comfortably illuminated area ahead.

And then, there he was. It was Denzel Jackson. Pushing a walker, but otherwise unaided, he was on his own two feet, positioning himself in front of the camera. The cumbersome brace was still wrapped around his neck and head, but it didn't keep him from offering a wink and a smile to the entranced members of his audience.

"Hello everyone," he said. "I'm not there with you yet, but my heart is, and I look forward to that day when I do walk out onto the field with all of you once again. I'll be watching you tonight. Play hard. Play clean. Play to win. But win *or* lose, you're still my guys." Denzel turned slowly away from the camera, and rolling his walker before him, he faded back into the shadows from which he had emerged.

Henry Debbie's assistant switched on the lights, but the slam, bang, rustle, jibes, and sighs of relief that usually signified that the meeting was over were absent on this occasion. The misty-eyed players filed quietly out of the room.

■

The Pioneers players had filed quietly out of their meeting room that morning, but after the game at Mile High Stadium that night, it was the Denver Broncos fans who were filing quietly out— into the parking lots. The Pioneers had stunned them into a state of silence. The scoreboard told the story:

PORTLAND: 30   DENVER: 20

It may have been quiet in the parking lots, but it sure wasn't quiet inside the Pioneers dressing room. It was raucous. By having just clinched the top seed in the NFC playoffs, they earned a bye in the first round of the upcoming elimination process. After that, they'd be playing at home against an opponent that would have to have played and won a playoff game while the Pioneers were enjoying that invigorating week of rest. Then, if the Pioneers could win that game, they'd be at home again the following week hosting the NFC Championship Game. Win *that* one, and—SUPER BOWL, HERE WE COME.

■

Several minutes after the Pioneers game was over, the locker room doors were opened to admit the credentialed media. Pioneers Director of Media Relations Lynn Denney directed the television cameramen to a location in front of where all the players were facing, and as the cameras began to roll, the players, all holding aloft their bottles of Gatorade, bellowed out in unison, "Coach Denzel, this one's for you!" And then they each poured the contents of the bottles they were grasping onto the head of any teammate standing within range. Back home in Portland, watching on television, Denzel Jackson choked back tears.

■

While joy prevailed in the Pioneers locker room, they were not the only team celebrating that Monday Night. The Los Angeles Leopards had reason to chime in just as heartily because when the Pioneers captured the top seed in the NFC by virtue of their win over the Broncos, that outcome also propelled the Leopards past Denver into the top seed in the AFC. The results of Portland's victory determined who was going to have home field advantage throughout the playoffs in *both* the NFC *and* the AFC. Now that qualifies as "A Big Win."

CHAPTER FORTY-TWO

    While all that excitement was swirling around on the fields of play during the march towards the Super Bowl, Brant Gilbert, like Mel Herbert, was becoming increasingly uneasy about some of the weird happenings that were occurring behind the scenes.

    Wasn't it unusual, he felt, that at least two of the Leopards' opponents over the past two seasons had star players come down with food poisoning on the day of the game? Screwed up wiring in the coach-to-quarterback communication system seemed to happen only to the other team. And wasn't it remarkable how often the Leopards came rallying back after the halftime break to pull out those home field victories? Enough for them to have gone undefeated when playing at home; that's how often. Enough times for them to have earned the right to be at home again as the playoffs were about to begin.

    Or had they *earned* it? That's what Brant was wondering.

    Brant and Mel visited with each other often during their regular forays into the press box and at the media sessions after practices and games, and it was on the day after the final game of the regular season that Brant asked a seemingly innocuous question.

    "Mel, isn't it amazing how these guys have been able to bounce back the way they do in the second half of all their games?"

    "Not *all* their games," Mel responded.

    "Well, every time they play at home, anyway."

    "Ah, you noticed, huh?"

    "In other words, so did you. Right?"

    "Yeah. Do you know that in every single game at home this year, they've outscored the other team in the second half, and that they've had to come from behind after halftime in order to win four of those games?"

    "Of course I know that," Brant answered. "I read all about it in Jordy Nerdmann's columns."

    "Brant, I know what we're both thinking; or maybe I should

say, 'fearing.' Let me ask you something. What is in that space right behind Joe's equipment room out at the stadium?"

"It's been empty since day one. It was meant to be available for extra storage if needed, but we never had to use it. Why are you asking me about that?"

"What's on the other side of the far wall in that room?"

"The visitor's locker room."

"I guessed that's what you might say was there," Mel said, and then he filled Brant in on what Joe Skoronski had told him about how assistant coaches Denny Koontz and Milo Becker always disappeared into that storage area at halftime and how they would emerge several minutes later with some device that they would then take immediately over to Randy Dolbermeier and the two coordinators.

"Has Joe ever gone in and scouted out that room?" Brant asked.

"Only Denny and Milo have keys to get in there, and once when Joe inquired about it, Randy called him aside and told him it was none of his damn business and that he better not ever try to go meddling in there."

"You don't think they're bugging the other team's locker room, do you?"

"Do you?"

"I asked first."

"Right," Mel said. "Tell you the truth, I think they may be doing a lot more than that. You know Dolbermeier better than I do, Brant. Would he do anything that contemptible?"

"It wouldn't surprise me one bit. But Mel, let's be careful. We may be jumping to some dangerous conclusions just because of this guy's lovable personality. Another thing, unless we know something for certain, I think it would be really unfair to the fans to swing their attention in that direction when they're all so excited about the team and the playoffs."

"I know that," Mel said, "and I agree. I don't want to be unfair to the players on this team, either. They've worked their tails off to get this far, and I know their concentration has to be on getting ready to play and not on having to deal with some rumors. Unless something develops that erases any doubts about it, I'm not going to do that to them."

CHAPTER FORTY-THREE

Mel Herbert needn't have worried about being the person responsible for diverting the players' attention. There was already a feeling of restlessness among many of them, and it had been growing in intensity as the result of some tactics that they were being encouraged by the coaching staff to employ.

Some of those "instructional pointers"—such as how to interfere with the opposing quarterback's cadence calls—were surreptitious methods for skirting the rules, while others were designed specifically for the purpose of inflicting injuries on key members of the opposing team.

While most of the Leopards players didn't like it, there were a few who went along. Linebacker Buster Stones, for instance, was rewarded with a tidy bounty payment (on the q.t., of course) for his dive-at-the-knees tackle that put Cincinnati Bengals quarterback Bjorn Gustafson out of the game—*and* into a leg cast—for the rest of the season.

When Bjorn's backup, Wayne "Macho" Gunzlinger, came in, he was way off target. He completed just eight of the 27 passes he attempted before being benched in the fourth quarter after throwing his third interception of the day.

Third stringer, Lewis "Zoomer" Simonson came in to relieve Macho, and he went 0 for 3 passing. It might have been 0 for 5 except that he got sacked on the other two occasions he dropped back.

By that time it really didn't make much difference since the Leopards had overcome a seven-point deficit, turning it into a 38–10 romp that had their fans hoarse from bellowing out repeated choruses of "Hooray For Hollywood" while the scantily clad cheerleading team known as the "Leopards Lovelies" gyrated in tune with the melody as it was pumped in from the loudspeakers attached to the flashing Jumbotron that was featuring up-close shots of the Lovelies' most captivating attributes.

Although Buster Stones was not alone when it came to savoring those opportunities to reap some extra income, his compatriots were few in number, and so one day after practice during the week of preparation for their regular season finale against the Minnesota Vikings, a committee of six players who represented all those who didn't like it approached Randy Dolbermeier and asked to meet with him in his office.

"Why?' Randy asked.

"It's something, Coach, that we'd really rather discuss with you in private," Colin Fitch answered.

"Okay, come in tomorrow morning before the team meeting, but I sure hope that this has something to do with our getting ready for our game against the Vikings this weekend. The last thing we need right now is to start screwing around with stuff that steers us away from what's really important."

"We all feel it's important enough for us to meet with you," Sammy Kurtask chimed in, "or we wouldn't be asking for such a meeting."

"If it's that important, why not tell me now?"

"Coach, we'd rather do it in private," Chase Banks said.

"Okay, if that's what you really prefer. But what in the devil is all this secrecy about? I never keep any secrets from you guys. You know that."

Silence.

"Alright, see you in my office at eight tomorrow morning. Don't be late."

■

At 7:45 a.m. the next day, the six players were waiting outside Dolbermeier's office. Randy showed up at 8:10.

"C'mon in," he said, "but let's make it quick. We've got a game to get ready for."

The players filed in and found places to sit in the cluttered office.

"Okay. What?" Randy said.

Five of the players turned their eyes toward Glenn Grabowski, making it apparent that he was the one they had appointed to be their spokesman. "Coach, I'll get right to it," he said. "A lot of our players are concerned because we keep getting instructions to do things that are outside of the rules, and it's gotten to the point where we felt it necessary to make our feelings known. We've all been discussing how we ought to approach this thing, and we finally decided it would be best if we came directly to you. That's why we're here."

"For heaven's sake, Glenn, is that what this is all about? We've got a huge game coming up, and you fellows are in here questioning how we go about getting ready to try and win it? We're doing everything we can to help you guys be winners, for crying out loud."

"We want to win, but we don't want to play dirty football. We want to do it in a way that lets us be proud of how we did it," Glenn responded.

"First you've got to win the doggone game. That's what should really be making you proud. We need every single damn advantage we can get. That's the way you wind up winning games in this league. And I'll tell you something else. The other teams are doing everything they can come up with to try to beat us."

"We believe that almost all of them are trying to do it while playing fair," Glenn said.

"If you guys believe that then you're a bunch of dummies," Randy said as he shifted in his seat and glanced at his watch.

A few of the other players sensed that it was time to come to Grabowski's aid. Sammy Kurtask was the first one to jump in. "Coach Dolbermeier, we are not dummies, and we do believe that by far the great majority of players and coaches in this league play 100% by the rules."

"Sammy, you are one helluva football player, but you sure are a lousy mathematician. Can you honestly name even one coach who is a stickler for this lily-white adherence to what you guys are trying to call 'clean football'?"

"I think I can name lots of them, Coach. In fact, I think a better answer would be 'most of them,'" Sammy said.

"I'm asking you again. Name one." Now it was Chase Banks's turn to speak up.

"I'll name one," he said. "How about Coach Bobby Russell? We aren't the only ones who know that. You were here, too, while he was coaching us. You know how he always preached, 'Don't be dumb, and don't be dirty.' We liked it, and we believed it."

"Bobby Russell! How many championships did he ever win? I am not going to coach the half-assed way he did. I want to win. And I want men on this team who want to win as much as I do."

Three of the players in the room folded their hands, closed their eyes, and lowered their chins. The other three sat there wide-eyed and open-mouthed. None of them had any more to say.

Randy let it seep in for another several seconds, and then he steered the meeting to its conclusion. "Okay fellas, I'm going to say this one more time. You all know that old adage that 'all is fair in love and war,' don't you? Well, football may not be love, but *it is war*! And we are going to do whatever it takes to win it. Remember that. You guys may not know it now, but there is going to come a time when you all wind up being grateful as hell when you realize that everything we are doing is keeping us on track for that ultimate goal—win the damn war!

"We've already used up a lot of valuable time talking about it in here this morning," he continued, "but if you leave here with a better understanding of what it takes to be a winner, it will have been worth-while. Right now, though, it's time for us to get back to work. Let's go."

Six usually energetic and extroverted young men shuffled out of Dolbermeier's office staring straight ahead and without murmuring a sound.

Down the hallway, several of their teammates were standing around waiting for the committee of six as they emerged from the meeting with Randy. "How did it go?" Ronnie Tubbs asked.

No one answered. They just shook their heads.

"See, didn't I tell you?" Kelsey Marco said. And then they all straggled into the team meeting room. It was time to begin going over the short yardage and goal line plan for the game against the Vikings.

CHAPTER FORTY-FOUR

The growing concerns expressed by Brant Gilbert, Mel Herbert, and many of the players on the team were being felt by three other people, as well.

Two of them, Joe Skoronski and Zig Zag Zizzo, were present in the locker room where it was impossible for them to miss the chatter among the players. Sometimes the topic was girls; sometimes it was night clubs; sometimes it was about pass coverage schemes or audibles to use against the blitz; sometimes it was about music or maybe it was about pizza or about tomorrow evening's scheduled meeting of The Fellowship Of Christian Athletes; sometimes it was about automobiles or about contract matters; and sometimes it was about something else. Most of the time those "something else" topics were short lived.

Recently, however, Joe and Zig Zag were being exposed to a growing number of rumblings from players who were objecting to "dirty tricks," and, as the players became less reluctant to sound off when Joe or Zig Zag were in the area, the Two Mustachekateers became more uncomfortable about what they were hearing.

On their one day off during the bye week prior to their first playoff game, Joe and Zig Zag joined Mel for one of their frequent dining adventures at The Nate 'n Al Deli Restaurant on Beverly Drive.

After browsing through the eight-page menu, Joe gave vent to some mounting frustrations relative to his two favorite subjects: food and football.

He began by speaking about the one that, for him, was always primary.

"Mel, tell me again, willya, what's da difference between dem knishes and dat keplach?"

"What do you care?" Mel said. "You never order either one anyway."

"Well, maybe den it's just dat I wanna be smart about important tings like dat."

"Tell you the truth," Mel said, "I don't know the difference myself. I'm still trying to figure out the difference between smoked salmon and lox."

"Hey!" Zig Zag interrupted. "What's with you two? We've got to be thinking about playing the winner of this Sunday's game between the Bills and the Raiders, and you guys are all wrapped up talking about things to eat." Before giving either Joe or Mel a chance to respond, Zig Zag called out to their server: "Yo, Millie, don't forget to bring me some cream cheese and jam for this bagel."

"I know all about keepin' an eye on dat Bills/Raiders game," Joe said as Millie, while balancing a tray loaded with cheese omelets, pancakes, sunny-side-up fried eggs, hash browns, waffles, bacon, sausage, French toast, sweet rolls, and syrup, nodded her head and then veered around the corner of the end booth with a move that would have made running back Gunner Gaines envious. "But ya know," Joe continued, "I'm really startin' ta worry about dat udder ting dat da players keep talkin' about a whole bunch lately."

"And what would that be?" Mel asked.

"Dey're not real happy wit da way da coaches are tellin' 'em ta do tings ta da guys on da udder teams, and dey're really gettin' upset about it all."

"Do they talk to you about it?" Mel asked.

"No, but I hear dem alla da time. Come ta tink of it, dough, Glenn Grabowski and Jon Feeney, dey was in da car wit Zig Zag and me da udder day, and dey was talkin' about nuttin' else but dat. Dey was even askin' us some questions."

"Why were they in the car with you two?"

"Well, it was cause sumpthin' went wrong wit da transition on Grabo's car, and he couldn't get it goin' after practice. Feeney had hooked a ride ta da stadium wit him dat mornin', and now Glenn had ta go pick up his sister—she was flyin' inta da airport ta visit for da weekend—and when Zig Zag saw dey was havin' a problem, he offered ta drive dem dere. I came along, too, cause Zig Zag and me, we was plannin' ta go ta da Lakers game dat night."

"That was really nice of you fellows," Mel said.

"Hey, let me tell you," Zig Zag said, "it wound up being a lot of fun for all of us. Glenn's sister was really a knockout, too. She sure caught Feeney's eye."

"And you know how smart dat Glenn is, don't cha," Joe added. "Well, Kimberly—dat's his sister—I'll betcha she's even one step up on him. She's studyin' for some kinda Mistress of Arts degree at da U of Chicago."

"It's Master of Arts!" Mel said.

"It's his sister; not his brudder. His brudder's da one wit da Master degree. Dey told us he has what dey call an MBA, whatever dat is."

"And what is Kimberly majoring in?" Mel inquired.

"I tink she said it was Rainy Science Art or sumpthin' like dat."

"If she's as smart as you said, I'll bet she could really soak that up," Mel said. "Did she have any opinions about the discussion the players were having?"

"Naw, once she got inta da car, all dat Feeney wanted ta talk about was places where dey could all go ta have a good time dis weekend. I was sorta gladda dat. I was gettin' real fidgety about what dey'd been talkin' about before she got inta da car. Dey began ta ask me some tings about stuff happenin' around the locker room, too, just when we was close ta da airport, and den when Kimberly got in dey dropped dat subject."

"Is there anything more you can tell me about this?" Mel asked.

"Mel, right now I'd radder not get myself all wound up in dis ting. Randy walks around pissed off at me mosta da time anyway, and I gotta watch it."

■

There was that third person, in addition to Joe and Zig Zag, who had gotten drawn in because of something he, too, heard from one of the players. That person was Cedric B. Medill.

It wasn't until late in the week following the Leopards' win over the Vikings that Cedric B. first learned of the players' concerns. It had been a fantastic season. Come-from-behind victories. Getting to watch players like Q.T. Pye, Gunner Gaines, Chase Banks and Sticky Fingers Lavell—men for whom Cedric B. himself had campaigned so fervently on draft day—perform like the great athletes and leaders he had envisioned them to be. Seeing how the fans packed the stadium and how a ticket to a Leopards game had become such a coveted commodity. He had done everything right the day he named Randy Dolbermeier his head coach, hadn't he?

It seemed so. But that was until what transpired on Friday during the bye week. He was at his studio offices, his mind on other business, when his secretary, Laura Norder, buzzed him and said that a Mr. Glenn Grabowski was at the security gate requesting an opportunity to meet with Mr. Medill. She explained that the officer at the gate knew who this person was, otherwise he wouldn't have bothered them with this call.

"The security guard asked me to apologize to you, Mr. Medill, if this is an unwanted intrusion," Laura said, "but he felt it would have been presumptuous for him to send the young man away if you really did wish to see him."

"I'm glad he did call, Laura. You can tell him that for me. And then please have him get someone to bring Glenn to my office."

Ten minutes later Glenn Grabowski walked in, all six feet, five inches, and 297 pounds of him, but it was apparent from their contrasting demeanors that he was the more intimidated—not intimidating—of the two.

"Man, you're even bigger than I thought you were," Cedric B. said with a chuckle, hoping that that might help relax his guest. "This is a pleasure, Glenn. I don't get to visit enough on a person-to-person basis with the fellows on the team. I really have admired the way you play and what you've contributed to all the success we're having this season. And that we're going to continue to have, I hope."

"Yes sir. That's something we all want, too."

"I know that's not the reason you've come here today to see me, though, is it?"

"No, sir. It's about something else, and it's sort of difficult for me to find the right way to get started."

Something flashed through Cedric B.'s mind, and with a more reserved tone in his voice, he posed a question. "This is not about your contract, is it?"

"Oh no, Mr. Medill. That never even occurred to me. Honestly, that's the last thing I'd be bothering you with right now. Believe me, I'm here for a reason that I think almost all of our players would agree is way more important, especially at this stage, than something like that." Glenn was beginning to feel more relaxed now.

"Good. What is it then, Glenn?" he asked.

"Mr. Medill, we are being asked to play dirty football."

"What do you mean 'dirty football'? By whom?"

"By Coach Dolbermeier and by some of the other coaches, too. They keep showing us ways to get around the rules, but worse than that, they want us to do things designed to injure the top players on the other team, to put them out of the game."

"Glenn, are you sure you're not misinterpreting some of Coach Dolbermeier's exuberance? Even I know that he can come up now and then with some off-the-wall comments. That's just him being himself."

"Yes, sir, I am sure. And so are almost all of the other players. We've been talking about it a lot, and finally they asked six of us to go speak personally with Coach about our concerns."

"Did you?"

"Yes, we did."

"And?"

"He just blew us off. Told us to get our minds back on winning games and on doing what they teach us to do in order to win those games."

"That's all?"

"Yes, sir. Then he showed us the door, and, honestly, we left his office even more frustrated about it than ever. We didn't know what to do next until Ronnie Tubbs suggested that rather than making a public fuss about it, maybe one of us ought to come directly to you. They asked me to carry the ball on that one. That's why I came today, and I do want to thank you, Mr. Medill, for being kind enough to listen."

Cedric B. asked Glenn to be more specific about what he meant by "dirty play," and Glenn filled him in on a number of instances whereby opposing players on whom Randy had placed a bounty had to leave the game with injuries. He also advised Cedric B. of other dubious "coaching pointers" that Randy would refer to as part of the team's "arsenal for victory."

Cedric B. had heard enough. He didn't want to believe what Glenn was telling him, but he was having difficulty discounting it. This wasn't some disgruntled troublemaker talking to him, and he knew it. He was aware that Glenn Grabowski was one of the smartest and most team-focused players on the Leopards roster. Cedric B. wished that he did have some sound reasons for doubting what he was hearing. He'd just have to hope for now that Glenn was mistaken. But what if he wasn't?

"Glenn," he said, "this is a matter that does need to be investigated further, and I promise you that I will be looking into it immediately. I hope when I do, though, that I find out you've misjudged what is happening, but I am not going to jump to that conclusion or to any other one until I learn more. And I sure don't want to do anything foolish that throws us off course just as the playoffs are about to begin."

"Neither do I, Mr. Medill. All our players, including me, really debated about whether any of us should come to you at this time, but we felt we had no other options left. We want to win. We want to go to the Super Bowl. We want to win the Super Bowl. But we want to do it the right way. We all believe that you want to do it that way, too, and that's why I'm here. And, once again, I want to thank you for allowing me to come in and for listening to what I had to say."

"You're welcome, Glenn. And, just so you know, when I speak with Coach Dolbermeier, I am not going to mention to him that I spoke with you or with any specific individual about this subject."

"I was hoping you would approach it that way, sir. I'm sorry we had to dump something like this in your lap right now, but I really do hope that only good things result from all these talks."

"So do I," Cedric B. said. But he doubted it.

CHAPTER FORTY-FIVE

As Cedric B.'s chauffeured limousine, with wiper blades going full speed, splashed into the parking lot of the Administration Building at the Leopards practice facility, Randy Dolbermeier was gazing out his office window. After spending a full day sitting at his desk viewing game tapes, he needed a break.

Randy squinted through the raindrops streaming down the windowpane and watched the limo head for the canopied parking slot located at the front door of the building. It was the one reserved for Cedric B. However, earlier that morning when Randy came to work, it had already begun to rain, and since Cedric B. never came to visit on Fridays anyway, Randy decided to pull his SUV into that reserved spot.

Now, as Randy watched, the limo eased over to the far side of the lot and squeezed into a space designated for compact cars. Cedric B. struggled to slide out of the small opening he had created by pushing open his car door into the side of the vehicle parked next to him. The rain intensified as he struggled to open his umbrella, and just when it finally popped open, a gust of wind provided enough force to blow the top of it inside out and then rip it from his hands, sending it twirling across the soaked asphalt.

Cedric B. and his driver scampered after it, and as they both bent to pick it up, they collided, causing Cedric B. to tumble into a puddle. Fortunately, he wasn't injured, but after his driver helped him to his feet and brushed off some of the water, mud, and soggy vegetation from his pinstriped suit, Cedric B. slogged across the parking lot to the front door in an even worse mood than he had been in when he departed from his studio offices 30 minutes earlier.

Randy scrambled back to his desk, shoved an Oakland Raiders videotape into the machine, placed his left elbow on the desktop, wrapped the thumb and forefinger of his left hand around his chin, and peered at the game film. His mood wasn't any more upbeat than Cedric B's, but you never would have known it by how he reacted when the boss walked into his office.

"Hey, Cedric. What a pleasant surprise," he exclaimed. "I sure wasn't expecting to see you out here today."

"That's apparent from where you parked your car," Cedric B. said.

"Oh, my gosh, that's right," Randy said. "That's the first time I ever parked there. Gee, I wish you had called before heading this way. I would have moved it. In fact, I'm going to go out there and do that right now. Boy, what a stupid thing I did!"

"No, just stay here," Cedric B. said. "I came to talk, but I didn't want to distract you by calling ahead of time knowing how busy you are getting ready for your playoff game."

"Any time, Cedric. I always get a kick out of talking football with you. You know that."

"Right. Anyway, I wouldn't be bothering you at this time unless I felt it was important."

Rather that responding, Randy just sat up in his chair and directed a quizzical look at Cedric B.

"Randy, I'll tell you why I'm here. I've received a report that you and some of the other coaches have been instructing our players to do things that are in violation of the rules. What's more, I hear that a lot of what they're being coached to do is for the purpose of injuring the other team's players."

"What! Who told you that?"

"I'd rather not mention any names, but I can tell you that it was a reliable source."

"Cedric, if there is some guy on this team who is unhappy with me because of his lack of playing time or for any other crazy reason, he can come running to you with any kind of cockamamie story. I'd like to talk to that young man. Please tell me who it is."

"I'm not going to do that. It was someone who certainly should know, and since he informed me that a substantial number of the players feel the same way, I'd rather not divulge any names. What I do want to know from you, however, is why would so many players be of the same mind if it weren't true?"

"Cedric, doggone it, we teach tough football. Football is a tough game, and the teams that understand that are the teams that are going to win. Tough doesn't mean 'dirty.' Maybe some of those players interpret hard play that way. Maybe some of these guys are finding out for the first time what it really takes to be a winner. And I am convinced, based on what you are telling me now, that they are overreacting."

"I hope you are correct, and the one thing that I do want to avoid at this critical time is creating some stir that throws everything we've accomplished so far, and everything we are still hoping to accomplish, into the trash bin. Nevertheless —"

"And neither do I," Randy interrupted.

"Let me finish. I want to make it clear that I will not tolerate having the Los Angeles Leopards play dirty football. Our players are not to be taught or urged to use any gimmicks that can be interpreted as such. Do you understand?"

"Of course, I do, Cedric, and I am sorry that someone who I feel is way off base has caused you to be so upset. I understand your concerns, however, and I respect them. You watch. When we get ready for these playoff games, there is not going to be anything we ask the players to do that could possibly be thought of as dirty play."

"For all our sakes, Randy, that has to be true."

After Cedric B. departed, Randy kicked his wastebasket half-way across the room. Then he settled down. "Fine," he told himself, "we won't be instructing the players to do anything that involves bending the rules. I know some even better ways to outsmart those other guys."

CHAPTER FORTY-SIX

The bye week was over. The Leopards were deep into preparations for the team's first post-season game ever. The Buffalo Bills, winners in their playoff game against the Oakland Raiders one week earlier, were coming to town. The Bills had done it the hard way, having traveled cross-country to Oakland where they drubbed the Raiders on the previous Sunday.

After returning home to Buffalo, weary and battered, the Bills underwent a short week of practice before turning around and flying all the way back out to the West Coast, this time for a Saturday matchup against the rested and ready Leopards. Hard as they prepared and hard as they tried, it was too much for the Bills to overcome.

The score was tied at halftime, but in the second half the Leopards pulled away. When it was over, the Leopards were still undefeated on their home field, winning there for the ninth consecutive time that season. One week hence they would be playing in the AFC Championship Game, and that one, too, would be in their own backyard. The challenge that confronted them this time, however, was more formidable than any they had faced all season.

Still standing in their way were the Denver Broncos, defending Super Bowl champions, fresh from their own playoff victory over the Baltimore Ravens. It would be Denver at L.A. for the AFC Championship. Winner goes to the Super Bowl.

■

It was remarkable. In just their fourth year of operation after coming into the league as an expansion team, the Leopards were but one victory away from making it to the Super Bowl. What made it even more remarkable was what was transpiring at the same time in the NFC where the Portland Pioneers, the NFL's other four-year-old expansion franchise, were matching them step for step.

The Pioneers' road to glory was no less rocky, because in their first playoff game they had to compete against one of the three teams that had defeated them during the regular season. Back when Bobby Russell took over as interim head coach early in the year, his first game had been on the road against the Tampa Bay Buccaneers. The Bucs won it, 13–10, and went on to have an outstanding season. Not quite as good as the Pioneers did, however, so the playoff game was played in Portland.

It was a long trip out there for the Buccaneers, and it was an even longer trip home because Portland won it, 21–10.

The NFC Championship game was next, and for the second year in a row it would be the Pioneers vs. the New Orleans Saints, fresh from their playoff victory over Dallas. At stake? The crown and a trip to the Super Bowl.

■

Would Napoleon meet her Walter Lou once again? Jordy Nerdmann predicted that she would.

This time he was right *and* he was wrong. Lilly Napoleon did meet Walter Louis. They were friends. They admired and respected each other. They exchanged cordial conversation in the press box before the game, and they did so again after the game was over. That's how Jordy was right. Where he was wrong, however, was in predicting the outcome of the game. He said the Saints would—as they had the year before—send Napoleon and her troops into exile. They almost did.

With three minutes remaining in the game, the Saints, trailing 21–17, forced the Pioneers to punt. New Orleans took over at its 32-yard line. Seven plays and a minute and 45 seconds later, running back Donnie Brooks barreled into the end zone from four yards out for the touchdown that put the Saints ahead, 23–21.

The fans in New Orleans may have been going wild, but the crowd in Portland's Bekins Van Lines U-Haul Stadium became quieter than they had been at any time during the season as the Saints kicking unit jogged onto the field for the routine process of adding the extra point.

Even when Saints backup quarterback, Phil Andurrer, who was their holder on PAT attempts, bobbled the snap from center, the Pioneers fans' momentary cheers turned quickly to groans when Phil picked it up and sprinted to the corner flag at the goal line and dove into the end zone inches ahead of all pursuers. Instead of adding just one point, the Saints had lucked into tallying two. They led 25–21. Even if the Pioneers managed to get into field goal position before the game's final minute and 15 seconds expired, it would be to no avail. A field goal meant nothing now. They needed a touchdown.

■

While the long break set aside for television commercials dragged on, the players huddled on the sidelines waiting impatiently for the action to resume. This was not a time for any complex strategy discussions. Since the beginning of training camp six months earlier they had drilled and prepared for these kinds of situations.

And so they waited. They weren't interested in what was going on up on that noisy, flashing Jumbotron. That was for the fans. Commercials, statistics, and an occasional shot of a cute girl wearing a Pioneers jersey dominated the big screen.

Pioneers quarterback Kelly James wasn't really looking at the Jumbotron either, but as he fidgeted along the sidelines with his teammates, something up there caught his attention. The camera was focused on the open window of the press box suite reserved for the Napoleon family and their guests. Kelly stared for a moment to be certain that his eyes were not deceiving him. They weren't.

Normally, Kelly James was *not* a man of few words. This time he was.

"Hey!" he called out. His teammates' heads snapped in his direction, and they saw Kelly pointing up at the Jumbotron screen. And that's where they saw Denzel Jackson, standing there, on his own two feet, clean-shaven, wearing a coat and a tie, his head no longer encumbered by that neckbrace. Somehow aware that the players were looking at his projected image, Denzel signaled them with a double-pump of both fists. The players all looked at each other, and when they did, Kelly James repeated the gesture. They all knew what he meant.

The whistle blew, and the teams streamed back onto the field. Only the producers of ESPN CLASSICS could have written the script for what happened during the next minute and 15 seconds of play. The Pioneers returned the kickoff to their 33-yard line. Kelly James went to work. So did running back "Touchdown Tommy" Thurber, receiver Reed Andreas, and their supporting cast of teammates. They moved the ball, but the clock was moving, too. There were only 25 seconds left when Thurber was spun out of bounds at the Saints' 1-yard line after weaving 20 heart-stopping yards through their defense following his reception of a screen pass.

It was first down and goal to go. The Pioneers lined up in their goal line power formation, and they gave the ball to Tommy once again. The Saints stuffed him for no gain. The clock was running, so the Pioneers called a timeout. It was their final one.

Play resumed. The ball was snapped, and it appeared the Pioneers were sticking with what had worked so well for them all season long—hammer it in by giving the ball to Tommy on a power plunge. Tommy exploded into the line of scrimmage, but he was unable to force his way into the end zone.

But wait! Tommy didn't have the football. Kelly James had pulled it out, and for a split-second he just stood there watching Tommy give an Academy Award performance as Best Supporting Actor in the game. If Tommy got the Best Supporting Actor Award, then the one for Best Performance In The Role Of Leading Man would have to go to Kelly James. While the pile of bodies in front of him continued to tangle and grunt, Kelly lofted a soft pass to backup tight end, Rollie Butcher, who had slipped into the end zone. Rollie caught it, and the referee raised his arms into the air. Touchdown.

The Pioneers didn't screw up *their* extra point attempt. They made it, and with only 14 seconds remaining, they were back in front,

28–25. It still wasn't over, because on the ensuing kickoff, even though their special teams star, "Crazy Lou" Scannon, made the tackle at the Saints' 36-yard line, he was guilty of waving off the old "Don't be dumb, and don't be dirty" admonition they heard so often from Coach Bobby Russell.

What Lou did wasn't dirty, but it sure was dumb. After nailing the Saints kick return man, Lou jumped up and went into a celebratory dance so outlandish that the officials interpreted it as being unsportsmanlike conduct. Flags flew, and the Pioneers were penalized 15 yards.

Only four seconds remained—time for just one play—as the Pioneers lined up at the Leopards' 49-yard line for what had to be that desperate last-play-of-the-game "Hail Mary." It was.

Saints quarterback Manning Archibald let fly, and the ball sailed toward the throng of receivers and defenders congregated near the Pioneers goal line. It descended into that jostling crowd, got tipped a time or two, and then fell to the ground. The game was over.

No! Wait! What was that yellow flag lying on the ground all about? It was about pass interference on Pioneers defensive back Eric "Diddy" Dewitt, that's what. None of the Portland players, coaches, or fans had seen the infraction, but so what? The guy in the striped shirt had, and he called it.

There was no time left on the clock, but the rulebook states that the offended team is allowed one additional play when a penalty of that nature occurs even though time has expired. And so, at the Portland 4-yard line, the Saints lined up for a chip shot attempt at the field goal which, if they made it, would tie the game at 28–28 and send it into overtime.

Snap. Hold. Kick. Around the corner of that impregnable human fortress of protectors for the kicker, a solitary member of the opposition came streaking. It was Lou Scannon, and he was heading for a single blade of grass located exactly 12 inches in front of where the foot of Saints kicker Joel "Goal" Post would meet the ball and send it on its journey skyward.

Crazy Lou accelerated. Then he dove at his target, parallel to the ground, while pushing his arms *forward*—not up!—as far as he could extend them. A few moments earlier, Lou had not remembered to "Don't be dumb," but now he did remember everything he had been drilled to do so many times when it came to trying to block a PAT or field goal attempt.

Don't go at the kicker; go at the pinpoint block spot. Don't raise your hands; slide them out; thrust them out still more. Don't even look at the kicker; stare through your stretched out fingers at that block spot using your eyes to urge them forward even farther. Lou remembered it all. Why not? He'd done it in practice more times than he had said "Oui, monsieur" whenever Yves or René Napoleon asked him if he was having fun. And so it wasn't just snap, hold, kick. It was snap, hold, kick—*thunk!*

Lou blocked the kick. The ball hit the ground, and—oh, for heaven's sake, it *still* wasn't over! The Saints Phil Andurrer scooped it up, and the chase was on as Phil zipped around changing directions while trying to find an open receiver. After sprinting to his left, then to the right, and then back again to his left, he spotted his tight end, E. Z. Pickens, jumping up and down all alone in the end zone.

Phil cocked his passing arm, and then whipped it forward, but just as he did, a Pioneers player, the one who had been in relentless back and forth pursuit during Phil's desperate journey, came crashing into him. It was Bill Hanlon, the Kickasska from Nebraska. The football popped into the air, and then it fluttered to the ground, out of bounds.

The whistle blew. There were no flags. The fans in the stadium went berserk, although "*Not* So Crazy Lou" Scannon exerted unparalleled discipline by restricting himself to a polite smile. This time the game really was over. So was the New Orleans Saints' season. But it wasn't over for the Pioneers. They were going to the Super Bowl.

CHAPTER FORTY-SEVEN

The production executives at CBS Sports were as delighted as the Portland fans were that the game would not be going into overtime. CBS was televising the AFC Championship Game played later that afternoon between the Los Angeles Leopards and the Denver Broncos, and those execs were anguishing over the possibility that their pre-game show telecast might have to go up against a Portland vs. New Orleans overtime on Fox Sports. Think what that would do to the ratings!

Lou Scannon and Bill Hanlon saved them from that fate. By virtue of their heroics, Lou and Bill clinched not only a Super Bowl berth for the Pioneers, but they also assured themselves of high praise from the CBS panel of experts. If Randy Dolbermeier had been watching, he would have been miffed. Randy was down on the field, however, and so was Denver coach, Norb "Headstrong" Armstrong. They weren't watching TV; they were watching their teams warm up for the big game.

Big game it was, but in many respects it was just like every other game. The players and coaches reported to the locker room two hours before the scheduled kickoff. They spent the first hour getting taped and putting on those damned uncomfortable uniforms, and during the next 45 minutes they were out on the field going through a warm-up procedure that had become as routine as a visit to the men's room. Then, it was back to the locker room to spend the final minutes of the longest two hours of the week.

The players were rarely subject to any additional instructions during that interminable pre-game ritual. They'd been preparing all week. Now it was time to put it to work, and on the very first series of the game, the Leopards came up with a remarkable display of game planning brilliance.

It was third down and six yards to go for the Broncos. Denver's quarterback, Elroy Jonathan, lined up six yards deep in a shotgun formation. Standing next to him was his star running back, Darius "Paycheck" Danning.

The center snap went to Elroy, and he handed the ball to Darius who took it and sprinted out to his right. The fastest man on the Broncos team was off and running on a surprise end sweep, and all of the Leopards defenders had to shift into pursuit. That, at least, is the way Fred Cantrell, the Broncos offensive coordinator, had envisioned it when he introduced this bit of trickery to his players during the practice week leading up to this game.

Most of the Leopards defensive unit did take off in that direction, as did all of the Broncos blockers. There was only one player on the Broncos who did not head toward the right flank, and that was Elroy Jonathan. Elroy drifted to the left. Then he streaked down the left side of the field. Darius pulled to a stop, then flung the ball back across and down the field toward Elroy.

In anticipating that *all* of the Leopards defenders would pursue Darius, Cantrell came up a tad short of being 100% correct. Although eight of them did go flying after him, the remaining three—cornerbacks Odell Nathan and Kirby "Psychiatrric" Ward, plus linebacker Colin Fitch—went the other way, sizzling along step for step with Elroy. Kirby ran in front of Elroy. Odell ran with him, elbow to elbow, and Colin trailed him by a step or two.

When Darius's pass arrived at its destination, it wasn't the intended receiver who caught it. It was Odell Nathan, and after his grab, Odell raced the other way—70 yards into the end zone. The game was less than three minutes old, and the Leopards had taken the lead, 7–0.

The battle continued. Denver answered with a touchdown, but when they kicked off after that score, Sammy Kurtask, behind some outstanding blocking by the front five on the Leopards kickoff return unit, ran it all the way back for the score that put the Leopards back in front, 14–7.

Late in the first half, Denver took a drive deep into L.A. territory. On a fourth and seven-yards-to-go situation at the Leopards'

15-yard line, they lined up to kick a field goal. They didn't get those three points, but it wasn't because the kick was no good. It was because they never kicked it.

When the Leopards stacked all 11 of their defenders at the line of scrimmage, as they had done on several all-out rush occasions during the season, the Denver PAT and field goal holder, Crane Neal, called the audible they had prepared for such a situation. That audible alerted his teammates that the field goal would be faked and that Crane would roll out with the intention of tossing a pass to tight end Pete Metzger, whom they expected to be wide open.

The ball was snapped, but none of the Leopards players seemed to be making any attempt to block the kick. Four of them—two to the left and two to the right—took wide contain paths in order to shut off any attempt by Crane Neal to roll to the outside. Six of the Leopards defenders dropped back into pass coverage positions. Unheard of!

When Crane tried going wide, he couldn't, and so he pulled up. Frantically, he looked for an open receiver. They were all covered. He was tackled, and the Broncos came away with no points. At halftime it was still Los Angeles: 14, Denver: 7.

■

During the halftime break, Norb Armstrong made a bold decision. Having noted how the front five players on the Leopards kickoff return unit had gone sprinting back deep into their own territory to provide blocking for Sammy Kurtask when he returned Denver's only first half kickoff for a touchdown, Norb told his team they would begin the second half with a *surprise* onside kickoff. The way that the Los Angeles front five had vacated their up front area left them vulnerable to this tactic.

In the other locker room, Randy Dolbermeier dispensed some key strategic information to his team, but he didn't do it until after assistant coaches Denny Koontz and Milo Becker came rushing back from the empty storage area to which they always retired at the beginning of halftime. They beckoned to Randy to come join them in a quiet corner of the locker room, and although you could see them whispering, they were doing it in an unusually animated fashion.

Randy listened. And then, with a nod of his head, a wink of his eye, and a smile on his face, he pointed a finger, first at Denny and then at Milo. After that, he turned back in the direction of the players, called for their attention, and told them what they were going to do on the kickoff at the beginning of the second half.

■

When the Broncos kickoff coverage unit came charging forward to begin the second half, the players on the Leopards receiving team didn't drop back to provide blocking for Sammy Kurtask. Instead, their front five drove forward in an immediate attack mode. Five other Leopards players also moved swiftly forward. The Leopards wound up with 10 men in place to cope with the "surprise" onside kick.

It was no contest. The Leopards weren't surprised; the Broncos were. Tucker Wren, the Leopards special teams standout, recovered the bouncing ball at the Broncos 42-yard line. Four plays later Sticky Fingers Lavell caught a 12-yard touchdown pass from Q. T. Pye. The shell-shocked Broncos trailed 21–7.

Even the press box was abuzz.

"How in the crap are the Leopards always one step ahead of our guys?" Archie Pelligo of *The Fort Collins Colloquy* asked Rick O'Shea from *The Denver Prattler*. Rick responded with a grimace and a shrug of the shoulders. Sitting nearby, both Mel Herbert and Jordy Nerdmann overheard Archie's inquiry, and both of them did have an opinion on that subject.

"I think I know," Mel said, but he was talking only to himself. "It's almost as if he had tuned in on the Broncos halftime instructions. Wouldn't that be something?"

Jordy felt no hesitancy about being more vocal. "It's because Randy Dolbermeier is one smart dude," he said. "It must be embarrassing to all the other coaches in this league to have him always be so much sharper than they are."

No one else in the press box commented. Their focus was on what was happening on the field below.

Down 21–7, the Broncos didn't have time to diddle. They needed to take some chances. They knew it. The keen minds in the press box knew it, and the Los Angeles Leopards knew it. All of that sounded exciting, but it also meant that it would be much easier to predict what they would be doing in their efforts to narrow the gap.

They'd be passing the ball more, going for the big yardage, time-conserving plays. On defense, they'd be stacking the line of scrimmage and blitzing their linebackers—and even a defensive back on occasion—in an effort to force turnovers. Sure, it was risky, but that's what they did.

And that is what the Leopards wanted them to do.

It didn't work. The Leopards turned one interception into a touchdown, and they came away with a field goal following a second one. The Broncos tried blitzing, and the Leopards, seeing it coming, called an audible that put Chase Banks one on one against cornerback Scott Chansota. Fifteen yards downfield, Chase broke away from Chansota, snatched the pass that Q. T. Pye threw his way, and sprinted the remaining 60 yards for another Leopards touchdown.

The Broncos did manage to squeeze out a field goal late in the third quarter and a meaningless touchdown as the game was ending. When the final gun sounded, it was Leopards: 38, Broncos: 17. Starting with that pivotal recovery of the onside kickoff, the roof fell in on the previous season's Super Bowl champions. The Leopards out-scored them 24–10 in the second half. It was the type of scene that had been taking place in the friendly confines of the Leopards home stadium all season long.

The Broncos were not going back to the Super Bowl this year. Two weeks from this day it would be the Los Angeles Leopards vs. the Portland Pioneers for the Super Bowl Championship.

CHAPTER FORTY-EIGHT

"Coach, how were you able to respond so well to Denver's onside kick at the beginning of the second half?" Helen Gaughan of the *Newport Beach Beachcomber* asked at the start of the post-game press conference. Several of the other writers scratched that one off the list of questions they were planning to ask.

"They took a big chance, and it just didn't work for them. That's all," Randy said.

"Yeah, but you had almost all of your players moving forward even before their kicker actually contacted the ball," Helen said.

"Call it intuition, I guess."

"Was it also intuition on that fake field goal of theirs when your guys pulled off and played for the fake rather than rushing the kicker?" Ken Nahora of *The Honolulu Hullabaloo* asked.

"Hey, don't forget, we were leading 14–7 at the time. A field goal still would have made it only 14–10. I took a guess, and it paid off."

"It seems as if you made a lot of correct guesses at crucial times today," Ken said.

"Well, thank you for the compliment. That's what it's all about, isn't it? It's a physical game, but it's also a mind game, and I'm proud as can be, not only of our players, but also of how well my coaches and I made the sharp and alert moves we did in order to win this game. Sure, you've got to outplay the other team, but, doggone it, you've got to outsmart them, too."

■

During the first week of the two-week break between the conference championship games and the Super Bowl, the teams practiced at their home facilities. Although members of the media were allowed only limited access to the practices, they were present in abundance in the media headquarters at those sites, and at the daily post-practice interview sessions the writers and broadcasters probed the players and coaches about what it would take to emerge victorious on Super Bowl Sunday.

Mel Herbert's suspicions about what Randy Dolbermeier thought he had to do in order to assure such an outcome had grown. He hoped he was wrong. He feared he was right. He had to find out. But how?

Mel didn't want to jeopardize Joe Skoronski's job status by subjecting him to any more questions on the matter, but he knew he needed to do something. Maybe Zig Zag Zizzo could help.

The morning practice on Friday was a short one, and so, rather than hanging around for a reprise of the press conferences that had been taking place all week, Mel told Zig Zag he would treat him to lunch at Factor's Famous Deli on West Pico Boulevard.

"Sounds great to me," Zig Zag said. "Some fellow I met at the off-track betting parlor told me that one time when he went to Factor's, he saw Tommy Lasorda and Sandy Koufax eating there. Is the food any good?"

"You'll love it. Let's go."

■

After they were seated and placed their order, Mel spoke first. "Zig Zag, when we're out at the stadium, I see you go wandering off into all the different areas a lot. Can I ask you a big favor?"

"Whaddya mean? Of course you can. What is it?"

"Do you ever go over to where the visiting team's locker room is?"

"Yeah, I bop around all over the place. I keep discovering lots of new and interesting things when I do. Why do you ask me that?"

"Because I think it's possible that you might find something extremely interesting in there. Make that, I'm *afraid* you might. I hate to say this, but I believe that Coach Dolbermeier may be employing some very underhanded methods in getting his team ready to play their games."

"What do you mean by 'underhanded'?"

"I guess that was just a nice way of saying that there is some out-and-out cheating going on."

"I thought that's what you meant, and I've got to tell you, Mel, you're not the only one thinking that way."

"You, too?"

"Not just me. The stuff I keep hearing from a lot of the players makes me real antsy. Joe and me, we talk about it all the time, and Joe is getting even more nervous about it. Joe—"

Zig Zag stopped in mid-sentence. He was gazing up at something in the aisle, just a foot or two above and behind where Mel was sitting. Mel forced his arthritic neck to turn his head toward the object of Zig Zag's stare. There stood Joe Skoronski.

"How come youse guys dint invite me ta come witchas?" Joe asked.

"How come you knew we were here?" Mel asked in return.

"Coupla da players in da locker room, dey told me dey heard Zig Zag say he was goin' here witcha for lunch. I taught maybe you taught I'd be too busy ta make it, but I got everythin' wrapped up fast, and so I decided ta come join da fun."

"Joe, I really didn't want to ask you to be with us," Mel said, "but it was for a darn good reason. I'm asking Zig Zag to give me some help on a rather touchy matter, and I felt it would be best for your sake if we did not involve you. You work for the team. Zig Zag doesn't. He works for the paper and for me, and there are some issues that I just have to look into. It's best if you're not drawn in."

"I tink I gotta good idea whatchas probably talkin' about," Joe said. "I'll just go up dere ta da counter and sit wit myself and let you two guys gab wit each udder. I brought sumpthin' wit me ta read, anyway. Grabo told me dat a lotta da players are goin' on a cruise early next summer, and he invited me ta tag along. He gave me dis pamphlet ting ta look over dat tells all about it. He told me dey're gonna get on a boat on da Alaska mainland and den go sailin' all around da Illusion Islands. Sounds like fun."

Joe headed for a seat at the counter. When Mel was sure that Joe had settled in, he turned back to Zig Zag.

"Okay. I have some good reasons to believe that Randy arranged to have the visiting team's locker room wired. If so, he's devised a way to listen in on any pre-game instructions they get or on any halftime adjustments they make."

"Geez, do you think he'd really do that?"

"Yes, I do. But I might be wrong. It would be terrible if I made such an accusation and it wasn't true, but it would be even more terrible if that is what he is doing and he gets away with it. I know you love this game, too, Zig Zag. That's a big reason I'm going to ask you to help."

"How can I do that?"

"Well, since the team will be practicing at the stadium tomorrow and you usually roam all over the place anyway when we're out there, how about roaming into that visitors' locker room and seeing if you can find anything in there."

"Like what?"

"Like any hidden mikes. You know that's what I mean, don't you?"

"Yeah, Mel, I do. I have a pretty good idea where to look, too. My uncle Carmie was an electrician, and when we were growing up he used to show me and my brother Eugene a lot about that kind of stuff."

"I hate to ask you to do the snooping for me, Zig Zag, and I hope I'm not asking you to do something you feel is wrong. If it is, let me know. I'll understand."

"It's not wrong. It's right. And if that's what's happening, I don't like it anymore than you do."

"If you get caught, Randy may see to it that you never get back into the stadium or the team locker room again," Mel cautioned.

"I'm not afraid of that, and if no shenanigans are going on, then Randy's got nothing to be afraid of."

■

After practice on Saturday, Mel eased himself into the passenger seat of his car. After settling in, he turned to Zig Zag who was sitting in the driver's seat, but before either one of them spoke, Mel knew the answer to the question he was so eager to have answered. He read it by looking at Zig Zag's tightened lips, at the fire in his eyes, and at his reddened cheeks and twitching nose.

"Damn it!" Zig Zag growled. Then they drove off, and after they pulled into the Albertson's Supermarket parking lot 10 minutes later, Zig Zag filled him in.

"There are eight of them. Mikes, that is. They're planted up there in the ceiling with some kind of a mesh covering over the holes, but it's the type of material that would let any sound come through. They look like they might be up there to spew out water in case there's a fire or something like that, but they're what I said they are. I can't believe it."

"I didn't want to," Mel said, "but now I do. I've got another question. Have you ever been into that area that attaches off the back of Joe's equipment room out there?"

"No. I asked Joe what was there, but he told me he's never been in it and that it's always locked up and that he hasn't got any key for it."

"Right," Mel said.

"Oh, Oh, I gotcha. Well then, how are we going to get in there?"

"That's what I'm trying to figure out."

■

Many miles to the north, the Portland Pioneers also spent the first week of preparation for the Super Bowl Game at their home facility. Bobby Russell sought to keep the meetings and practices as similar as possible to what they were like throughout the regular season and the playoffs, although he knew there were a few special items that needed to be addressed. He reminded the players that for the tens of thousands of spectators who would be at the game and for the millions of fans worldwide, this was the occasion for one hoop-dee-doo of a party. Not for the players. They were going for a different reason.

"The biggest distraction with which you will have to deal," Bobby told them at their Monday meeting, "will come from family and friends who will be using up all your cell phone minutes with requests for tickets to the game. All of that needs to be handled this week, period! Not next week."

On Wednesday there was a distraction. It was one that the players and coaches welcomed. Five minutes after the meeting was scheduled to begin, Bobby Russell was still not in the room. "Coach Russell's not on time!" Sylvester Simmons bellowed. "This is the biggest upset in the history of the NFL." No one disagreed.

Moments later, when the door to the room opened and Bobby, looking back over his shoulder, entered, numerous cries of "Fine him! Fine him!" erupted. And then, when the person trailing Bobby appeared in the doorway, the clamor ceased immediately. It was Denzel Jackson.

Bobby and Denzel, walking slowly and smiling at the stunned players, moved together to the front of the room. Bobby indicated who would speak first by stepping aside, and extending his arm toward Denzel.

"How proud I am of all of you," Denzel said. "How fortunate I am to be standing here in front of you today. It may be a while before I get back out onto the practice field again, but because of the love and support I've been getting from people like you, that day is going to come. It won't be this season, but even though I won't be down on the field with you as you practice for and then play in the Super Bowl, my heart—and my spirit—will be there with every one of you."

When Denzel finished his remarks, a 10-minute recess ensued, enough time to allow every person in the room to exchange a few words with Denzel. Bobby then called the meeting back into session.

"Any final words, Denzel?" he asked.

"Yes, Coach Russell. I want to address the issue of your being late for today's meeting. You are hereby fined in the amount of 25 cents, U.S. currency. Any players wishing to contribute something to a fund that would help you in your efforts to meet this obligation are encouraged to contact your agent in order to make any such arrangements." Then, a happy Denzel left a room that was filled with happy Pioneers players and coaches.

The fun for today was over. Even more fun lay ahead.

CHAPTER FORTY-NINE

During the week prior to leaving for the Super Bowl site, both the Leopards and the Pioneers practiced outdoors. Saturday of that week was the last time they did that, however. The Super Bowl Game was to be played indoors in Indianapolis's Lucas Oil Stadium, and all the practices after the teams arrived in the frigid Midwest were scheduled at indoor venues. The Leopards drilled at the Indianapolis Colts athletic complex. The Pioneers were assigned to hold their practices at Lucas Oil Stadium.

While running backs plowed through the line every day at those *indoor* practice sessions, the only plowing being done *outdoors* was by the city trucks that were clearing away the snow so that the team buses could make it from their hotels to the practice locations. The weather was lousy, and although players from other teams in the NFL may have been enjoying vacations in Hawaii or the Bahamas, the players getting ready for this game didn't envy them at all. They were where they wanted to be. Let the snow pile up. They didn't care.

■

It did pile up, and the only things that piled up faster during that hectic week were the questions from the media and the obligations placed on the players and coaches to respond, for the umpteenth time, to the same questions. Some of the players hated it; some of them loved it; most of them tolerated it.

Reporters and broadcasters from all over the world poured into Indianapolis. Some served a USA audience whose knowledge of football exceeded their knowledge of history or math. Other journalists came from far-off lands to convey to their entranced countrymen the fervor that a mere sporting event elicited from so much of the American populace. How could so many people, the foreign readers and listeners wondered, be so engrossed in an activity that was only a game. After all, it wasn't soccer, you know.

Appearing along with the cadre of media regulars, there were many newcomers in attendance at the daily question and answer sessions, and it was the nature of their interests that added spice for the fan who thought he had heard it all before.

There was the routine query, of course, voiced this time by one of the usual suspects, Mason Blue of *The Burbank Bulletin*. "Have you given any thought, Coach Dolbermeier, to surprising everyone by starting Toby Eggleston at quarterback?"

"Why in the world would we put Q.T. Pye on the bench?" Randy responded.

"Well, my research shows me that you won all four games when Toby was the starter at that position. That's why I asked you that one."

"Toby did well, but doggone it, Mason, are you forgetting that we won nine games with Q.T. as our starter?"

"But all five of your losses came with him in there, too," Mason said.

"Hey, pal, if it'll make you happy, go ahead and say that we won't announce who our starting quarterback is until just before kickoff. How's that?"

That suited Mason Blue just fine. The lead line for his column the next day was: "Toby Or Not Toby? That Is The Question."

"Next question?" Randy asked, pointing to a woman reporter he didn't recall having seen before. It was Consuella Schlepkowitz of *The San Fernando Valley Outlet Mall Shopping News*.

"Will your players be wearing any special make of sweat socks, T-shirts, or head bands that you feel will enhance their performance *and* appearance?" she asked.

"You know, as busy as we've been, I haven't had a chance to decide about that one yet, but just as soon as I do, young lady, I will be pleased to bring you and your readers up-to-date," Randy said with a wink at a few of the more familiar faces in the audience.

Many of the European journalists seemed more interested in the personalities of the men who would be playing in the game than they were in the intricacies of the Leopards Fun and Shout offense or of the Pioneers defensive schemes. When Stavros Giannopoulos of *The Athens Marathon* learned that Leopards backup running back Gillespie "Dizzy" Davis had spent some time in Athens while on vacation the previous spring, he asked Dizzy if he had visited the Parthenon and the Acropolis.

"No, I didn't go to no night clubs when I was there," Dizzy answered.

For British scribe Phineas Huckleberry of *The Liverpool Linguist*, the player that captured his attention was 6'8", 375-pound offensive tackle Maurice "House" Zanzibar of the Pioneers. Phineas dedicated his daily columns to accounts of House's intake of calories, to describing the size of his apparel (especially his size 17 EEE shoes), and to expressing disbelief about the weight of the barbells that some of House's teammates told Phineas that "their man" could hoist.

After spending most of the week trailing around after House and his XXXL-sized offensive linemen teammates, Phineas—at 5'7" and 143 pounds—suggested that perhaps, instead of calling them the Portland Pioneers, it would be more fitting to refer to them as "the *Portly* Pioneers." Blimey, but you should have seen how all the lads and lassies at the Firkin Pheasant Pub in Liverpool had such a jolly good laugh upon hearing about that one.

If, over the course of the long season, the players and coaches had become weary of hearing the same-old from the stateside media, then the foreign press provided some refreshing variety.

"Herr Russell," Ernst Weil of *The Berlin Braubeiter* asked, "will your team be introduced before the game in numerical or in alphabetical order?"

"Don't know yet. We'll be discussing that at our staff meeting this evening," Bobby answered.

"Danke!" Ernst said, and then he turned his furrowed brow back to scrutinizing the flip card that contained all the roster information on both teams.

The press conferences for each team during that interminable week were held separately. That changed on Saturday, the day before the game, when, in accordance with league protocol, the head coaches of the two teams stood side by side at the microphones. Randy Dolbermeier and Bobby Russell smiled at the gathered throng. When they glanced at each other, their gazes turned into glares, but they didn't exchange words.

The NFL's Director of Media Relations, I. L. Gregorio, opened the meeting for questions. Randy's answers usually dragged on, leading to impatience on the part of those writers waiting to ask their next question. Bobby's responses, many of the assembled group felt, weren't detailed enough.

Thirty minutes later, Gregorio made a stab at bringing the session to a close.

"One more. Last question," he said.

"This question is for Coach Dolbermeier. Coach, how big of a challenge is it for you to be going up against the number-one ranked defense in the NFL?" asked Everett Glades of *The Tallahassee Talisman*.

"Hey, buddy, what the hell do I care? How many times do I have to hear about their defense? Defense! Schmeefense! We've got a pretty damn good *offense*, you know. You just watch. When our Fun and Shout gets going, *we'll* have the fun, and when *they* shout, it'll be 'Ouch.' We've got a defense, too, remember? And it's a damn good one. They'll find that out. But let me tell you, this game is about moving the ball. It's about razzle-dazzling the other guy until his head starts to swim. It's about out-smarting him and out-hustling him. Those are the things we plan to do better than anyone who has ever played in this game. Those are the things that we want to do so damn well that it'll make the other guys whimper. That's what we're going to do. How's that?"

"Coach Russell, how do you respond to that?" Everett asked.

"We'll be there, and we'll be on time," Bobby said.

CHAPTER FIFTY

This wasn't the first Super Bowl that Mel Herbert had covered. He'd been to them all, and he was as excited to be here now as he had been for every one of the others. Some things about this one sure were different, however.

It wasn't his *first* one, but it was going to be—in accordance with what Mel had known since that first day of training camp—his *last* one. When this season ended, Mel was going to announce his retirement. It has been fantastic, he told himself, but there is a whole world out there away from the athletic fields that Frannie and I have yet to explore.

When the playoffs began a few weeks earlier, Mel finally told Frannie about his plan to retire. Any doubts or hesitancies that concerned her when she heard the startling news were allayed when Mel told her they would celebrate the start of this new era in their lives with a vacation in Italy.

"When we are there," Frannie told him, "I want you to call me 'Francesca.' In fact, why don't you start doing that now? Will you?"

"For you I will do anything," Mel said, "but pretty soon, I'm not going to know who I'm with. When I met you, you were Frances; then it was Fran; next you're Frannie; and now it's going to be Francesca. I'll try to keep it straight. But only if you promise that you won't tell anyone that I'm planning to retire."

The secret did remain just between the two of them. Three days before Mel departed for Indianapolis, however, he felt obliged to let Sports Editor Carroll Blumenthal know of his intentions. Carroll, taken aback, sought to dissuade him, but Mel didn't waver.

"Carroll, I've thought about it for a long time, and I made this decision even before the season began," Mel said. "It is what I plan to do, but I felt it only fair to tell you now. Other than Francesc—er,

Frannie—you are the only person who knows, and I ask, please, that you not say anything about it to anyone else until after the season is over."

"Okay, Mel. We'll talk again after the Super Bowl."

That wasn't all that was different about this year's championship game. Mel's hometown team was playing in this one. Great! But what about the unrest and the apprehension that was tormenting him? How can I keep my focus on this game, he wondered, when there is something that must be addressed, something more important than who wins it and who loses it?

And how do I go about carrying out that task, especially when, at the last minute before heading here to Indianapolis, it turns out that my top aide isn't able to be here with me?

■

At midnight on Saturday, just 10 hours before the Los Angeles Leopards and the hometown media were scheduled to depart for Indianapolis, Zig Zag Zizzo—Mel's driver, his buddy, his support —telephoned him with some startling news.

There was a fire.

There was a fire late that afternoon at Zelda's animal shelter, and although Zelda, through her heroic efforts, succeeded in saving all of the dear animals in her care, it was she who needed rescuing by the firemen who rushed to the scene several minutes later. They pulled her from a blazing wooden structure into which she had ventured to see if any of the panicked creatures were trapped inside. They weren't, but she was.

The firemen did it. They got her out before the flames seared her flesh, but she was in a dire state suffering from smoke inhalation. They rushed Zelda to the hospital.

"I'm here with her now, Mel," Zig Zag said. "I've got to stay with her, too."

"Of course. What's her condition? How's she doing?"

"Thank the Lord. She's doing better now. She's regained

consciousness and she's breathing the right way again, but she's so worn out that all she wants to do is sleep."

"Oh, I'm so glad to hear that," Mel said.

"Mel, I'll try to get back there and drive you around just as soon I think it's okay to leave her, but I've really got no idea when that might be. And besides that, I've got to do all the taking care right now of Amigo and Paisan. Zelda's assistant is looking after things at the animal shelter."

"Zig Zag, don't you worry about me. You stay there with Zelda. She needs you."

"So do you, I think," Zig Zag said.

Boy, do I ever, Mel mused to himself, but he didn't say it to Zig Zag. Instead, he said, "I'll manage. I'll find myself a driver somewhere."

"I know how to help you out with that, Mel. My cousin, Bruno, lives in Indianapolis. He knows all about you. He'd be thrilled to do it. Besides that, he knows about sports almost as much as I do. You'll like him. He knows how to get a job done."

And so they worked it out. When Mel's plane arrived in Indianapolis, Bruno Banducci was there to meet him.

Bruno was all that Zig Zag said he would be. He was always on time. He knew every twist, turn, and shortcut needed to maneuver their way through the traffic during that week of bustling activity. Besides that, Bruno entertained Mel by treating him to numerous recitations of the previous season's batting average for every single player on the Chicago Cubs baseball team.

Having Bruno as his driver turned out to be fine so far as getting around this relatively unfamiliar city was concerned, but Mel still missed not having Zig Zag on hand to help him with the issue that was now his foremost concern. Without Zig Zag there to help him do some investigative work, Mel felt he would be unable to nail down the evidence that would allow him to reveal how tainted—he was becoming more certain—the Leopards road to the Super Bowl had been.

But then again, what if he *was* wrong.

CHAPTER FIFTY-ONE

Super Bowl Week was so packed with activities that it took until Friday evening before Mel and Joe Skoronski finally found time to meet for a relaxing dinner in Indianapolis. Joe recommended that they dine at St. Elmo's restaurant after being advised by Colts equipment manager, Dick Taffone, that any dessert he ordered there would be delicious beyond description and of a size that would challenge even Joe's vaunted capacity to consume it.

As concerned as Joe was about selecting the proper dessert, it did not deter him from inquiring, immediately after they were seated, about Zig Zag and Zelda. "I miss havin' dat guy here, ya know, but I unnerstan' dat he's gotta be dere wit her. Ya heard any more about how she's comin' along?"

"She's making steady improvement," Mel said, "but they've got to monitor her closely because that breathing problem was a very serious thing."

"Yeah, I know. I heard dat she inhaled somma dat carbon peroxide poisonin' or sumpthin' like dat."

"It was smoke inhalation."

"Oh, dat was it, huh? I can't tell da difference. I never had eadder one a dem myself. Boy, I really like dis menu here. I tink I'm gonna get me one a dem glutton-free pasta dishes dey say is so hellty for ya. Whaddaya gonna have? Ya know yet?"

Mel knew, and so they ordered, ate, chatted, and enjoyed this respite from all the game-related frenzy that had commanded their attention since their arrival in Indianapolis.

One hour and a hefty quadruple-digit number of calories later, it was time for dessert. Mel, after getting Joe to promise that he would not tell Frannie about this transgression, went for the cheesecake drizzled with strawberry compote. Now it was Joe's turn. He ordered the macadamia nut-battered mashed banana bundles served with warm Hawaiian chocolate toffee syrup and crème anglaise for dunking.

Joe was about 30% (give or take) through his assault on that splendiferous concoction and showing no signs of fatigue when Mel asked what he felt to be an innocent question. "How about you, Joe. Tell me what's different about getting ready for a Super Bowl Game compared to all the other games?"

Joe wiped some of the chocolate syrup off his chin, getting half of it on his napkin and the other half on the collar of his shirt. "Same old stuff, mostly," he said. "Washin' da laundry, gettin' da balls out onta da field before practice, and den roundin' dem up and gettin' em back in after. And den washin' more laundry. Dat's about it."

"Come on, Joe. That's your routine, I know. But give me *one thing* that's different for the team. Think. Let's see if you can come up with something. Anything. Tell you what. If you do, I'll buy you another dessert."

Joe stopped eating. He licked first one side and then the other side of the spoon that had served him so well up to now. While retaining his grip on that essential utensil, Joe plunged himself into a thinking process over the next 30 seconds that he interrupted just one time in order to glance down and make certain that that neglected bowl of nutrition sitting in front of him was continuing its patient wait for his return.

"Okay, here's one," he said, "and I won't even take ya up on dat offer for anudder one a dem desserts. You can donate it ta charity if ya want or even give it ta dat little kid sittin' over dere wit his Ma and Pop."

"That's very noble of you. Let's hear it."

"We're taking way more films of our practices for dis game den we have for any udder one all year long."

"That's it?"

"Yeah, dat's it. And dat's why, I guess, we even hired dat extra camera guy ta help out more."

"You needed an additional video man? That's crazy. Phil Maecker does a terrific job running that department, and he already has three full time assistants working with him, doesn't he?"

"Yeah, he does, but dis new guy must be some kinda specialist or sumpthin' because he always delivers his stuff direct ta Coach Dolbermeier right dere in da locker room."

"That's unusual," Mel said. "As I recall, the video staff always went back to their studio and prepared the tapes of practice so that they'd be ready for the coaches to review after the coaches showered and returned to their offices."

"Dat's what dey're doin' here, too, 'cept for dis one guy."

"Have you spoken at all with that fellow?"

"Only once. After da first day's practice here, he came inta da locker room lookin' around, and I asked him if I could help him wit sumpthin'. He had one a dose passes hangin' down from his neck dat allows him ta come in dere. Anyways, Randy wasn't dere yet, and so da guy gave da tape ta me and told me ta tell da coach dat Chick Peasley—dat's da guy's name—brought it dere for him. Just right den, dough, Randy walks in da door and sees da guy handin' da tape to me, and Randy really lays it on him. Tells him dat he gives dose tapes to nobody but Randy himself. Man, he was really steamed. Anyways, all da resta da week when dat Chick guy comes in and Randy ain't dere yet, he just waits around til Randy shows up and den he hands it straight to him."

"Joe, if you're able to find out any more about this Peasley fellow, let me know, will you? Be very careful, though. You never know how Randy will react if he thinks you're being too inquisitive."

"I'm afraid he's already dat way, Mel, cause he wasn't only mad at dat udder guy, but you shoulda seen somma da dirty looks he was sendin' my way."

"On second thought, Joe, forget it. I don't want to put you in that kind of position. I'll figure it out."

■

The following morning at the media headquarters, Mel strolled up to the table where Brant Gilbert was sitting. "How's the coffee?" Mel asked.

"That's what you walked all the way down the hall to ask me, Mr. Ace Reporter?"

"The world awaits that news, Mr. Wise Guy. No, what I really want to know, Brant, is how well do you know Phil Maecker?"

"How well? I hired him. Good man. Does a great job. We still talk now and then. Why do you ask?"

Mel filled Brant in on his conversation with Joe.

"Uh, oh here we go again," Brant said. "Am I thinking that what I'm thinking, you're thinking, too?"

"I think so."

"You know what?" Brant said, "I'm going to ask Phil who this guy is and what all that 'locker room only' crap is all about."

"I guess we *are* thinking alike, Brant. That's what I was going to see if you would do, and I was hoping that it could even be before tomorrow's game. When do you think you'll have a chance to talk with Phil?"

"I've got Phil's cell phone number. How about right now?'

"Sounds good to me."

Brant dialed, and Phil Maecker answered.

"Maecker here," he said.

"Hey Phil, Brant Gilbert. You busy?"

"Always, but never too busy for you, Brant. What's up?"

"May sound like a crazy question, Phil, but when did you add that new man to your staff?"

"New man. What new man? What're you talking about?"

"One of our people told me that you've brought in another assistant, and I was wondering if he's replaced one of the men that's been working with you or if he's just a special assignment guy for the Super Bowl."

"That report's all wrong," Phil said. "Jimmy, Chris, and Dave are still here. There's no one else. We're operating just like we always do. Where did your man come up with that one?"

"The guy who told me said that he spoke with the fellow personally. Said his name was Chick Peasley."

"Chick Peasley! You're kidding. That guy has been after me for a couple of years now looking to get hired. He's some freelance video addict who is obsessed about getting a job with an NFL team. He's not with us. He lives back in L.A."

"He may live there, but he's here now. The person who told me about it is very reliable."

"No matter what, Brant, any story about him working for our video department is not true. That's about all I can tell you."

"Okay, Phil. I was just curious. That's why I called you. I won't keep you any longer. I know you've got more important things to do than talk to some rumor monger from the media."

"With you, anytime, Brant. Always a pleasure."

Brant closed his phone, clipped it back onto his belt, and turned to Mel. "I guess we didn't learn much from that call, did we?" he said.

"Quite the contrary."

"That's what I meant. You know what I think?"

"What?"

"Hang on. I think Randy's the man who hired Peasley, and I think he hired him to sneak into the stadium and videotape the Pioneers practices. It's not that hard to do. He just needed to get a pass somewhere. Randy could have arranged that."

"We still keep thinking alike, don't we," Mel said.

"What are we going to do about it?" Mel didn't respond to Brant's question, and so Brant repeated, "What are we going to do about it?"

"I'm thinking. I'm thinking."

"Well, while you're thinking, I'm going to get in touch with Mr. Medill and let him know what we've learned. He'll be mortified, but, knowing him, I'm sure he'd rather be made aware if anything this despicable is being carried out by someone representing an enterprise of his."

"I can understand that," Mel said.

"I hope I can get through to him. Between his new movie and having his team in the Super Bowl, he's so darned busy that it's really tough to catch up with him."

CHAPTER FIFTY-TWO

Every day after he arrived in Indianapolis, Mel placed a telephone call to Zig Zag in order to be kept abreast of Zelda's progress. The news he received was encouraging. By Tuesday, Zelda was allowed to begin walking the corridors at the hospital. By Wednesday, she was showing signs of her old perkiness, and on Thursday, she was released from the hospital with the admonition to not rush back into full activity. Friday's news continued to be upbeat, and so on Saturday, Mel decided there was no need to bother Zig Zag with another call. But late that night it was Zig Zag who called Mel.

"Hey, Mel, guess what!"

"What? Is Zelda okay?"

"She's real good. You talked to Joe at all today?"

"Not today. We had dinner together last night, though. Why do you ask?"

"Well, Joe buzzed me early this morning and said that Mr. Medill had called Mabel at the switchboard over at the Leopards practice facility and asked about how he could get some team jerseys and caps for his two grandsons. The kids are going to a big Super Bowl TV party at their high school auditorium to watch the game tomorrow. Anyway, Mabel called Joe back there in Indianapolis to find out how they could take care of Mr. Medill's request, and then Joe got in touch with me. You still listening?"

"Yeah. Go on."

"Joe asked me if I could go by the equipment room and pick up that stuff for Mr. Medill's grandkids and then bring it over to him at his office. Mr. Medill has been real busy out here in L.A. all week with a new movie that's coming out, and he wasn't going to be traveling to Indianapolis until this evening. I told Joe I'd be glad to do that for him. And besides that, it sure sounded like fun to me."

"So, was it fun?"

"More than you can imagine," Zig Zag answered. "When I got to Mr. Medill's office and his secretary told him I was there with the goods, he came right out his door and thanked me in person. Then, when he asked me my name and I told him 'Zig Zag,' he said, 'I know who you are. Come on in.' Turns out that Brant Gilbert, when he was the GM here, used to say some things about me to Mr. Medill, and I guess most of them were pretty good."

"That's nice," Mel said. "What did you fellows talk about?"

"That's why I'm calling you now. You aren't going to believe this."

"Try me."

"Okay. We talked about tomorrow's game, naturally, and he even told me a little bit about his new movie. It's going to be called *Ale's What's Good For You.* And then, right out of the blue—you could've knocked me on my butt—he says to me, 'Zig Zag,' he says, 'I know you hang around this team and the players a lot. Have you ever seen or heard anything about dirty play or cheating on the part of our team? I've got to know.'"

"He asked you that? Did he say where he heard those rumors?"

"Nope. He just sat there looking at me real intense and waiting for an answer, and I've gotta tell you, Mel, I felt it would be all wrong for me to tell him a lie. I didn't mention you at all, but I did tell him about all the wiring I found in the visitors' locker room at the stadium."

"Wow! How did he react?"

"Well, first he just asked me why I went in there."

"And?"

"Well, I told him about how me and Joe talk about a lot of things and how Joe kept saying to me that some of the coaches at halftime of the home games go into that storage room and come out of there with what looks like some kind of a recording machine that they always take right over to Coach Dolbermeier."

"What did Mr. Medill say to that?"

"He just says, 'Are you sure?' and I said back that I was sure of what Joe told me, and that it made both of us sort of suspicious. That was why, I told Mr. Medill, I got curious and decided to meander over to the visitors' locker room to look around."

"Go on."

"By that time, I was getting real nervous because I could see how angry he was looking. I thought maybe it was me he was mad at, but that wasn't it at all because he told me right away how much he appreciated my being so straight with him. Then he wanted to know if I ever went into that storage room where the assistant coaches went at halftime."

"And what did you tell him?"

"The truth. I said that no one I knew had the key for it and that I heard no one else was allowed to go in there. Then wait til you hear what he said next."

"I *can't* wait. Tell me."

"He asked me if I would be willing to go to the stadium and check that room out. If I'd agree to do that, he said, he'd call the people in charge out there and tell them that I was to be admitted."

"You agreed to do it, didn't you?"

"You bet I did. And after that, Mr. Medill arranged for me to meet Casper Schmotz out there, first thing tomorrow morning. He's the head guy in charge of all the electrical setups at the stadium. He's out of town until tomorrow morning, but Mr. Medill wants him to be there with me when I go in to look things over."

"But by then Mr. Medill will be here, won't he?"

"Yeah, he's on his flight heading there right now, in fact, but he told me that he wants us to call him tomorrow morning first thing after we come out of that storage room. I hope we can get it all covered in time for me to get back home before the opening kickoff, you know."

"You're going to call me, too, aren't you?"

"Count on it. That's the main reason I'm letting you know now what's happening. That and reminding you to be sure you don't turn off your cell phone like you always do."

"Good advice," Mel said. "Be talking to you. Have fun."

CHAPTER FIFTY-THREE

It was Super Bowl Sunday morning. Mel checked his cell phone. No calls yet. Rather than trying to fight his way through the pandemonium in the packed hotel lobby to get to the restaurant for breakfast, Mel orderered room service. They told him his breakfast would be delivered in approximately one hour.

Fifteen minutes later there was a knock on Mel's door. He couldn't believe that room service would ever be that early. He was right. When Mel opened the door, there stood Brant Gilbert.

"Got any coffee?" Brant asked.

"It'll probably be here by halftime," Mel said. "Come on in."

"You know why I'm here, don't you?"

"I don't think it's for coffee."

"I was hoping, but there's another reason."

"You've spoken with Mr. Medill, haven't you?"

"I finally got to him at the airport just before he was boarding his plane in L.A. on his way here last night. I told him what we heard about Chick Peasley and about what I suspected it might mean."

"How did he take it?"

"This will surprise you. He *wasn't* surprised. He was damn angry, though. More than I can recall his ever having been."

"That does *not* surprise me," Mel said. "When I spoke with Zig Zag last night he told me Mr. Medill had invited him into his office and asked him whether he'd been hearing any rumors about dirty play or cheating. When Zig Zag told him about discovering wiring in the visitors' locker room, Mr. Medill asked Zig Zag and Casper Schmotz to go into that empty storage room area early this morning to investigate whether anything's amiss in there."

"Did they find anything?"

"I don't know. Zig Zag or Casper was going to call Cedric B.

today just as soon as they got out of there. Zig Zag was going to call me, too, but I haven't heard anything from him yet."

"You're not the only one waiting," Brant said. "I couldn't talk real long last night with Cedric B. because I caught him just when his flight was about to take off. He did say, though, that he was going to speak with Randy today about that Peasley matter. He said he'd be back in touch with me after that, but I haven't heard anything yet."

"Let's try to stay in touch, okay?" Mel said.

While Mel continued waiting in his room, he checked his cell phone again to be certain that he hadn't missed hearing it ring. There was nothing from Zig Zag.

Noon. Still no calls. Mel took the initiative. He dialed Zig Zag's number. No answer. Another hour passed. It was time for him to leave for the stadium.

CHAPTER FIFTY-FOUR

I've got to keep my mind on what's happening out there on the playing field, Mel kept reminding himself as Portland Pioneers place kicker Trey Pointer sent the opening kickoff into the air. The Super Bowl Game was on.

At the end of the first quarter the score was tied, 7–7, and Mel still hadn't heard from Zig Zag. Five minutes into the second period, the Leopards were facing a fourth-and-10 at the Pioneers' 17-yard line. The stadium was rocking, and just as the Leopards field goal team came trotting onto the field, Mel's cell phone broke out in a bouncy musical rendition of "You Are My Sunshine."

Following a few shouts of "Hey, turn that damn thing off!" from some fellow inhabitants of the press box, Mel jumped up from his seat, and while he was ducking into the more quiet confines of the men's room, Uprights Updyke was nailing his field goal attempt. The Leopards took the lead, 10–7.

■

"Zig Zag. What's the deal? Where have you been?"

"It's what we suspected, Mel. That storage room has a speaker outlet right in the corner, just above floor level. It looks like it's a vent or something like that, but Casper Schmotz was with me, remember? And he figured it out right away. And man, was he teed off."

"What did he say? Anything meaningful?"

"Yeah, he—" Zig Zag started.

"Hold it, Zig Zag," Mel interrupted. "Some guy just flushed the damned toilet, and I can't hear anything." Twenty seconds passed. "Okay, go on. No! Wait! Now he's got that stupid hand dryer making all the noise. What's wrong with this guy? There. At last. Go ahead."

"Like I was saying, Schmotzie wanted to see what was in the visitors' locker room, too, so we went over there, and I showed him how that place was all wired up. By then, he was calming down a little, and he told me that he had a pretty good idea about who the person who may have done the work was."

"Did he tell you who?"

"No, he didn't want to say any names until he was sure, but he did say that the guy he suspected is on the regular staff out there at the stadium."

"Have you spoken with Mr. Medill about all of this?"

"Yep. I just hung up from talking with him a few minutes before I called you. He's at the game, you know, so it was sort of hard to talk. But he's got Casper's number, and he was going to call him right away."

"OK, thanks," Mel said. Then he hung up and headed back to his press box seat. The scoreboard showed that the first half was coming to a close, and that the Leopards were leading the Pioneers, 17–10.

■

Mel directed his attention to analyzing the play-by-play and statistical information that was distributed to the journalists in the press box.

Mel always hated the halftime ceremonies at the Super Bowl. They went on endlessly. To the good football fan, they were meaningless. C'mon, let's get the teams back on the field. Let's play ball! That's what Mel—and the true fans of the game—preferred.

This time, however, Mel was grateful for the 45-minute halftime hiatus. He needed that time to catch up on what he had missed while he was on the phone with Zig Zag. After all, reporting on the Super Bowl was the main reason he was here, wasn't it? Mel felt guilty because of how he had neglected those duties so far, but he also felt a sense of responsibility that conflicted with the devotion he had for getting the account of the game right. What to do?

■

He tried calling Brant Gilbert. All he got was some recording instructing him to press 2 to page this person, to press 3 for a list of services available, to press quatro por Español, to press 5 for further instructions, to press 6 to return to the main menu, or to wait for the tone to leave a message. Mel waited for the tone. After a few seconds the call disconnected. Mel hung up and continued his review of the halftime stats.

The teams came back onto the field. Thank goodness. Let's play some football.

CHAPTER FIFTY-FIVE

Late in the third quarter it was still 17-10, and the Leopards were backed up at their own 11-yard line, facing a third and one-yard-to-go situation. That's when Randy Dolbermeier told his offensive coordinator, Moe "Longball" Marks, to surprise the hell out of the football world.

"Never mind a stinking first down, Moe," he yelled. "They're going to be stacked at the line of scrimmage.   Let's go for a big one."

"You make it *fun* when you *shout*, Coach," Moe responded. Then, with a lowered voice, he spoke into the mouthpiece of his headset. "Q.T., run Trips Right 989 and look for Chase on his Go route." Q.T. Pye stepped out of the huddle and directed an incredulous wide-eyed stare at Moe. Moe nodded his head twice, and then, after a pause, once more.

Seconds later the ball was snapped, and while Q. T. executed a quick five-step drop into his protective passing pocket, Pioneers defensive right end Sylvester "Sackmaster" Simmons came zipping around the corner on Q. T.'s blind side. Bam!

Q. T., knocked sideways by Simmons, went flailing to the ground. Sylvester landed more gracefully, clambered to his feet, and began spinning around in search of the ball that he was almost certain he had seen separate itself from Q. T.'s grasp. There it was: bouncing, rolling, and twisting its way toward the Leopards goal line.

While Sylvester was having trouble locating the ball, many players on the field knew exactly where it was. Diving, shoving, bumping each other, and at times actually touching and nudging the ball along on its unpredictable course, none of them was able to gain control of it. More than once it squirted out of someone's hands, and then it crossed the goal line and accelerated its progress toward the back of the end zone.

As it continued moving to within a yard of the back line, Portland's "Kickasska from Nebraska," Bill Hanlon, dove at it, and, while his momentum kept him rolling in that direction, he pulled the ball to his chest. Touchdown, Pioneers!

No! The officials ruled that Hanlon did not have control of the ball until after his body had crossed the back line. No touchdown. It was a safety, worth two points. The score was now: Los Angeles: 17, Portland: 12. That's the way the third quarter ended.

◼

During the first 10 minutes of the final quarter, the defenses from both teams continued to dominate. They exchanged punts twice. Boring? No way, especially when Pioneers special teams standout Mark Spikes is racing down the field covering those kicks, because, after that second punt, when he applied a jarring tackle on Leopards punt return man, Chaz Chombly, the ball came loose. The Pioneers recovered it. Sixteen yards away lay the Leopards goal line—and the Super Bowl Championship.

The Pioneers offense went nowhere, except backwards, from there. Three plays later, it was fourth down and 12 yards to go at the 18-yard line. There were three minutes left to play. Bobby Russell flashed a signal to quarterback Kelly James, directing him to call a timeout.

Bobby needed that timeout. He had a decision to make. Should I try—against heavy odds—to gain those 12 yards for a first down, thereby keeping alive our opportunity to score a go-ahead touchdown? And, what are our chances of picking up the first down? Slim, I think. And if we do, we still need to score that touchdown.

What if, instead, we kick a field goal? We're still behind, but by only two points. We can try an onside kickoff after that, and if we recover it, we're not too far away from getting a shot at a game-winning field goal. But what if we don't recover that onside kick? Then we've got to stop them and count on our two-minute drill to pull it out. What if? What if? What if?

Bobby made his decision. He sent the field goal team onto the field. Kicker Trey Pointer and his holder, Hank Wright, waited quietly until the referee blew the whistle signifying it was time to resume play. The kick was good. Los Angeles: 17, Portland: 15.

There were two minutes and 54 seconds remaining in the Super Bowl Game. Time for a commercial break.

■

"We're back," television play-by-play announcer Hal Merkels said after the commercials. "We're ready for the final chapter of this thrilling game. And there it is, just like we predicted! An onside kickoff."

The scramble was on, and when the game officials finally dug to the bottom of that squirming pile of humanity at the Pioneers' 43-yard line, there was Sammy Kurtask of the Leopards cuddled up with the ball in his arms.

The Leopards didn't come out with any Fun and Shout pass-the-ball bravado this time. On first down, they ran for a one-yard gain. The Pioneers called their second timeout. On second down the Leopards ran again. No gain, and then, for the next few seconds, the clock kept ticking until the referee's signal brought it to a stop for the two-minute warning.

That's when Mel Herbert's cell phone played its bouncy ring-tune again.

"Zig Zag, been waiting to hear from you. What's up?"

"Everything! That's what's up. I've been back and forth talking with Schmotzie so damn much that I ain't been able to see hardly any of the game. That don't make no difference, though, because I'm finding out that this whole deal is even worse than we thought."

"I'm hearing you, I think," Mel said. "It's noisy as hell right now, but I've got to stay here. What can you tell me? Speak loud."

"Remember when Schmotzie said he had suspicions about who wired the place? Well, he sure did. It was one of the guys on the crew that works there, Otto Mattick. Schmotzie used to see him talking with Randy all the time. Otto admitted it to Schmotzie. He said that Randy threatened him that he'd be fired if he didn't do what Randy said was in the best interests of the team."

"How was Schmotz able to get Otto to own up?" Mel asked.

"Well, after Schmotzie saw all of the secret wiring in the storage room and in the visitors' locker room, he went straight to Otto and confronted him. Schmotzie told me that Otto was almost relieved to finally get out from all the guilty feelings he was having, and then —you won't believe this."

"What? Quick! Tell me! They're about to start playing again."

"Okay. You know the Pemberton Hotel where the visiting teams all stayed the night before their games in L. A., don't you?"

"Yeah, so what?"

"Otto told Schmotzie that Randy arranged for another one of the guys to work weekends as the attendant that sets things up in the meeting room that the visiting teams use at the Pemberton."

"Did he say who it was?"

"He said it was Lupe."

"Lupe? Not Lupe Delloupe, the fellow who handles all those connections in the press box on game days? Hold it, Zig Zag, the game's starting again."

It was third down with nine yards to go for the Leopards. If they could pick up a first down, that would do it. After that, they could run out the clock. Q.T. Pye dropped back to pass. No one was open, and so he took off hoping to scramble for the first down. He got back only to the line of scrimmage where he was brought down by Bill Hanlon's shoestring tackle.

It was now fourth down with nine yards to go. The Pioneers called their final timeout. One minute and 52 seconds remained on the game clock.

"Zig Zag, you still there? Be quick."

"Okay. Yeah, that's the Lupe I mean. Anyway, Schmotzie got to him, too, and Lupe admitted that he set up a way of recording what was being talked about in the visiting team meetings at the hotel the night before the games and then getting that info to Randy."

"Lupe admitted it?"

"He knew he was caught, and like Otto, he just wanted to come clean. He even admitted that a couple of times during the season he did some things that screwed up the other team's communication system with their quarterbacks while the game was going on."

"Is Mr. Medill aware of any of this, Zig Zag?"

"I'll bet he is. Schmotzie said he was going to call him right away. I ain't heard nothing back from him yet, but I'll let you know if I do. Right now, though, I want to watch the end of this game."

"Me, too," Mel said, "Uh, oh, here they come. Talk to you later." Mel signed off. Their phone call was over. But the game wasn't.

■

Fourth and nine. Leopards' ball at the Pioneers' 42-yard line. The Leopards punted, and the ball rolled into the end zone for a touchback. It was now the Pioneers ball, first down at their own 20 with just a minute and 44 seconds—and no timeouts—remaining.

Two days earlier, at their Friday practice, the Pioneers had worked on their two-minute drill. They were ready now to put it into game-day action. They would be employing a package of plays and a player personnel combination that they practiced all season long, but had never used in a game. In the few two-minute drill situations they faced in games up to this point, they had utilized other parts of their arsenal.

In Friday's practice they were sharp and confident, and they took the field now still confident that if they did it right, they could move the ball at least as far as—maybe even farther than—the Leopards 30-yard line. Do that, and they'd have put themselves in position to attempt the game-winning field goal.

In the four plays that followed, they did move the ball, but it was for a total of just six yards. The Leopards were all over them. The only gain that Portland registered came on second and 10 when Kelly James, finding no receiver open, scrambled upfield for those six yards before stepping out of bounds to stop the clock. His receivers were covered on the next two plays, as well, and although he tried to drill the ball to one of them anyway, it was to no avail. Defenders batted both throws to the ground.

When Kelly's fourth down pass attempt fell incomplete, so did the Super Bowl hopes of the Pioneers and their fans. It was now the Leopards' ball with a minute and eight seconds left in the game. Twice in a row, they ran every coach's favorite play—the quarterback kneel down. The game was over. Los Angeles: 17, Portland: 15. The scoreboard told the story. Or did it?

■

Fireworks exploded. Sparkling confetti and glittering tinsel filled the air. Music thumped. Players on the Leopards sideline sprinted onto the field and embraced their teammates. Television sideline reporter, Allison Wundaland, oblivious to the dribbles of Gatorade spilling down onto her sleeve from Q. T. Pye's drenched shoulder pads, extended her handheld mike and screamed a question at him.

"So, Q.T., what do you feel was the turning point in the game?"

"The final gun, probably, ha, ha," he answered.

"There you have it," she said, as Q. T. raised his arms in an attempt to ward off a second soaking from his teammates. "I guess I got it, too," she giggled, as a healthy portion of the dousing messed up her meticulous make up.

On the other side of the field, the Pioneers players walked silently to the tunnel that led back to their dressing room. Bobby Russell, despite knowing how painful it would be, walked to the middle of the field intending to congratulate Randy Dolbermeier. When he noted that Randy was making no effort to get out there himself, Bobby, too, headed for the locker room, more grateful than upset about not having to exchange pleasantries with that guy.

CHAPTER FIFTY-SIX

The game was over, but Mel Herbert, still sitting in his press box seat, continued to gaze at the action taking place on the field below where Commissioner Paul Rogers, holding the Lombardi Trophy, was striding toward a microphone. Randy Dolbermeier, waving and grinning, was bouncing along beside him while a jovial throng of Leopards players, assistant coaches, trainers, and equipment room personnel milled about on the turf surrounding the presentation platform.

It was a scene similar to the ones that Mel had witnessed following every Super Bowl prior to this one. Or—wait a minute—was it?

Something was different. Where was the team's proud owner? Where was Cedric B. Medill? Why isn't he out there with the commissioner and Randy? Why isn't he there to receive that trophy? I know why, Mel told himself.

A press box attendant tapped Mel on his shoulder and handed him an envelope. In it was a note from Brant Gilbert. "Mel, been trying to reach you. Can't connect. Call me. Brant." In the note, Brant had written a contact number different from the one Mel had been dialing earlier. Mel called the new number. Brant answered.

"Mel, I've got to be quick. Our post-game show is back on in three minutes. Stupid me; I left my cell phone back at the hotel, and without it I didn't have your number. I'm on Howie Short's phone right now. I borrowed it."

"I understand. Did you talk with Mr. Medill?"

"Yes. That's why I'm calling. I went over to his booth and spoke with him right after he arrived here at the stadium before the game. I told him how we learned about Chick Peasley and how we suspected that he might have been videotaping the Pioneers practices here in Indianapolis."

"What did he say then?"

"Nothing at first. He just seemed devastated. But then he told me all about the reports he received that the visitors' locker room back in L.A. had likely been bugged. He said that Casper Schmotz was supposed to go check on that this morning. Cedric said he still hadn't heard from Casper, but now with this Peasley situation he'd had enough, and that he was heading down to the Leopards locker room right then to get some straight answers from Randy."

"How did that turn out?"

"I don't know. I've haven't heard from Cedric since then."

"Do you know if Mr. Medill heard back from Casper Schmotz yet?"

"Don't know that either."

"Well, I spoke with Zig Zag a little while ago. He was with Schmotz, and the rumors were all true. By now, I'm almost certain that Mr. Medill has been informed. I don't know if you've noticed, but he's not down on the field for the presentation ceremonies. Does that tell you anything?"

"A lot," Brant said. "There's not much doubt in my mind about what's been happening, but I still don't want to be the one who goes public with it yet. Coming from me it will just look like I'm trying to be vindictive over my departure from the team."

"Brant, there is *no more* doubt in my mind."

"I've got to go now, Mel. We're just about ready to go on the air. Talk to you later."

◼

And so there Mel Herbert sat, continuing to agonize over whether he could bring himself to be the one responsible for destroying the elation now being experienced by the Leopards players and fans. Why did he have to be the one who would turn their exultation into anger and humiliation?

With the deadline for his submission of tomorrow morning's column closing in on him, Mel remained tormented by indecision. And then, from deep within his subconscious, there arose some words; words that he himself had scribbled on a page in his tattered personal journal on a day more than half a century ago. World War II had ended, and 20-year-old Corporal Melvin Herbert of the United States

Marine Corps, a wounded, but thankfully recovered veteran of the Battle of Okinawa, was riding home on a troop train across the quiet South Dakota prairies. At last, he was heading home, and so were all those other "Semper Fi's" with whom he was sharing that joyful trip. But elated as he had been, Corporal Herbert still experienced a sense of melancholy that moved him, for the first time in his young life, to write, of all things, some lines of verse.

Long ago, Mel had placed his handwritten original version of that composition into a cardboard box that was stored, along with several other items of inconsequence, in a battered old valise that now slumbered in the quiet of his basement. The paper on which it was written had become fragile and yellowed, and the ink from the prehistoric pen he had used was faded.

As Mel sat there now in the distracting post-game atmosphere of the press box, the sentiments that he had expressed in his poem from so many years before came surging back to him. The lines paraded silently before him, and as he viewed them he experienced a serene release from the anguish that had been gripping him just a few moments earlier. His long-ago words resonated still:

> *I listen to all the laughter as I ride home on this train,*
> *But my thoughts are of many others. It's painful, but I'll explain.*
> *Some of them I knew, and some I never met,*
> *But I cannot allow them to become those whom we ever forget.*
> *They, too, were young and eager for the years that lay ahead.*
> *They, too, were loved and cherished, but now they lay dead.*
> *Those of us more fortunate who live in this brighter day*
> *Must represent them always by the things we do and say.*
> *Because of them we all still thrive in this land of the free,*
> *And to them we owe a debt that lasts for eternity.*
> *So let us honor their memory by virtue of all that we do,*
> *Not only by what we accomplish, but by deeds honest and true.*

Bang! That did it. His problem was solved. His decision was made. Mel began to type the lead to his story: "When the final gun sounded last night at the Super Bowl, the score was Los Angeles: 17, Portland: 15. For the Los Angeles Leopards it should have been a moment of euphoria. They were the winners. They were the champions. Or were they?"

■

Mel paused, and then resumed typing. "No, they were not," he wrote. "It was not the Los Angeles *Leopards* who came out on the long end of that score. It was the Los Angeles *Cheetahs*. Okay, make that the Los Angeles *Cheaters*."

The remainder of Mel's exposé provided detailed information about how the Leopards coaches had tuned in on their opponents' locker room discussions at halftime during home games and also on how they had taped what was being discussed at the meetings the visiting teams held at their hotel the evening before those games.

"Evidence of tampering with the other team's coach-to-quarterback-helmet communication system is emerging," Mel wrote, "and there are some shocking indications that Coach Randy Dolbermeier arranged for someone to secretly videotape all of the Portland Pioneers practices during the week leading up to the Super Bowl. There is more—much more—that still needs to be investigated."

■

And there was more—much more—that Mel needed to deal with before sending a story of this nature back to Sports Editor Carroll Blumenthal at the *Guardian*. Mel knew that this wasn't the type of story that Carroll was expecting. This wasn't what Mel's assignment to cover the Super Bowl was supposed to have been about. And this wasn't what an editor cleared for publication without feeling assured that his paper was not setting itself up for being sued for libel and defamation.

Mel realized he would have to deal with those issues, but right now the presentation ceremonies were concluding. In 10 minutes, in locations next to the locker rooms, the post-game press conferences with players and coaches from both teams were scheduled to begin. I've got to be there for that, Mel told himself. I might even learn more about this whole mess. Mel put his article on hold and headed for the elevators.

CHAPTER FIFTY-SEVEN

When Randy Dolbermeier came out of the locker room and swaggered to the microphone he was already wearing a brand new cap emblazoned with the words "Super Bowl Champions."

"Weeee—did it!" he called out as he reached the mike. The questioning began.

Jordy Nerdmann was first. "Coach, where did you come up with that miraculous defensive game plan?" he asked.

"That's why we're here, Jordy old pal. You've got to know how to do it if you want to win, and obviously we did."

"But," said Singh Galongh of *The Mumbai (India) Mystic*, "it was as if you had karma. Every move they made, you seemed so aware of how to counter it. I am so impressed."

"That's why we're the champions. I have to admit that they did a darned good job of coping with our Fun and Shout offense. Don't forget, though, that before I took over as head coach of this team, my specialty was defense. Coming into this game, remember how enamored everyone was with *their* defense. Well, what do you think about ours now?"

When no one responded to Randy, reporter Justin Case of *The Hollywood Harlequin* offered an observation. "Coach, many of us noticed that Mr. Medill was not on the field for the presentation of the Lombardi Trophy. Is he all right?"

Anyone looking closely enough would have seen Randy's jaw tighten. But then his eyes brightened a bit, and he said, "Oh, yes, he's fine. I guess he's just being modest and letting the players and coaches be the ones to stand in the spotlight."

"Has he come to the locker room to congratulate you all?" Justin asked.

"Gee, I don't know. I've been so busy taking care of other things that I really didn't notice whether he had come in there or not."

"You didn't notice if the *owner of the team* came into the locker room?"

"You heard me, dammit. Who else has a question?"

After a few more for Randy, it was time to bring in some of the game's star players. Sidney "Matzo" Ball, selected as Defensive Lineman of the Game by Fox TV Post-Game Show panelist Howie Short, was the first to be interviewed.

"Sidney, what was the key to the way you fellows were so effective in shutting down Portland's final drive?" asked Teresa Crowd of *The Louisville Lecturer.*

"No doubt about it," Sidney answered. "It was preparation. We were ready for them. On Saturday, we practiced against their two-minute drill like you can't imagine."

"Well, don't you practice your two-minute defense every week?" Teresa asked.

"Oh, sure, but, I'm telling you, this time we went over it even more than usual, and the way our coaches anticipated what they were going to do was unbelievable. In practice we worked against the exact plays and personnel combinations that they actually used. That's what I mean by preparation."

"I've covered their games all year," said Emanuel Love of *The Portland Plain Talker,* "and I don't ever recall their having employed the four-receiver combinations that they showed today."

"I wouldn't know about that," Sidney said. "I do know that we were ready for it, and we went against it a lot in practice."

CHAPTER FIFTY-EIGHT

When the post-game activities were concluded, it was time for Mel to turn his attention back to the most difficult task he had faced since his career as a journalist began. Perhaps the toughest part, he reflected, is going to be convincing Carroll Blumenthal that I have an even bigger and more meaningful story than the one he is anticipating receiving from me about the thrilling Super Bowl victory by "our" Los Angeles Leopards.

Mel knew there was only one way to accomplish that. He made the phone call to Carroll.

At first, Carroll dismissed Mel's shocking assertions, stating that he could not believe they were true. Mel remained persistent, and with each succeeding bit of evidence that he provided, Carroll's initial resistance gave way to a growing acceptance for hearing more. Then it became *a desire* to hear more, and not long after that, Carroll switched from his listening mode to *probing* for even more information.

By this time Carroll was convinced, but there were reservations that continued to bother him.

"Mel, I do believe now that what you are telling me is true, but I think it is too risky for us to come out with a story like this until we get sworn testimony that these actions actually did occur and that they were orchestrated at Randy's behest."

"If we wait until then, Carroll, there is a good chance that some other news outlet is going to beat us to the story. How do you feel about risking that?"

"You think it's all true, Mel. I believe it's true, too. But what if it isn't?"

"I don't *think* it's true, Carroll. I'm *convinced* it's true. And that's why I'm willing to risk staking my reputation on it."

"It won't be just your reputation that's on the line, Mel. It'll be mine, and it'll be that of the *Guardian*, as well."

"I know. But it's the right thing to do. Besides, there is such overwhelming proof that's going to come out once this story breaks that it will result only in enhancing the paper's reputation."

"And who is going to handle all of the aftermath? No matter how much and how many times I've tried to talk you out of it, you keep insisting that you're retiring right after the Super Bowl. That's really going to help lend credibility to what we publish, isn't it? Writer accuses Super Bowl champs of cheating. And then he wimps out and scoots off to the Italian Riviera."

Mel had no answer for that one. After a painful silence, Carroll came up with what he hoped was a solution. "Mel, tell me you'll stay on for another year—or for another 10 for that matter—and I'll take the gamble. I do believe you are right about this thing, but if you and the paper part ways right after the story appears, it is going to look like either we've fired you or like you are ducking out. I cannot go forth with the story for tomorrow's edition if you are going to be leaving the paper."

Mel understood Carroll's plight. He understood, too, the logic in what he had just heard. What to do? Forget about it and get away from it all? Or do the right thing?

"I gotcha," Mel said. "If you can put up with me for another year, boss, I guess I can put up with you, too."

"No changing your mind later, right?"

"I promise."

"That's good enough for me. Finish up your piece, send it in, and then join me in holding your breath."

Mel followed those instructions.

∎

Even before the sun rose Monday morning and while many of the Los Angeles Leopards fans were still on the streets and in the barrooms celebrating, the first editions of *The Los Angeles Guardian* were dropped off at doorways and at newsstands. The front-page headline screamed the news: CHEETAHS WIN SUPER BOWL.

Disbelief. Anger. Denial. Humiliation. An additional shot of hooch for some, and a quick sobering up for others. Those were but a few of the initial reactions from the L.A. fans. As the city awoke, its stunned residents, including those who cared nothing about sports, tuned in. Every newscast and every talk show buzzed with rumors and opinions.

Soon the entire nation was hooked. The national news dealt with almost nothing else. The President's scheduled address to Congress about his important new proposal on global warming wasn't even mentioned by most commentators.

At 10 a.m. Los Angeles Mayor Kelvin "Buck" Fundrayser announced that the Victory Parade originally planned for later that day on Wilshire Boulevard would be "postponed" until more information about the shocking accusations was made available. Mayor Fundrayser wasn't the only person who hungered to know more. Many commentators, the experts they interviewed, and hordes of irate fans on call-in shows expressed similar sentiments.

Everyone wanted to know: what did Randy Dolbermeier have to say about all of this? No one was able to reach Randy during the morning hours, and then finally, at 3 p.m., a spokesman for the law firm of Niasz, Carruthers, and Nicholson announced that Randy Dolbermeier would be available at a press conference at five o'clock in the auditorium of the building where their law offices were located.

CHAPTER FIFTY-NINE

By 4:45 p.m. the place was packed with writers, announcers, tape recorders, notepads, and cameramen. Mel Herbert was one of those present. At exactly five o'clock Randy and another man walked onto the stage where two podiums, positioned within a few feet of each other, were awaiting their arrival.

This wasn't the same Randy Dolbermeier that those in the audience had come to know over the past few years. This wasn't the Randy who always came bounding up to microphones in a baseball cap, wrinkled and smudged polo shirt, and sagging oversized trousers.

This Randy was wearing a navy blue suit, a starched white shirt, and a muted crimson tie with glistening gold stripes. Polished black leather shoes served as a replacement for the gym shoes or the flip-flops that usually adorned his feet. He was clean-shaven, and his hair was combed and plastered down. With measured stride, looking somber and resolute, he proceeded to the stage.

The man accompanying Randy appeared to be about 60 years old. He, too, exhibited taste in how he was dressed, beginning with his immaculate charcoal-colored suit. An abundance of thick, graying, wavy hair flowed over his ears and cascaded down the back of his neck. He was the first to speak.

"Ladies and gentlemen, thank you for coming here today," he said. "My name is Payne Niasz, and I am the senior partner in the law firm of Niasz, Carruthers, and Nicholson. I am here on behalf of Mr. Dolbermeier as he undertakes the task of dealing with and refuting the outlandish, ill-substantiated accusations that blemished the pages of today's *Los Angeles Guardian*."

Niasz nodded to Randy, who opened the notebook he had placed on the podium before him. He looked down and began to read the first page.

"It is with a great deal of disappointment on this day, less than 24 hours after our beloved Los Angeles Leopards experienced the exhilaration of realizing their almost impossible dream by emerging as victors—as Super Bowl champions—in America's premier sporting event, that I must now respond to the scurrilous attempt by isolated media sources to besmirch the heroic efforts of the young men who accomplished so much out there on the field of battle.

"The vast majority of you serve and inform the public with care and with honor. I know that, and I commend you for it. But let me say to everyone, in or out of the media, that the unsubstantiated and untrue accusations that appeared in this morning's *Los Angeles Guardian* are an insult to our fans and to those of you who adhere to higher standards. Thank you for being here today and for listening to my side of the story."

As Randy was closing his notebook, a barrage of indistinguishable questions erupted from the media. Niasz intervened. "Mr. Dolbermeier will take one or two questions now if that is your desire," he said. "Yes, that gentleman over there."

"Have you spoken yet with Mr. Medill about the article that appeared in the *Guardian*", Brandon Irons of *The Riverside Record* asked. Randy glanced at Niasz, who flashed four fingers at Randy while pointing the forefinger of his other hand at the notebook that Randy had closed a moment earlier. Randy reopened it, leafed to the fourth page, and then recited his response.

"I am in conference with several people regarding what actions I plan to take. I can assure you that *there will be* action forthcoming. At the present time, however, I feel it is in the best interests of all concerned that I keep confidential the names of those persons and the nature of the discussions which are now in progress."

Brandon Irons tried to follow up with another question, but Niasz directed the intern from his office whom he had assigned to manage the handheld microphone to "please give it to that young lady across the aisle."

"How can we help you, Miss?" he asked of Celia Layder from *The Inglewood Insider.*

"Coach Dolbermeier," she said, "in his article, Mel Herbert is very specific in identifying, by names, people who are quoted as saying that, under personal directives from you, they carried out acts which are obvious and blatant violations of rules and of ethics. How do you explain that?"

"Let me tell you something," Randy began to answer, but he glanced at Niasz, who held up three fingers. Randy, after inhaling a deep breath, switched his attention from Celia to page three of his notebook from which he reframed his response to her question.

"I do not plan to lend credence," he said, "to the defamatory claims made by anyone or by any entity by engaging in an exchange of diatribe with such perpetrators. As the true nature of the situation unfolds I will be fully vindicated, and you will be witness to how unfortunate it is that they have chosen to focus on some contrived allegations rather than upon the sterling accomplishments of our players, our coaches, our team, and our city."

Niasz signaled his intern to take the mike away from Celia, but she refused to relinquish it. "In other words, you are saying that Casper Schmotz, Otto Mattick, and Lupe Delloupe, to name just a few, are all liars. Is that right?"

"Dammit," Randy answered as he tossed his notebook to the floor, "you don't have to go that far to find liars. There are enough of you out there chewing on your pencils who qualify for that, and the biggest one is that old fart Mel Herbert sitting on his butt over there looking like he knows it all. What the hell have you ever done, you jerk ass?" Niasz stepped over to where Randy was giving vent, and he grabbed Randy's sleeve. Randy pulled his arm away and kept talking.

"You sit up in the nice cushy confines of the press box looking wise while the real men are down on the field doing battle. You don't have any idea of what it's like when the bombs are exploding down there. You just wait till all the tussling is over, and then you get smug and start to write some bull crap that's supposed to show how much smarter you are than anyone else, don't you? You think you know so much, but you really have no idea. Well, I've said it before, and I'll say it again, football is war, and you've got to treat it as such, you creep."

Celia Layder was standing just two rows in front of where Mel was sitting.

She spun away from the intern's outstretched hand, found a gap between two men sitting in the row behind hers, pushed the mike through, and handed it to Mel. He kept it brief.

"Coach Dolbermeier, although it was a long time ago when I was in high school and then in college, I have played football. And I have been to war. Believe me, football is not war." Mel handed the microphone back to Celia.

"Again, I ask," she said, "are the men I named liars?"

"I'll tell you what they are. They're part of a bunch of losers who don't really know what it takes to win. They're jealous. I know where some of those rumors started. They came from assholes in this organization who always got pampered by Bobby Russell when he was here, and they never did get over seeing Mr. Nice Guy get canned. They probably even wanted him and the Pioneers to win the game. Well, they didn't, did they? And then *The Guardian* and their number-one hit man, Herbert over there, just couldn't wait to dance out onto the streets with an 'Extra.' Talk about repulsive; that guy leads the league."

When Randy paused to take a breath, Niasz, who had been trying to intercede, was finally able to do so. "Ladies and gentlemen," he said, "you can see for yourselves the devastating toll that this misrepresentation has taken on my client's desire to keep this conversation civil. By virtue of this meeting, however, you are now aware of our position in this matter. It is our intention to employ vigorous measures in support of the ideals in which we believe. When appropriate, you will be apprised of what those measures are. That will conclude this meeting. Once again, thank you for your attendance and for your concern."

Payne then latched on to Randy's arm, and accompanied by two security guards who had stepped onto the stage during Payne's wrap-up remarks, they made a quick exit. The press conference was over. But the furor was just beginning.

CHAPTER SIXTY

By late that Monday night it wasn't just the media and the fans who were involved. Cedric B. Medill and NFL Commissioner Paul Rogers both issued statements expressing their shock and concern. Both stated that they would be taking immediate steps to determine the validity of the accusations; that they were committed to keeping the public informed about their findings; and that they would invoke whatever action and discipline appropriate in order to maintain the integrity of the game.

Cedric B., knowing that he needed guidance, turned to the person he trusted most in matters related to his team. He asked his former general manager, Brant Gilbert, to join him at his office as soon as he could. Forty-five minutes later, Brant was there. Cedric B. welcomed him with a solemn, "Thank you for coming."

"Brant, this stuff is true, isn't it? How much do you know?"

"Quite a bit, Cedric. I've already told you about Chick Peasley, the fellow I'm almost certain that Randy hired to videotape the Pioneers practices during Super Bowl Week. And Mel Herbert's contentions that the visitors' locker room and their meeting rooms at their hotels were bugged are based on very solid evidence."

"I am aware of that," Cedric B. said. "Casper Schmotz called me in Indianapolis yesterday morning. He told me that he had just finished investigating the locker rooms at our stadium, and they were wired. Beyond that, he told me that he confronted a couple of the men working there whom he suspected, and they admitted that they had done it and that Randy was the person who put them up to it."

"I heard that, too," Brant said. "Yesterday morning you told me that you were going to talk with Randy before the game about the Chick Peasley accusations. How did that turn out?"

"You should have been there. He went into a tirade about how a bunch of bleeping liars were trying to create a distraction before the most important game of our lives. He even blathered on about how he wouldn't be surprised if Bobby Russell was behind it."

"Yeah, sure. Where did you go from there?"

"I knew by then who the real liar was, Brant. There wasn't anything I could do about it just minutes before the kickoff, though. By that time I knew the real story. I knew it even before Mel Herbert wrote about it. That's why I didn't go down onto the field for all that post-game folderol. And I still haven't succeeded in getting in touch with Randy yet. I've been trying, although I can't stand the thought of even looking at him."

"I don't think you know *all* of the real story yet, Cedric."

"Oh, no. What else?"

"There is a strong likelihood that the food poisoning and substance-in-the-eyes that happened to some of the star players on teams we were playing against, were the handiwork of Randy. That may not be as easy to prove, but the league really ought to look into those situations, too."

"I will leave that part of it up to the league, as you suggest, but I can't sit still on those other issues. What a disgrace. What an embarrassment. How do I deal with it, Brant? That's the reason I asked you to come here this evening."

"The first thing I'd suggest is that we call in legal counsel to help us get formal statements from Casper and from Otto Mattick and Lupe Delloupe spelling everything out in detail. We should have those lawyers do whatever is required to allow them to question Chick Peasley. Phil Maecker, the team's video director, can tell us how to get in touch with him."

"What about the public in the meantime?" Cedric B. asked.

"Shoot straight. I know you. That's what you want to do, anyway. Beginning immediately, I'd let everyone know that you are not taking these charges lightly; that you are in the process of finding out the truth; and that as soon as you do, you will disclose what your investigation has uncovered. Then do it that way."

"Great. Then what?"

"Let's talk again then, Cedric. That's when we'll know better what the next step should be."

"And I fired Bobby Russell, let you go off to work somewhere else, and hired Randy Dolbermeier to run my team. Am I brilliant, or what?"

"Like I just said, let's talk about it again later."

■

Otto Mattick and Lupe Delloupe admitted to NFL Security that they had carried out the assignments Randy Dolbermeier had delegated to them, and Casper Schmotz disclosed the details involving the wiring of the visitors' locker room. They responded to all media questioning in like fashion.

Chick Peasley, after being assured by Cedric. B. Medill that he would not press charges against him if he told the truth about whether he videotaped the Pioneers practices during Super Bowl Week, told the *whole* truth. Not only had he videotaped the Pioneers practices, but two weeks earlier, he had been sent to Denver by Randy Dolbermeier, his mission being to find a way to videotape the Broncos practices as they prepared for the AFC Championship Game against the Leopards. It was a mission he accomplished.

Randy Dolbermeier reacted. "There is a damn conspiracy taking place, and it's being engineered by Bobby Russell," he proclaimed. "He couldn't take getting fired here, and now he's whimpering around because I beat his ass in the Super Bowl. *The Guardian* doesn't want the truth. This is too good a story for them to pass up, so they are happy to keep throwing fuel on the fire."

Randy went on to accuse Casper, Otto, Lupe, and Chick of being on Bobby's "payroll." Hardly anyone believed him—not even Jordy Nerdmann.

CHAPTER SIXTY-ONE

If there were any fans who continued clinging to the hope that Randy's denials were valid; that he was the subject, as he claimed, of a mean-spirited conspiracy; that their Los Angeles Leopards truly were the Super Bowl champions, their hopes were erased Wednesday afternoon.

Tuesday had been chaotic enough. That's when Cedric B. and Commissioner Rogers announced what procedures they intended to follow. It was the day when Otto, Lupe, and Chick admitted the roles they had played in carrying out Randy's instructions, and when Casper Schmotz told about the wiring he had uncovered in the visiting team's quarters. It was also the day on which Randy—despite cautioning from Payne Niasz to remain quiet—lashed out about Bobby Russell being the culprit.

But it was on Wednesday that the clincher took place. At 11 a.m., the Leopards players who were still in town assembled in the team meeting room at their practice facility. Glenn Grabowski, on behalf of the players attending, invited Cedric B. Medill to join them, and when Cedric B. said he would like to bring Brant Gilbert along, Glenn welcomed him to do so.

It took less than an hour for that gathering to reach a consensus, and they sent out word through director of media relations, Bert Scott, that they would all be on hand for an important press conference at their facility at 1:30 that afternoon. They broke for lunch, and when they filed back into media headquarters they noted that the buzz from the waiting journalists that greeted them was more intense than usual.

Grabowski stepped to the microphone. "My teammates and I are here for a sad reason," he said. "Naturally, we have all heard the accusations about how cheating tactics on the part of Coach

Dolbermeier and some of the other coaches were used in making it possible for us to emerge on the winning end of last Sunday's Super Bowl Game. As we look back on it now, we realize that the information they fed to us during the week of preparation was so precise that it could have been gleaned only by their having been able to tune in on Portland's practices.

"We'll leave the investigation of that up to those who are more qualified to do it," Glenn continued, "but we feel it is important that all of you, and all of our fans, and everybody who loves the game of football is made aware that the players on this team now know that the victory we thought we earned by fair play was unfairly won.

"On many occasions throughout the season, Coach Dolbermeier instructed players on this team to employ certain tactics against players on other teams that would cause injuries serious enough to put them out of the game. I'm proud to say that in almost every instance we resisted and refused to do it. We even complained to him about it, but he'd just brush it off.

"Today, unfortunately, we all stand up here, not able to be proud of having won the Super Bowl Game. Instead, we are embarrassed to have been the tools used to achieve a dishonest objective. We apologize to you all. We ask that you forgive us. We will go back to work, and we will conduct ourselves in a manner that can lead us to redeeming our own self-respect and to regaining the respect of all the people who love this game."

Following Glenn's remarks, several other players told how they and their teammates had been offered bounties if they succeeded in putting an opposing team's star players out of the game with an injury. When they finished their accounts, Glenn spoke again.

"There are a few players on the team—not many, I assure you —who actually did receive payoffs for such actions," he said. "Many of us suspected that anyway, and in the meeting we had earlier today, they 'fessed up. We all agreed that they would take it upon themselves to inform the Commissioner's office about what took place. They understand that some disciplinary action will be forthcoming. Please allow them to handle it in that manner rather than asking for names today.

"That's it from my teammates and from me," Glenn said, "but Mr. Medill, whom we invited to join us when we met this morning, has something he wants to add. Please know that we all agree with what he is about to tell you."

Cedric B. stepped forward. "This ought to be an occasion that we should still be celebrating," he said. "It isn't. It's quite the contrary. We did *not* win the Super Bowl. A few minutes before this meeting began, I telephoned Commissioner Rogers and told him that we would be returning the Lombardi Trophy. I told him that we should not be designated as the winners of this season's Super Bowl. All the players gathered here with me agreed that was the proper thing to do. The Commissioner said he understood and that he would move forward toward evaluating and, most likely, implementing my proposal.

"The Los Angeles Leopards will move forward, too," Cedric B. continued. "We will make the changes that need to be made. We will right the ship. We will begin anew an honest and an earnest pursuit of a *real* Super Bowl Championship. We will bring our fans a team they can truly be proud of. We didn't win a championship for them. We let them down. We owe them so much."

■

By Friday, Commissioner Rogers was convinced he had sufficient proof of the allegations for him to make a formal announcement.

"The National Football League has verified that a story that first appeared in *The Los Angeles Guardian* on Monday of this week was based on accurate information. The evidence we have uncovered during our investigation points to Coach Randy Dolbermeier of the Los Angeles Leopards as being responsible for engineering a complex and many-faceted cheating operation through which his team consistently gained unfair advantages over their competition. This includes his arranging for the illicit videotaping of opponents' practices, including those of the Portland Pioneers during the week leading up to last Sunday's Super Bowl.

"There are many more incidents involving shameful cheating activities on his part, and there are numerous other suspicious acts that we are in the process of looking into.

"As you probably know, team owner Cedric B. Medill and the Los Angeles Leopards players have expressed their vehement disapproval and their embarrassment over what has occurred. There is absolutely nothing that implicates any of them in the planning of what took place. Mr. Medill, with concurrence from the Leopards players, has asked that their Super Bowl Championship title be vacated. That is an action that I most likely will implement at such time when all the unresolved issues have been attended to."

CHAPTER SIXTY-TWO

On Saturday, six days after the Super Bowl Game, Mel Herbert knew he needed to unwind. He decided that the perfect antidote to the turmoil that had engulfed him would be to have breakfast with Joe Skoronski and Zig Zag Zizzo.

Mel and Zig Zag arrived 10 minutes late, and for a few moments they couldn't find Joe. He was camped behind a towering double stack of pancakes that he had ordered to keep himself company til his cronies showed up. After they found him, they spent the next 15 minutes talking about items on the menu and telling many of the same jokes they had exchanged countless times before. Zig Zag drifted in and out of the conversation; he was reading a copy of *Pro Football Weekly*.

Mel was enjoying getting away from what had occupied so much of his time and energy over the past several months. Then Joe put an end to Mel's vacation.

"You heard, dintcha, Mel?" Joe asked.

"Heard what?"

"Dat Randy's officially bein' fired from da job."

"What do you mean by 'officially'?"

"Well, on Monday when Mr. Medill gets back inta town from some business he has up dere in San Luis Abysmal, he's gonna make dat official pronouncement. Dat's what he told Casper Schmotz when he called him last night and told him ta pack up alla Randy's belongins. Den Casper told me to clear out all da stuff from Randy's locker room area. And—oh, geez, I forgot. Casper told me not to tell no one. If you go ahead and write about dat now, Mel, I tink me and him might both get da boot, too."

"Okay, Joe, don't worry. I won't say a word about it." Mel turned to Zig Zag. "You, too, Zig Zag, don't say anything to anyone."

■

By noon on Monday, as Mel had been alerted, it became official: Randy Dolbermeier was fired.

The National Football League announced that its investigation into the scandal was ongoing and that all steps required to re-establish the league's tarnished reputation would be taken, beginning with the mandate that Randy Dolbermeier was permanently suspended from holding any position in the league. Randy proclaimed his intentions to seek legal redress for having been made the victim of such "unwarranted vilifying measures."

CHAPTER SIXTY-THREE

The Leopards players, coaches, and fans were not the only ones feeling the pain. There was anguish in Portland, too. Everyone there believed that had the competition been honest, the Pioneers would have been the Super Bowl Champions.

Some members of the league's Competition Committee presented a proposal that the NFL should consider awarding the championship to the Pioneers by forfeit. Yves Napoleon, Lilly Napoleon, and the Pioneers players and coaches voiced strong objections to such a solution.

"Speaking for everyone in the Pioneers organization," Lilly said, "we believe the title should be bestowed only as a reward for an honest victory on the playing field." Lilly surmised that those sentiments were not just those of the team, but of the Pioneers fans, as well. She was right. The league office agreed with her, too. "There will be *no* Super Bowl Champion this year," they decreed.

As disheartening as the situation was for the Pioneers, they were able to take solace from the knowledge that they hadn't been the cheaters. Every one of the players knew that he was surrounded by tough, resilient teammates, and that when next September came they would be back out on the gridiron working their tails off but still having so damn much fun. After the heartbreak of losing in the Super Bowl, the pendulum began to swing in the right direction for the Pioneers: Denzel Jackson was back.

No more neck brace. No more walker. No more restrictions. Just the green light to coach football again. The Pioneers had reason to celebrate after all, and that they did, starting with a party attended by the Pioneers coaches and administrative staff, all of whom showed up wearing T-shirts with the words "Welcome Back Denzel."

Bobby Russell was among the many who addressed the gathering. "Denzel, you are back taking the heat, and I am back coaching defense. I couldn't be happier."

◼

Although Randy Dolbermeier wasn't at the party in Portland, he chimed in, nevertheless, about Denzel Jackson's resumption of his head coaching responsibilities. Randy did it in front of a much larger audience, however, since his comments came while he was appearing as the featured guest on the After Dark with Lionel Bitterman Show. After Bitterman recited a segment on "10 reasons why the L. A. Leopards should be invited to the White House," he put on a football helmet and then introduced Randy, who also wearing a helmet, came trotting onto the stage. They butted heads, and when the audience stopped laughing, Bitterman asked Randy about his take on Denzel's return.

"It's great for a lot of reasons," Randy said. "He's one of the top two coaches in the league in my opinion. Make that 'top *one*' now that I'm not coaching. Not, that is, until my lawyers clear the air and the league reinstates me."

"What are some of the other reasons?" Bitterman asked.

"It means that Bobby Russell isn't going to be a head coach anymore. He won't be hogging the spotlight and pretending like he knows what it takes to win football games. He now fades back into the shadows and everybody can just forget about him."

"What about you? Are you going to fade back into the shadows?"

"Are you kidding? My agent is negotiating a contract right now for me to write a book. You haven't heard the last from me. There's plenty more that I've got to say. You want to know what it takes to win, folks? Read my book."

◼

While Randy was busy talking to anybody who would listen, Cedric B. Medill elected to speak with just one person.

"Okay, Brant," he said, "remember when I told you that I was going to take some pretty drastic action? That was when I asked you, 'After that, what's next?' You told me we'd talk about it later. Well, it's later."

"Right. I figured that's why you invited me here. Let's talk."

"Good. I wasn't at all sure where I wanted to go at that time, Brant, but I am now."

"And that is?"

"First thing I've got to do is hire a real good general manager."

"Are you looking for advice from me on that subject?"

"No. I'm not looking for *advice* from you. I'm looking *for* you."

"That's what I was hoping," Brant said.

"So was I. How about it? Maybe you can just say that you wanted to spend less time with your family."

"I think I can find a better way to phrase it, Cedric, but I do accept your kind offer. In fact, I am overwhelmed by your kind offer. And just think, I already live here in L.A. You won't even have to reimburse me for moving expenses."

"Of course. Why do you think I offered you the job in the first place?"

"I thought it was because I have such a keen knowledge regarding the type of coach we need. That's why."

"No, that's not it. I already have someone in mind for that job."

"Are his initials B. R.?"

"Yes, and it's not Babe Ruth."

Twenty-four hours later the Los Angeles Leopards announced that Brant Gilbert had been rehired as the team's general manager. Forty-eight hours after that came another announcement: Bobby Russell was coming back to L. A. as the team's head coach.

"With these moves," Cedric B. Medill said, "our team will be heading in a new direction."

■

Denzel Jackson was back. Brant Gilbert was back. Bobby Russell was back. And so was Mel Herbert. I made a promise to Carroll Blumenthal, and I've got to keep it, Mel realized, but now, how do I break the news to Frannie, he wondered. She was so excited about that vacation in Italy. She's been taking those Italian language classes. She's getting so comfortable with being called Francesca. I'm almost getting used to calling her that myself. Poor girl, she's going to be crushed.

At first, Frannie was disappointed, but then she understood. "I guess I'm going to have to postpone being called Francesca," she told Mel after a second glass of wine one evening at dinner.

"I'll keep calling you Francesca, if you wish," Mel said as he raised his glass. "Here is a toast to my darling Francesca."

"You can call me any name you wish. Your voice is poetry to me any way you say it."

At dinner, one night later, again after their second glass of wine, Mel reached into the inside pocket of his jacket and pulled out a sheet of paper. "If, when I say your name, my voice is poetry to you, then your name, darling girl, is always poetry to me," he said. With that, Mel handed his latest composition to Frannie.

I AM IN LOVE FOUR EVER

Her name was Frances when first I met her,
And I knew at once that I had to know her better.
But then I had dinner with a girl named Fran,
And I fell so much in love. Wouldn't any man?
They were both so pretty, such fun, and so canny
That my head began to spin, and then I found Frannie!
Deciding between Frances, Fran, or Frannie is a task that
truly will test ya;
And to complicate it so much more, in walked Francesca.
With Frances, Fran, Frannie, and Francesca all on the scene
I pray to the heavens above that I meet no one named Francine.
Frances, Fran, Frannie, and Francesca; I love all of them so,
That I hope each one of them understands why I can't let
the other three go.

CHAPTER SIXTY-FOUR
(Super Bowl Sunday, one year later)

Here I am again, Mel Herbert reflected as he took his seat in the press box three hours prior to yet another Super Bowl. If I would have gone ahead and wrapped it up after last season like I had planned, he mused, I could now be strolling, hand in hand with Francesca along the ancient streets of Florence. But you know what? I'm glad I didn't. This is a Super Bowl that I don't want to miss. Oh, heck, I say that every year.

The warm-ups were over. The teams returned to their locker rooms. Ten minutes later they came back out for the introduction of the starting lineups. Along each sideline the players stood, helmets nestled under their right arms as they, and the nation, listened to opera star Bessie Mae Moucheau's stirring rendition of *The Star Spangled Banner*. The pre-game coin toss was next, and then it was time for the opening kickoff.

The referee's whistle blew, and, while glancing across the field at each other from opposite sidelines, head coaches Denzel Jackson of the Portland Pioneers and Bobby Russell of the Los Angeles Leopards exchanged a half wave/half salute.

The game was on. There was no doubt this time. The winner would be the true Super Bowl Champions.

ACKNOWLEDGEMENTS

I thought only football was a team game. That was until I decided to write this book. What a team effort this has been. From so many talented and caring people I have received guidance, insights, help, instruction, inspiration, and even, on occasion, a bit of criticism.

Sometimes it was wearying, but I will repeat now, in recognition of all those who have contributed to keeping me on track, some words that I often spoke to our players after a stirring victory out there on the gridiron—"I couldn't have done it without you."

How grateful I am to all my newfound friends at Ascend Books for helping to steer this 86-year-old rookie novelist in the desired direction. And it was my agent, Tony Seidl of TD Media, who helped steer me to those wonderful folks at Ascend Books. Thank you, Tony.

Publisher Bob Snodgrass, Publications Coordinator Christine Drummond, and Editor Lee Stuart at Ascend Books were among the best teammates I've ever had. Their expertise and their enthusiasm helped provide additional motivation for me. Not only that, they turned what started out for me to be one of those clichéd labors-of-love into a heckuva lot of fun. Thank you, Bob. Thank you, Christine. Thank you, Lee.

Also, without the love and support I received from Frannie, Kimberly, Angela, and Marilyn (those aren't my girlfriends; they're my family) during those seemingly endless days when I sat at my computer searching for the right word or phrase, this book would never

have become a reality. How can I ever thank them enough? I can't,
but I'm going to keep trying.

And to all those coaches and players who honor the game and
who play by the rules, I want you to know something—I couldn't have
done it without you.

ABOUT THE AUTHOR

Marv Levy has always been unlike any other football coach. A Phi Beta Kappa graduate—and holder of a master's degree in English History from Harvard—he has combined brains and brawn in a unique way.

After coaching in the college ranks at Coe College, the University of New Mexico, the University of California (Berkeley), and the College of William & Mary, Coach Levy won two Grey Cup championships with the Montreal Alouettes of the Canadian Football League. He then worked his way through the NFL ranks, eventually leading the Buffalo Bills to four consecutive Super Bowl appearances.

He was named Coach of the Year twice, in 1988 and 1995, and was inducted into the Pro Football Hall of Fame in 2001.

His legendary good nature and grand sense of humor are frequently on display in popular television beer commercials.

His biography, *Where Else Would You Rather Be*, reached *New York Times* Best-Seller status in 2004.

He lives in Chicago with his wife, Mary Frances. This is his first work of fiction.